THE MASKED MAN OF CAIRO

THE CASE OF THE PURLOINED PYRAMID

by **SEAN MCLACHLAN**

Copyright 2017 Sean McLachlan

Cover design courtesy Andrés Alonso-Herrero

This book is a work of fiction. Names, characters, places and incidents are either products of the author's imagination or used fictitiously. Any resemblance to actual events, locales, or persons, living, dead, or undead, is purely coincidental. All rights reserved. No part of this publication can be reproduced or transmitted in any form or by any means, electronic or mechanical, without permission in writing from the author or publisher.

All rights reserved

*To Almudena, my wife,
and Julián, my son*

CHAPTER ONE

Cairo, 1919

It was a day to be remembered on Ibn al-Nafis Street. Someone had finally purchased the old house of the Rifaat family, five years after the last elderly member of the family had died. The death of Umm Abdullah had been news all over the neighborhood, and her distant relatives had immediately started squabbling over the inheritance.

Now it appeared that those squabbles had finally been resolved. For the past few days, a small army of cleaners, painters, and carpenters had been up and down the house, making it fit to be lived in. The chatterers at the Sultan El Moyyad Café watched the men come and go and gossiped over their coffees as to what great family might be moving in. Perhaps some wealthy Greeks or Armenians from Alexandria? A merchant from the south, here to bolster his fortunes in Egypt's greatest city? Or perhaps the newly married son of an aristocratic Cairene, setting up house to start a family?

Each worker had been closely questioned, if not by the regulars at the café then by Bisam the water seller, who did good trade during the renovation work, or by Youssef the barber, who always had time to chat as he sat on his little wooden stool outside his shop waiting for customers. But none of the workers knew the name or heritage of the new owner, only that they had to be finished by the end of the week.

That the new owner had a fortune was beyond question. The Rifaat house was the oldest and biggest on the street, a fine three-story stone structure from the time of the great sultans. No one knew how old it was exactly, but people pointed to the tidy stonework, the complex wooden latticework mashrabiya covering the windows, and the great wooden and bronze double doors leading to the courtyard, cut with a smaller door for daily use, to show that this was one of the finest houses in all of Cairo. That it had fallen into disuse and disrepair had been a neighborhood scandal, and the news that it would soon be reoccupied brought cheer to the hearts of everyone who lived and worked on Ibn al-Nafis Street.

And now the day had come for the new owner to move in. The workers had all left. The mashrabiya had been repaired to ensure the privacy of the new owner's women, the exterior and the interior had been freshly whitewashed, and the great doors' bronze fittings gleamed in the morning sun. The stranger who would today become a neighbor was the only topic of conversation at the café, at the produce market, at the barbershop, and even among the dirty street boys who played and shouted and stole and generally made a nuisance of themselves wherever they went.

Everyone's first inkling that their new neighbor was someone out of the ordinary came when the police showed up.

These were not the usual neighborhood police, recruited from among the poorer class of Cairenes or fellahin from the villages to crack the heads of market thieves and to separate brawling drunks. No, these were colonial police, dark-faced Soudanese with their blue uniforms, red fezzes, tidy rows of bright brass buttons, and freshly polished black shoes. Even for colonial police they were unusual, for in addition to the stout stick that, like the local police, they were well practiced in using, each man had a holstered pistol hanging from his broad yellow belt. The idlers at the café dropped their conversation to a whisper. Youssef the barber sent up a quick prayer to protect himself, his business, and his family. The street boys stood as close as they dared and gaped.

Then came a commotion at the end of the street. Donkeys and pedestrians hurried out of the way as a long, rumbling column of carts piled high with crates approached the house. At its head walked several more police, a Turk everyone recognized as the solicitor who had untangled the legal troubles with the Rifaat residence, an old Egyptian man carrying a wicker basket, and . . . someone else.

He dressed like a European, with a suit and tie and one of those fine canes Europeans used even if they didn't need any help to walk. Indeed, the man appeared young and healthy and walked with a determined air, swinging his cane like a pendulum as if to launch himself forward.

But two details about the man kept the residents of Ibn al-Nafis Street unsure if their neighborhood was about to get its first European.

Firstly, the right half of his face was covered with a thin mask. It was molded to the contours of his head and even included a false ear. The mask matched the features of the other half of his face perfectly. Too perfectly. It made his face unnaturally symmetrical, and although the mask had been painted to match the hue of a European's skin, it had no blemish or mark like the normal part of his face did. That half of the face did, indeed, look like a European's, with blue eyes and northern features, although with tanned skin that made his mask look pale and sickly by comparison.

If that wasn't enough for everyone to become confused about the newcomer's origins, the second reason gave them even more reason to wonder.

The man spoke Arabic to those accompanying him, and not just a few shouted, mispronounced commands like some Europeans did, but as fluently as a Muslim.

The Arabic was strange, though, with an odd accent and some words that sounded unfamiliar. Occasionally the Turk or the old Egyptian with the basket had to ask his meaning, prompting the man to say it another way.

"He is a Moroccan!" Ali declared, thumping his coffee cup down on his usual table at the Sultan El Moyyad Café. Ali had been on the Hajj and had met Muslims from the Maghreb to Malaysia, so he knew these things.

"He doesn't look like a Moroccan," ventured Mohammed, the café's star backgammon player.

"Many Moroccans are as light-skinned as the Europeans," Ali said.

"Do they dress like Europeans?" Mohammed asked.

"Not that I have seen," Ali admitted. "Perhaps he is a diplomat from Rabat or Tangiers."

"Then why doesn't he wear a fez?" asked Anwar, the waiter whose aged father owned the café and was even now nodding off in the back corner.

Ali had no answer for that.

"Ah, I know that Egyptian with him!"

This was from Mohammed al-Hajji, the muezzin from the mosque at the corner of the street. Unlike all the others at the café, he had no glass of coffee or tea in front of him. He drank only water or the syrup sold by some of the street peddlers, saying it helped keep his throat smooth. He never bought anything at the café, although he spent much of his day there. Anwar didn't object because of the man's respected position, and while it was unheard of for a man to avoid tea and coffee, Mohammed al-Hajji's voice certainly did sound like paradise had opened up and the angels were singing.

"Who is it?" Mohammed the backgammon player asked.

"He is Sheikh Moussa el Hawi," Mohammed al-Hajji replied.

Everyone fell silent and stared at the old man with the basket, who just now arrived at the front door with the man in the mask. Sheikh Moussa el Hawi was a snake charmer whose fame had spread across all of Cairo. Whoever this newcomer was, he was wise to hire the sheikh to clear out the house after it had been vacant for so long.

The strange newcomer and his group stopped in front of the door. His carts took up almost the entire street, although prying eyes couldn't see any of their contents, their being all stowed away in crates. One man in the crowd studied the carts with more interest than the others—a lean, muscular young tough in a grungy jellaba. His head was shaved, and he had sharp blue eyes and light skin that showed he was the descendant of a Circassian slave. His features could have been handsome except for the permanent scowl on his face and the knife scar down one cheek. His name was Hassan, and the whole neighborhood feared him.

The Turkish solicitor, a small man with a pencil-thin mustache, a European-style suit, and a fez, unlocked the door and handed the keys to the man in the mask. As a pair of policemen pushed open the doors, their hinges groaning, Sheikh Moussa opened up the basket and turned it upside down.

"He wants us to see that he doesn't have any serpents hidden in there," Anwar the waiter said unnecessarily.

The snake charmer entered the building, wielding a three-foot-long stick of strong palm wood that was forked at the end. Those crowding on the street could see a wide entrance hall that led to a large central room and beyond that a small courtyard with a fountain. Doors and hallways led off in all directions.

As the curious throng pushed in to watch, the police shoved them back, shouting angrily. When one from the crowd tried to slip between the cordon, a policeman barked an order at him, pulled out his truncheon, and hit him.

The man shouted angrily and raised his hands. Just as the policeman was

THE CASE OF THE PURLOINED PYRAMID

about to swing his truncheon down again, the newcomer with the mask stepped forward and grabbed the policeman's wrist.

Everyone fell silent. The masked man's knuckles grew white, and the policeman gave out a little cry, either in shock or in pain it wasn't clear. Perhaps both.

The truncheon clattered to the ground. The masked man picked it up and put it back in the loop on the policeman's belt without saying a word.

Instead he turned and addressed the crowd.

"Please step back and allow the learned sheikh a chance to make my home safe from serpents."

Dumbfounded, the crowd moved back a little.

"He must be a European," Mohammad the backgammon champion said with conviction and took a sip of his tea. "No one else can treat a policeman like that and keep his limbs intact."

The others nodded in agreement, except for Ali, who objected. "A diplomat from the sultan of Morocco could get away with it."

Ignoring the scene on the street outside, Sheikh Moussa stood at the center of the room and made some clucking noises with his tongue, followed by a loud and lengthy recital from the Koran. The more learned among the watchers, once they recognized the surah, recited along with him.

The sheikh struck his stick gently on the flagstones. A gasp rose from the crowd as a long black serpent slithered out from a dark corner.

As the serpent approached him, the snake charmer's voice fell, and he started muttering in a low, quick voice words that the onlookers could not hear. The snake drew closer, then stopped when the old man pointed two fingers at it as if he were a Christian giving benediction. The snake raised its head, flicking its tongue in and out. Calmly, Sheikh Moussa took a step forward and grasped it just underneath its head. The snake slowly coiled around the sheikh's arm. He then carried it to the basket and placed it inside. The sheikh put the lid on the basket and went back into the house. He turned a corner and passed out of view.

The strange man with the mask and the Turkish solicitor stood waiting, ignoring the stares that were now directed at them.

A few minutes later, Sheikh Moussa emerged carrying another snake, which he placed in the basket with the first.

"I knew there would be snakes in there," Anwar said as he wiped an empty table clean with a cloth. "You can't leave a house abandoned for years like that. I bet they hid because of all of the bustle and noise the workmen made, but they would have come out for him the first time he tried to sleep in his new house."

"May God grant the sheikh success and protect our neighbor," Mohammed al-Hajji declared.

"God is great," several of the café goers added.

"What if it turns out he really is a European?" Anwar asked.

"Then God preserve him from what is coming," Ali said in a low voice.

"No politics right now, Ali, there are police in the street," Anwar whispered.

"I would never raise a hand against a neighbor, no matter what his faith," Ali said, "but as for others . . ."

Ali finished with a shrug.

Sheikh Moussa came out a third time with another snake and placed it in the basket with the previous two. He fastened the top of the basket by shoving sticks through loops on the lid and the sides and then lashing them all together with a thick rope. Despite his age, he worked the rope with strong, gnarled hands that were sure of their work. Once he had finished, the masked man pulled out a wallet like the Europeans used and handed him some notes. The sheikh bowed in thanks, lifted the basket on top of his head, and walked down the street, the street boys following him.

"Oh, Sheikh, may the Almighty's blessings be upon you!" Mohammed al-Hajji called with his sweet muezzin's voice. "Come join us. Let me have the honor of inviting you for a cup of tea and to make your acquaintance."

Anwar's eyebrows shot up. Was Mohammed al-Hajji actually going to order something, even if only for someone else? This was indeed a day to remember!

After the snake charmer had been made comfortable and the street urchins had been shooed away, everyone introduced themselves and asked after each other's health and family. Hassan sat down at a table far enough away that he wouldn't be obliged to take part in the conversation and near enough that he could hear it. He gave Anwar a scowl that brought the waiter hurrying to his table. Hassan ordered a tea and then looked off into the distance, pretending to watch the passersby in the street while actually listening to what the sheikh had to say about the rich newcomer.

THE CASE OF THE PURLOINED PYRAMID

The greetings, of course, took some time, so it was a good half hour before the regulars got to ask the question foremost in their minds.

"So who is this man? Where is he from? And why is he wearing a mask?"

"His name is Sir Augustus Wall, and he is an Englishman. I do not know why he wears that thing on his face, and I thought it impolite to ask."

***

Others had no such reservations. A couple of hours later, the small door to the main portal of the Rifaat house opened, and the Englishman stepped out. Ignoring the stares of everyone on the street, he locked the door behind him. Then he made his way down the street, swinging his cane in time to his steps.

Within moments, he was surrounded by a crowd of laughing boys.

"Do you really speak Arabic?"

"Yes," the man said, not looking at them.

"He does! Where are you going?"

"To see someone."

"Who?"

"None of your business."

"Why do you have that on your face?"

"None of your business. Go away."

The Englishman sped up, but the boys kept pace. One of the shopkeepers shouted at the urchins to leave him alone, but they didn't listen. The Englishman cut between a donkey and a fruit stall to avoid them, but they tailed him, some ducking under the donkey. One boy scampered under the table and snatched an apple as the vendor stopped another boy from doing the same.

The boy who took the apple, who seemed to be the leader of this grubby little band, cut in front of Augustus. He looked about twelve, clad in a filthy and patched jellaba that might have been white at some early point in its history. He had wavy, unkempt black hair that stuck out in all directions. Like the other boys, he was barefoot.

"What is that on your face?" he asked, munching on the apple.

"It's a mask, you little idiot."

"I am not an idiot! I'll show you!" he shouted, and then switched to broken English. "Hello, what country?"

"England."

"I am English!" the boy said in badly mispronounced English.

"No, 'You are English,'" Augustus corrected.

"Your name is Faisal. What is my good name, sir?"

Augustus switched back to Arabic. "Lesson over. You've failed your exam. Now go away, the lot of you."

The boys all laughed at Faisal, who stuck his tongue out at them.

Augustus cut down a side street that would lead him to his destination. It was quieter here, with no crowd, and the boys were able to surround him. They started getting underfoot, and Augustus had to take care not to stumble.

The boys laughed. Faisal offered Augustus some of the apple by shoving it in front of his face. Another boy used the distraction to reach into the Englishman's pocket, only to get rapped on the knuckles by his cane.

That only made the boys laugh harder. Dancing around him, they grabbed at his pockets and his watch. It was all the Englishman could do to keep them from taking anything.

Someone tripped him up, and as he stumbled, Faisal snatched the mask away from his face.

And immediately dropped it, backing against the nearest wall in wide-eyed terror.

The face beneath that mask was missing. Where the cheek should have been was a cavernous pit of scar tissue, leaving the eye, surrounded by a thin strip of flesh and poorly healed burns, almost hanging suspended. Veins stood out red and livid, and the flesh around where the ear should have been was pockmarked and crisscrossed with the scars of sutures. Part of the cheek was gone, and the man's teeth, which were too white and perfect to be anything but false, were exposed to view like those of a skull.

The boys screamed and ran off as Augustus Wall got to his knees and grabbed his mask. Faisal stood frozen with his back to the wall, his little fist against his mouth.

CHAPTER TWO

"The little bastard cracked it."

Sir Augustus Wall examined a tiny fissure in the bottom edge of his mask and hoped the whole thing hadn't been weakened. He'd have to go all the way to France to get another. A team of artists had made the masks as gifts for seriously disfigured veterans at the end of the war, using old photographs to guide them. His own, he had to admit, was a good job, but it made him look like some circus freak. But at least he could go out in public. If he went out without it, the entire street would run off as quickly as those boys.

Augustus grunted, put the mask back on, and uncovered his mirror. He examined his reflection. No, the crack wasn't too visible. After combing his hair, he covered the mirror again and went out into the main hall.

The spacious room was filled with antiquities. Statues and mummy cartonnages took up much of the space, some of them still in their packing cases. Long shelves along two of the walls held smaller artifacts such as ushabtis, amulets, and weapons. Another long shelf and the floor beneath it were dedicated to inscriptions and sculpture fragments. A couple of mummified crocodiles hung suspended from the ceiling. Coptic textiles covered the walls in various spots. One corner was dominated by the prize of his collection, a perfectly preserved eight-foot statue of a crocodile-headed god with a hieroglyphic inscription inscribed along the side and around the base. Augustus gave the statue a friendly nod and got busy unpacking the rest of the crates.

The pounding of the heavy brass knocker on his front door stopped him an hour later. Cursing under his breath at the interruption, Augustus checked that his mask was in place and went to answer it.

He opened the door to see an old beggar and the street urchin who had knocked his mask off. The boy stood on tiptoe, his head at an angle as the beggar held his ear in a tight grip. In the beggar's other hand was a gnarled old cane.

The beggar did not focus on Augustus. His eyes were clouded with blindness.

"Peace be upon you," the beggar said. "I hear you speak God's language."

"I do," Augustus replied curtly, unwilling to return the traditional courtesy.

"I am Osman ibn Akbar ibn Mubarak al-Hajji. This boy's name is Faisal, and he has come to apologize."

The beggar twisted the child's ear a bit more. Augustus stared in fascination. He didn't think an ear could be manipulated in such a fashion without coming off.

"I am terribly sorry, sir," the boy said, his voice coming out strained. He kept his eyes down.

"I hope that teaches you not to get too curious," Augustus grumbled. "You bring shame on your grandfather by acting this way."

The blind beggar snorted. "God is compassionate and merciful. He would never curse one of his faithful servants by giving him such a grandson."

"I am sorry to make presumptions on your noble family, sir," Augustus replied in his politest Arabic. "Thank you for making the boy see right."

The beggar let go of the boy's ear and swung his cane down with startling accuracy on the boy's backside, bringing forth a yelp.

"Making this boy see right would be like moving a mountain, but he meant his apology."

"Well, apology accepted then," Augustus said, turning to the boy.

But the boy was already gone.

Augustus gave the man a coin—which the beggar accepted by bowing and touching it to his brow—closed the door, and got back to work. He wanted to open for business within the next couple of days, and he had much to do. The front hall, main room, and courtyard would act as his showroom, with the side rooms on the ground floor as storage. The first floor was for his own use, while the second he would leave vacant. He hadn't really needed such a large house, but its fine architecture and remoteness from Cairo's European quarter had appealed to him.

After several hours of work, he went out for his customary evening stroll. The men in the café across the street stared, and hidden behind their latticework windows, the women of Ibn al-Nafis Street no doubt stared too as Augustus started on a brisk walk through the neighborhood, swinging his cane in long sweeps ahead of him and tapping it on the flagstones. Only the newer quarters of Cairo had electric streetlamps. The main streets here still used gas. Their soft light illuminated the intricate facades of the Bahri Period mosque at the end of the street with a soft glow and turned the dark wood of complexly latticed windows of the homes a deep golden brown. For a time, he relaxed, admiring the beauty of the scene and wondering what lay down the dark side streets and alleys. There were some architectural jewels in this quarter, and he looked forward to studying them.

His serenity was interrupted by a young voice beside him.

"Where are you going?"

It was that urchin again.

"Oh, it's you."

Augustus quickened his pace, looking around to see if the brat had brought along his pack of little monsters. He didn't see any. Nevertheless he kept an eye on doorways and the openings of alleys in case some of them leaped out and tried to rob him. This one, at least, was keeping a respectable distance.

"I'm Faisal," he said.

"I believe you mentioned that."

"I'm sorry," Faisal said, putting on a glum face.

"So you say."

"Thank you for not beating me."

"I was sorely tempted. Trust me."

"Osman ibn Akbar gave me a good thrashing," Faisal grumbled, kicking a stone so that it skittered down the street.

"Glad to hear it," Augustus replied with a satisfied nod.

"Where are you going?" the boy asked.

"That is none of your concern."

"Why don't you live in the European quarter?"

"Because there are too many Europeans there."

"Yes, that's why they call it the European quarter."

Augustus turned and faced the boy, who stopped and took a step back.

"I live here because I want to be left alone."

Augustus continued his walk. Faisal paced him.

"Then why don't you live in the desert?"

"I can't run my business in the desert."

"What is your business?"

"Selling annoying little boys to the Turks."

Faisal laughed. "You don't really do that!"

"I might start."

Faisal didn't reply for a time. Augustus glanced at him out of the corner of his eye. The boy bore a serious look.

"You should be careful in this neighborhood. There are many thieves."

"Yes, you and your friends tried to rob me this afternoon, remember?"

"Oh, we only did that because you are European. But we won't try again because you are different than the other Europeans."

"I wasn't always," Augustus murmured.

Faisal blushed. "Oh, I didn't mean that. I meant because you are a Muslim."

Augustus cocked his head. "Why do you say that?"

"You speak Arabic."

"I'm not a Muslim. I learned Arabic from a Moroccan officer in the French service while we were both convalescing in hospital. I taught him English in exchange for his teaching me Arabic. I also spent a year in Alexandria. People didn't leave me alone there so I came here."

Another long pause. Augustus began to hope the boy would get bored and leave. Faisal stared at him with big brown eyes that seemed to absorb his every detail.

"Did you get attacked by a jackal?"

"No."

"Did a bandit cut you with a sword?"

"No."

"Did you—"

Augustus rounded on him. This time Faisal took two steps back.

"A German shell exploded in the trench my friends and I were hiding in. They were all killed. I was less fortunate."

Augustus turned back around and continued his walk. To his greatest annoyance, he noticed Faisal still dogging him.

"The Germans are very bad people," the boy declared.

"Are they now?"

"Very bad people!" Faisal repeated, this time emphasizing his point with a loud spit. "I hate them."

"Have you ever met a German?"

"No, but they are bad people because they kill the English, and the English are very good people. I hate the Germans."

"Well, I don't hate them."

"But they are your enemies!" Faisal cried in obvious astonishment.

"Not anymore."

Faisal stopped abruptly and grabbed the Englishman's wrist.

"Unhand me!" Augustus shouted, pulling away.

"Shh. Look."

Augustus followed the boy's frightened gaze and noticed a shadow move back and merge with the darker obscurity of an alleyway ten yards ahead.

Augustus glanced around, suddenly aware that they were alone on this street. Being alone on a Cairene street in the middle of the night was not a healthy situation.

No, not alone. There was that shadow in the alley ahead, and the faintest sound of movement in a doorway behind.

Augustus gripped his cane in both hands. He moved to push Faisal to the cover of a shuttered shop entrance but found him already there, looking uncertainly in either direction.

"You stay there, boy," Augustus said, moving to shield him and glancing in either direction to try to watch the alley and the other doorway at the same time.

Silence, just for a moment.

Then the shadows burst into motion. Three Egyptian men leaped out of the alleyway and charged him, while a fourth, a tough-looking brute with a shaved head and a scar down one cheek, came out of the doorway behind him. All carried knives or cudgels. They didn't bother to brandish them, obviously thinking their mere appearance would make their intended victim throw his money to them and flee in panic.

That did not happen. Augustus ducked to the left and lashed out with his cane, tripping the foremost attacker and making the man just behind him fall over his friend. Then the Englishman swung his cane in a vicious backhand that cracked the third man on the back of the neck and sent him crashing down onto the other two.

Augustus spun to face the fourth man, the one with the scar. The attacker came in slow and cautious, his knife at the ready. Augustus grasped the end of his cane, twisted, and withdrew a hidden blade a full two feet long. In the same motion, he brought the other part of the cane, which acted as a metal scabbard, smacking down onto the skull of the most awake of the three thugs at his feet. The impact made the man crack his forehead against the ground.

Augustus chuckled and looked at the thug facing him. "Perhaps you might like to reconsider?"

The thief said nothing. He feinted to the right and then made a quick lunge to the left. Augustus spotted the movement just in time to parry, the two metal blades screeching as they ground along one another. The Englishman circled his blade, which while thinner was longer. The blades screeched again as Augustus twisted his sword cane into position and thrust for his opponent's head.

The Egyptian ducked out of the way and immediately ducked again to avoid a swing from the metal shaft of the cane, nimbly circling around his foe. He hacked at the blade of the sword cane, trying to break it, but it was made of strong, high quality steel and didn't even chip.

But it did lower enough to allow an opening. He slashed at Augustus's wrist, and the Englishman barely managed to move his hand in time.

Augustus backpedaled, jabbing his blade into the hand of one of the downed men as he tried to rise. The fellow hissed in pain and fell back to the ground, but the thrust left another opening for the gang leader, who dove in to slash at the Englishman's throat.

Augustus was ready for it and with a nimble movement slapped at the man's hand with the shaft of the cane and made his knife fly into the wall with a clang, missing Faisal by inches.

Augustus brought the tip of his blade up to the leader's throat. The man froze, but he did not tremble.

"If you kill me, Englishman, my friends will avenge me."

The sound of quickly receding footsteps did not make that threat seem imminent.

"Your friends just abandoned you."

"They will be back when you are not so ready. They will watch you and follow you and bring more men with better weapons. My cousins will come too, and since they are family they will not rest until they have killed you slowly. This little goat turd here can tell you the truth of that."

Faisal nodded, his eyes wide. "Everyone knows Hassan's cousins are killers."

"So Hassan here has a bit of a local reputation, has he?"

"His family will take vengeance," Faisal said, "and they already know where you live."

Augustus's blade didn't falter. "But if I don't kill him, how do I know he won't come back for a second try?"

Faisal shrugged.

Hassan's mouth curled in disgust. "I promise."

"Swear by God," Augustus demanded.

"I swear by God."

"You did that too quickly. I suspect you're even less of a believer than I am. Swear by your mother's name."

Hassan's eyes narrowed.

"I swear by my mother's name."

"That's one thing you can always rely on with Arabs," Augustus said with a grin, "even the lowest street thug is a mama's boy."

The Englishman pulled back the tip of the blade from Hassan's throat and sank it an inch into his shoulder. Hassan grimaced, gritting his teeth to keep from crying out.

"Something to remember me by. If you cross me again, I'll kill you. If I catch you loitering near my house, I'll kill you. Be out of my sight by the time I count to three, or I'll hunt you down and kill you. One."

Hassan fled so quickly that Augustus didn't bother continuing to two.

After Hassan was safely out of sight, Faisal leaped into the air with a whoop.

"That was magnificent! No wonder the English win every war."

Augustus gave Faisal a smile. "We generally win because of our native allies. Thank you. I might not have seen them but for you."

Faisal grinned and scooped up Hassan's knife, admiring the keen blade. Augustus snatched it out of his hand.

"That's not a toy for a little boy."

Faisal puffed himself up.

"No, it is a weapon for a man."

"That's precisely why you shan't have it. And don't pick up that other knife either."

"I helped you! I deserve both of them," Faisal whined.

"Out of the question."

"OK, only one."

"Here." Augustus fished a few coins from his pocket.

Faisal raised his hands. "Oh no! I can't take money, not this time. I was bad to you. Now we are even, so the next time I save your life you can pay me."

"That seems fair enough." Augustus chuckled and then grew serious. "Did I do wrong in letting him go?"

Faisal thought for a moment before shaking his head. "I don't know. Both choices were dangerous."

A long, mournful wail lilted through the night air, bringing words of flowing Classical Arabic from a voice as pure and as beautiful as the paradise it promised.

"Allah is most great. Allah is most great. I testify that there is no god except Allah . . ."

Faisal's eyes widened. "I nearly forgot. It's time for the night prayer! I need to lead Osman ibn Akbar to the mosque. Don't get into any more danger tonight; I can't save you until tomorrow!"

With that, Faisal ran off in the direction of Ibn al-Nafis Street. Augustus watched him go, then gave a little shrug and collected the other knife, which he put in his pocket before continuing his walk.

CHAPTER THREE

It was breakfast time at Shepheard's Hotel, and the guests were taking it on the terrace, both to see the passing scene in the street beyond and to be seen by any important Europeans walking past. The breakfasters were mostly British officers and civilians with a sprinkling of rich or well-placed Americans or Australians there on sufferance and one boisterous group of Italians who had obviously misread their guidebook. The guests dug into the eggs and bacon or sat back and enjoyed their coffee, clapping when they needed more from the native waiters dressed in immaculate red vests and matching slippers, with billowing white pantaloons that when the wind blew made them look like the sails of the feluccas that plied the Nile. The waiters wore fezzes as well, a tradition born from the time before the war when Egypt was run by the British but still nominally under the rule of the Sublime Porte in Constantinople.

The terrace stood several feet above street level, and an ornate railing separated the natives on the street from the whites on the terrace, their only contact being when souvenirs were passed through the bars in one direction as piastres went in the other. At the moment, a portly Egyptian in a voluminous brown jellaba was trying to interest the Italians in a fly whisk, while another older man waved a mummified crocodile over his head hoping someone would notice him. The Italians seemed more interested in a boy with a dancing monkey in a red vest and miniature fez. The monkey performed a somersault that made the Italians forget themselves and break into a loud applause and shouts of *"Ancora! Ancora!"* that earned them scornful looks from the British and even some of the Americans. Oblivious, the Italians kept cheering, and when the monkey doffed his fez and presented it through the bars, they dropped some coins into it.

"If only all the street urchins were so gainfully employed. We could put them in some remote quarter of the city and be free of both underage thieves and Italians," Augustus said.

"They quite often come to the same thing, old chap."

This was from Sir Thomas Russell, commandant of the Cairo police, who had invited him to breakfast. Augustus was good at refusing invitations, but no one, not even he, refused an invitation from Sir Thomas Russell.

"So any trouble in the new neighborhood?" Russell asked.

"None at all."

"I wish you had picked a house in Esbekiyeh or Kasr-el-Dubara," the police commandant told him. "This independence movement is picking up steam, and things might get a bit unpleasant before long."

"Is the government going to let Sa'ad Zaghloul and his delegation go to the Versailles Conference?"

"Of course not!" Russell scoffed.

"We did lead the Egyptians to believe they'd have a chance to discuss independence after the war. They were supposed to have an official delegation at Versailles."

Sir Russell dismissed the idea with a wave of a hand. "Those statements were completely unofficial. I suppose we did lead them on a bit, but what could we do? We were fighting for our very existence. We needed Egyptian grain, Egyptian cotton, and Egyptian labor. Why can't the natives understand that?"

"I think they understand that they've been tricked."

"Well, too bad for them," Russell said. Then he leaned forward and lowered his voice. "Now I wouldn't normally say this to a civilian, Wall, but you're living in a rough patch, and I think you should know. I've been getting signals from London—nothing concrete mind you, straw in the wind—that I'll receive orders to arrest Zaghloul and his pals before long and ship them far enough away that we'll never be troubled by them again."

"I'm sure the natives will just roll over and give up at that point," Augustus said, sarcasm lacing his voice.

Sir Russell either ignored his tone or was oblivious to it. "There'll be protests, of course, and perhaps some unfortunate incidents. I'll try to give you a warning if I'm given the time myself. Oh, there's polo at the Ghezireh Sporting Club this Saturday. Good group of chaps. I'm sure they'd lend you a horse. I heard you played at Oxford."

"I did."

"Well, if you'd like—"

"That's quite all right."

Russell chuckled and lit a cigarette. "Davison told me you were a bit of work."

Davison was the police commandant in Alexandria.

"Davison is a good man in his way, but he's damned hard to shake," Augustus said.

"You're not supposed to shake a police officer. Look here, Wall, it's bad enough that you're living in the Old Quarter, but that's no reason to go completely native."

"I'm not one for showing my face at social events."

Russell shifted uneasily in his seat, then put on a smile. "I know something you would like. Have you met Pierre Dupris? He's excavating a mastaba at Giza and has found quite a bit of note. He sent a message this morning that he wants to see me. There's been a theft."

Augustus must have betrayed a flash of interest because the commandant's smile broadened. "Ah, two bull's-eyes in one, eh? I heard how much you helped Davison out of a tight spot."

"He would have solved that case without me."

"I daresay he would have, but perhaps the khedive's jewels wouldn't have been recovered in time. That was more than some little police matter you untangled. Unfortunately, this case is merely routine, but since I wanted to see the diggings in any case, and I know you do, would you care to join me? My driver is waiting."

"So what's missing?" Augustus asked.

Sir Russell set his cigarette in an ashtray and rummaged around inside his jacket. The ashtray was adorned with the Shepheard's logo showing the silhouette of an Arab on a camel in front of the pyramids, now smudged with the ash from the policeman's cigarette. Augustus had noticed one of the Americans pocketing an ashtray a few minutes before. He hadn't bothered to speak up. The management at Shepheard's assumed their ashtrays would be stolen. They adorned drawing rooms from Nice to New York. It was a form of advertising.

Russell retrieved a notebook from inside his jacket and flipped to a page. "A slab of highly polished white limestone carved with some hieroglyphs. The inscription is fragmentary and obviously part of a larger text. No one has offered you anything like that, have they?"

"No. What did the inscription say?"

"Dupris didn't say. By the way, about that matter with the khedive's jewels, I meant it when I said the government was in your debt. Enough in fact," the policeman said, lowering his voice, "that I won't make a fuss about your living here under an assumed name."

Augustus lit a cigarette and studied the policeman for a moment, then exhaled the smoke slowly. "I suppose you would have found out eventually. I'm not on the run from the law."

"I know. I checked."

"I want to be left alone. That's all."

"I think I've heard you mention that before."

"Sometimes I feel like I say it all day," Augustus muttered.

"Look here, Sir Wall, and I shall call you 'sir' because I checked on your knighthood, and it's certainly more real than your name. You are part of the British community here whether you choose to be or not, for the simple reason that the natives see you as such. We must be a bastion, my good fellow, a bastion against the anarchy that threatens to engulf this country. Zaghlul Pasha and his independence cronies badger the high commissioner every day for permission to go to Versailles, but London simply isn't interested. The prime minister listens to his colonial officers, and he knows that if we give these people an inch of rope, they'll only hang themselves with it, and us too in the bargain."

A waiter bent over him. "More coffee, Russell Pasha?"

"No, thank you. And put this on my account," Sir Russell said, waving him away. "Now as I was saying, you have to stand with us. All the British do. One of the only good things to come out of the Great War is that we finally wrested Egypt away from Johnny Turk once and for all, and we're not about to give it up to a bunch of Mohammedans who will be too busy cutting each other's throats to keep up the cotton exports."

The police commandant glanced at Augustus's hands. He followed his gaze and saw he was gripping his chair, knuckles white. Augustus forced himself to let go and fold his hands on his lap. Sir Russell quickly changed the subject.

"Let's go see that excavation. Even an amateur such as I finds such things interesting, and perhaps Dupris will have a few little knickknacks to sell you."

"It's illegal for him to sell any of his finds without first getting permission from the Egyptian courts."

Sir Thomas Russell laughed. "I only fight real crime."

Augustus jabbed his cigarette into the ashtray with some force.

As they got up, Sir Russell asked, "By the way, howsoever did you get a false listing in *Debrett's Peerage*?"

"Their pay isn't at a parity with their reputation."

The policeman looked shocked. "I thought they were incorruptible."

"Everyone's corruptible."

Sir Russell clicked his tongue with disgust. "Don't be ridiculous."

***

The road to Giza was barren and dusty. The sprawl of Cairo came close to the plateau on which the famous pyramids stood but did not quite reach it before breaking up into scattered villages and fields. Fellahin toiled in the fields while their children tended herds of sheep and goats.

At the wheel of Russell's vehicle sat a colonial policeman who honked at the lines of donkeys and camels carrying European visitors toward the pyramids. The policeman seemed to enjoy driving as close as possible to the animals and letting out a sudden blast with his horn, inevitably making the animals buck and shy.

"Mind that you don't kill anyone, Aziz," Russell told the driver.

"Mind that you do," Augustus said.

The driver turned around in his seat and grinned at him.

"Does the good sir not like European tourists?" Aziz asked.

"They are Moses's final curse on Pharaoh. You might want to watch the road, my good fellow."

The driver turned back just in time to spot a tiny donkey carrying a fat, sunburned blonde woman in a white sundress and parasol. Aziz twisted hard on the wheel and missed the woman by inches. She disappeared in a cloud of the car's dust.

"Good show, Aziz. Carry on," Augustus said.

Sir Thomas Russell shook his head in dismay. "Davison warned me about this. Must you hate everyone?"

"I don't hate Aziz. I think he's a splendid fellow."

Pierre Dupris's excavation lay in the very shadow of the Great Pyramid of Cheops, just to the east of the pyramid of Queen Hetepheres, the famous pharaoh's mother. The three main pyramids were only a part of a much larger funerary system, which included numerous temples and several smaller queen's pyramids, plus smaller tombs called mastabas for the high nobility. These took their name from the Arabic word for *bench*, because the rectangular structures, not much taller than the height of a man, looked like oversize benches of the kind Egyptian farmers put outside their front doors. A whole field of mastabas lay in orderly rows next to the Great Pyramid. The desert sands had covered up most of them, and years of excavation by British, German, French, and Austrian Egyptologists had uncovered several. Others were only visible as low hummocks in the sand, awaiting exploration. Like their greater cousins the pyramids, most mastabas had been looted in antiquity, but they still offered up interesting bas-reliefs and wall paintings, plus the occasional stray find of value.

A team of native workmen had uncovered about half of the mastaba Russell and Augustus had come to see. The top was entirely exposed to about the top three feet and showed the mastaba to be eight feet wide and about twenty long. The entire northern part had been uncovered, and a row of fellahin hacked away at the sand on one side with hoes, quickly filling straw baskets that were removed by a long line of village women in voluminous robes, who carried the baskets on their heads about a quarter of a mile to dump them well away from the site. Aziz stopped the car far enough away that he didn't send a cloud of dust into the faces of his countrymen.

"That's all right, Aziz. We can walk from here," Sir Russell grumbled.

Aziz stayed with the car as Russell and Augustus got out.

As they walked away, the police commandant said in a low voice, "A good man, Aziz. It's all right to grant him a bit of fun."

A young, petite, energetic Frenchman with a bandaged right hand was overseeing the work on the mastaba. Despite a broad pith helmet, his face was red, highlighting his blond hair and bright blue eyes. When he spotted his two visitors, he waved and walked over to meet them.

THE CASE OF THE PURLOINED PYRAMID

"Sir Wall, I'd like you to meet Cavell Martin, Dupris's assistant director," Sir Russell said in passable French. "Monsieur Martin, this is Sir Augustus Wall, an antiquities dealer."

"Pleased to meet you, sir. I hope you forgive me for not shaking hands," Cavell Martin said, smiling sheepishly and raising his bandaged hand.

"In the process of mummifying yourself, are you?" Augustus asked. His French was perfect.

"Ah no, a little accident with a shovel. Occupational hazard, as you Englishmen say."

"So what have we here?" Augustus asked, pointing to the mastaba with his cane.

"A fine discovery. Come. Let me show you the entrance."

They approached the mastaba, a low limestone structure a bit taller than a man. Many of the stones were missing, probably from ancient or medieval quarrying. It was common for people of later periods to use the prepared blocks of earlier structures for their own use, rather than going through the trouble of creating new ones. This generally did not happen until medieval times, when the religious system of the ancient Egyptians had broken down and people no longer revered the cults of the pharaohs or respected their relations and prominent officials. To steal stones from a mastaba in ancient times would have been a sacrilege punishable by death.

Despite the missing stones, the mastaba's portal was well preserved, standing exposed at the bottom of a great hole the workers had excavated in the sand. A narrow, low door was topped by a lengthy hieroglyphic inscription on the lintel.

Augustus studied the inscription, slowly working out the words.

"Idu, son of Qar. Inspector of the um, something, priests—"

"Wab-priests," Martin interjected.

"Thank you. For the pyramids of Pharaohs Khufu and Khafre and um—overseer? inspector?—of scribes."

"Overseer. So you read Old Kingdom hieratic!" Martin said, obviously impressed.

"Not as well as I should. Ironically, my work takes up so much of my time that it keeps me from making a proper study of it. I'm afraid I don't know what a wab-priest is, for example."

"A wab-priest was responsible for the purification of any objects such as sistra or vessels used in religious ceremonies," the Frenchman explained. "There were several subclasses involved in various parts of the ritual process. It appears our man Idu managed all of them for the pharaoh."

"An important post then. I congratulate you on your find. What's this inscription on the doorjamb? I can't quite puzzle it out," Augustus said, pointing to another hieroglyphic text above the figure of a guardian carved in low relief into the jamb on the right-hand side. The guardian stood facing out, toward anyone entering, and held a staff in his hand as if to bar the way. Augustus had seen this figure on numerous tombs.

"Ah, it's a curse! It says, 'As for every man who shall enter this tomb, without purifying himself as the purification of a god, one shall make for him a painful punishment.'"

"Charming. May we go inside and see if it still works?"

"You are most welcome, and have no fear of any curses," Martin said with an easy laugh. "I was the first to enter the mastaba when we uncovered the doorway, and so the weight of the curse will fall heaviest on me."

The Frenchman ushered them through the narrow doorway and turned on an electric torch so they could see. Augustus fished another out of his pocket and added some more light.

The doorway was made of thick slabs of stone. Both the right and the left were carved with the figures of guardians, straight-backed men holding tall staves who were supposed to protect the tomb for all time.

"Excuse us, gentlemen," Augustus said, passing between them.

There were a couple of steps down, and they entered a long, low room. Sand crunched under their shoes, and a heap of it against the back showed the mastaba hadn't yet been fully cleared. Augustus shone his torch on the right wall and saw more hieroglyphic inscriptions above a depiction of Idu himself seated in front of a table piled high with the offerings that would sustain him in the afterlife. Various carvings showed typical scenes for a tomb such as this—men slaughtering bulls, servants carrying food to Idu, and similar images. Beyond was a false door for his *ka*, his spirit, to pass in and out of the tomb. Unusually, the tomb had a second carving of Idu, this one almost fully in the round, facing toward the inside of the tomb with his arms outstretched, palms up. On the left wall stood a series of statues in little niches. The paint was remarkably well preserved in spots, with the copper red of the statue's skin especially clear.

THE CASE OF THE PURLOINED PYRAMID

"Not a bad place to end one's days, eh?" Augustus said.

"Bit gloomy, but more elaborate than a coffin I suppose," Russell sniffed.

"So what do you think you'll find beyond this?" Augustus asked Martin.

"Just the rest of this room. As you can see, it takes up most of the space already, so there aren't any more rooms on this level. Once we've cleared it, we'll break through the floor and search for the burial chamber."

"You think perhaps it's undisturbed?" Augustus asked.

Martin shook his head sadly. "Unfortunately no. The paucity of the finds so far indicates it was looted in antiquity. The reliefs alone, though, make for a fine discovery."

"Indeed. You'll have tourists snapping pictures here a hundred years from now," the antiquities dealer said.

Sir Russell cleared his throat.

"Well, this is all very interesting, Cavell, but we best get down to business about that theft," the police inspector said.

Martin's eyes brightened. "Ah, we already have identified the culprit, a big buck of a Soudanese foreman named Moustafa. He doesn't suspect we know his game. So let us surprise him, eh? Then we can recover the piece that he stole."

"How do you know it's him?" Russell asked.

"He was caught in the find tent when he shouldn't have been there, and even worse, he was spotted coming out of Monsieur Dupris's tent."

"Sounds like our man. Let's go see your boss and have a talk with this Soudanese fellow."

Martin shook his head as he led them toward a cluster of large tents on a low rise overlooking the excavation. "It's a pity. He was a good foreman and quite bright for a native, but he had a habit of talking back. I can't say I'm surprised it was him."

They went up to the find tent and met the dig director, Pierre Dupris, a tall, spare man in his late forties with a calm and serious demeanor. He sat at a long table examining several broken bits of masonry and taking notes while a young French draftsman sketched the more important pieces. A few native workmen sat in a circle cleaning artifacts nearby. A wink and a nod from Martin told the Englishmen that the large black man directing them was the foreman he had mentioned.

Augustus studied the Soudanese man. He was tall and powerfully built, a hulk of a man, although Augustus got the impression that not an ounce of it was fat. He had an intelligent, open face and seemed entranced with his work.

Augustus's attention then had to shift to the Frenchmen. Augustus was already vaguely acquainted with Dupris from a lecture series the Egyptologist had held in Alexandria the year before. The draftsman he did not know. He was a studious younger man who greeted them with quiet courtesy and immediately went back to work. The four remaining men spoke in French. After the usual pleasantries, they got down to business.

"So, Monsieur Dupris, your assistant says you have discovered the thief," the policeman said in a low voice.

"Indeed we have. It's that fellow over there. Don't look or he might suspect something. Let us continue in French, if you please. The foreman speaks English but no French. We can switch to English for the cross examination."

Augustus glanced at Moustafa and saw he had slowed down his work and appeared to be listening. Augustus wondered if the Soudanese might understand French after all.

Sir Russell nodded. "Before we clap him in irons, can you tell me how you know he's the one?"

Martin answered the question. "We found the missing inscription the day before yesterday. I and the thief were overseeing the workmen as they uncovered it. Quite an odd piece, I must say, with very large writing for some sizeable monument. Our foreman seemed most interested in it for some reason and asked me all sorts of questions about it. I was preoccupied with my work and didn't pay much notice to his behavior. I didn't think until too late that he had been seen on numerous occasions lingering around the find tent when he was not on duty. I should have been suspicious, but I'm afraid neither I nor Monsieur Dupris thought much of it."

"That's true," the dig director said. "He's always been an eager one, and I wrote it off as simple animal curiosity. I didn't realize he had a more sinister motive."

Augustus glanced at Moustafa. The man's work had slowed almost to a halt, and he was obviously eavesdropping. No one else seemed to notice.

At least no one European. One of the other workers said softly in

Arabic, "What's the matter, Moustafa?"

"Quiet, I'm listening," Moustafa whispered back.

"This morning I came in before dawn to get the workmen ready," Martin said, "and I discovered that the piece was missing. It was quite a large piece, and thus I noticed its absence immediately. It had been there the previous evening when I left so it must have been stolen at night."

"Where was it exactly?" Russell asked.

"Sitting just there at the edge of the tent. It was far too big to put on the table."

"If it was so large, why do you say it was carried off?" the police commandant asked.

"It must have been almost a hundred kilos, but that's nothing for such a big fellow. I've seen him lift heavier stones than that without breaking a sweat. Oh, and he was the last to leave last night. Instead of heading back to the outskirts of Cairo where he lives, he was loitering around the village just over the hill. We saw him as we drove back to Cairo. So he was here after we left."

"What did the night watchman say?"

"He has disappeared. No doubt our crooked foreman paid him to walk away."

"Couldn't the watchman have taken it?"

"He wasn't nearly strong enough and showed no interest in our finds."

Augustus glanced at Moustafa, who was glowering at the group of Europeans. When Moustafa caught him looking, the antiquities dealer turned away.

"Something about this doesn't make any sense," Augustus said. "Why would he take an inscription fragment? You have dozens lying around here, most of which are far more portable and easier to conceal. Plus, there are the other artifacts. Surely those would fetch a higher price."

"The better artifacts we lock up or take back to Cairo," Dupris said. "You are correct that some of these hieroglyphic inscriptions are worth more, but you have to familiarize yourself with the African mind. It equates size and weight with value. Just look at the clunky jewelry that they burden their women with, and just look at the size of the women themselves! Grotesque things. Our foreman picked the biggest fragment because his simple mind decided that would be the most valuable."

Augustus didn't look at Moustafa. He knew the expression he'd see.

"What's going on?" the Egyptian worker asked Moustafa in Arabic.

"They're claiming I stole something last night."

"You? Of all people! Besides, you were with us all night at Khayyam's wedding."

"And they're saying I paid Abdul to look the other way."

"Ridiculous. What happened to him anyway?"

"He must have gone back to the Fayyum."

"Without saying goodbye?"

"I guess someone really did pay him to look the other way, but not me."

Augustus focused on the European conversation once more. The police commandant was speaking.

"So your evidence is that he is strong enough to carry it away, he showed interest in the inscribed pieces in general and this one in particular, and that he was here last night. So far, so good. But that's not enough to convict him. We can certainly bring him in for questioning, but it would be best if we had something a bit more solid."

Martin nodded. "When Monsieur Dupris and I passed through the village yesterday evening, I noticed our foreman there. Monsieur Dupris did not. He was at the wheel and focusing on the road. You know how essential that is! I happened to glance in the rearview mirror and noticed the foreman get up from where he was sitting and head back toward the excavation site. You'll notice he's wearing a brand-new kaffiyeh today."

Everyone looked, and Moustafa did, indeed, have a brand-new kaffiyeh wrapped around his head.

Russell nodded. "We'll soon get to the bottom of this. Call him over."

Monsieur Dupris switched to English. "Moustafa, could you come over here a minute please?"

The foreman put on an innocent face. "How may I help, sir?"

Augustus noted that the foreman's English was excellent, almost without an accent.

"Do you know anything about a missing inscription?" Russell asked.

"A missing inscription?" Moustafa looked around. "Something has gone missing?"

"Yes, and Abdul the night watchman has gone missing too," Dupris said.

"He has? I thought he was sick."

"No, he's gone," Dupris snapped, his tone hardening. "As you well know. You paid him to leave while you stole the inscription."

Moustafa narrowed his eyes. "I did not."

"You asked for a raise last week, and I refused. Is this your way of getting back at me?" Dupris asked.

"I asked for a raise because I have a family to support."

"Don't you all. And what about your new kaffiyeh?"

"Are only Europeans allowed to have nice things?"

"It was you! Don't deny it!" Martin said, pointing his bandaged hand at the Soudanese.

Augustus clamped down on Martin's wrist with an iron grip and used his other hand to unwind the bandage. The little archaeologist protested and struggled, but he couldn't come close to matching the Englishman's strength. Martin clenched his hand, but Augustus forced the fingers open to reveal a livid rope burn on the palm.

"An accident with a shovel, eh? More likely the rope slipped when you were tying that stone onto the back of a donkey. It wasn't Moustafa at all. It was you! And you paid Abdul to leave his post and never return."

"What? That's a lie!" the archaeologist sputtered.

Dupris's face darkened. He studied the rope burn and then turned to his assistant.

"Cavell, I know you have gambling debts . . ."

"This is insane! I would never steal from you! It was Moustafa. He's been acting suspiciously. You said so yourself. Didn't you catch him in your tent once?"

Dupris looked uncertain. "That's true."

Augustus turned to the foreman. "I admit I can't explain that. Why did you enter Monsieur Dupris's tent?"

"To study his books on hieroglyphics," Moustafa replied.

Dupris, Martin, and Russell all burst out laughing.

Moustafa snarled and moved toward the table.

Russell whipped out a pistol. "Easy there, boy."

Moustafa gave him a contemptuous look and picked up a fragment containing a cartouche.

"This is the cartouche of the pharaoh Khafre," he said and put it down.

He picked up another fragment and read. "'To the glory of Amun, he riseth in the east, overlooking the lands of . . .' And the inscription breaks off." He put the inscription down and picked up another. "'In the fifth year of the pharaoh's reign, he sent trading boats to Lebanon for cedar, carrying with them gold and . . .' I don't know this word. Can you translate it for me, Monsieur Dupris?"

The Europeans all stared at the foreman, stunned. Dupris blinked, examined the inscription, and replied, "Ah, that's the sign for turquoise."

Moustafa looked surprised. "I thought there were two circles on the upper right register for turquoise."

"Um, no. That's true in New Kingdom hieratic, but this is the older form."

"I see. Thank you for the language lesson, Monsieur Dupris. I wouldn't make such mistakes if I had regular access to books."

All eyes turned to Martin, who blurted out, "So the ape reads hieroglyphics. What of it? All that shows is that he knew what he was stealing!"

"He was with the other workmen at a wedding last night when the theft occurred," Augustus said.

"How could you possibly know that?" Dupris asked.

Moustafa looked equally mystified.

"They were speaking about it while Moustafa eavesdropped on our conversation. He understands French. I suppose no one else here is fluent in Arabic? No? I didn't think so. And before you ask, no, they were not making up an alibi. Your foreman is innocent."

All eyes turned to Martin once more. The little Frenchman slumped.

"Forgive me, Monsieur Dupris. It was my gambling debts, as you say, and a woman in Cairo. My creditors were hounding me, and I had to do something. A collector showed interest in that particular piece and offered me a good price."

Dupris shook his head in disappointment. "Cavell, pack your things and get out."

Moustafa looked from Russell to Dupris to Cavell Martin and then back at the police commandant.

"What? You're not going to arrest him?"

Russell looked to Dupris. "If you don't press charges . . ."

Dupris shook his head. "It's enough that he's ruined. His career is over."

"I'm so sorry, Monsieur Dupris," Martin pleaded. "Since it was a stray find and not associated with the mastaba I didn't think its loss would be so important."

"Oh, but the loss of my honor wasn't important, either, you son of a dog!" Moustafa bellowed. "I have a wife and five children to feed, and you were going to let me rot in prison for your misdeeds!"

Martin shrugged. Moustafa rounded on Dupris.

"And you were going to let the police take me away without a shred of evidence! It was Martin's word against mine, and that was good enough for you!"

Dupris put out his hands in a calming gesture. "There, there, Moustafa. It's all over now. Why don't you go back to work?"

"Work? Work for you? Bah!"

Moustafa threw his hands in the air and stormed off. They watched him go. The foreman made it only about ten yards before he stopped abruptly, nodded as if he had decided something, and spun back to face them.

He then launched into a tirade against Dupris in French of a fluency worthy of a graduate of the Sorbonne.

The content, however, was more worthy of a sailor from Marseilles. For sheer ferocity, variety, and creativity, that seedy French port had probably not heard the like for at least a generation. Indeed, upon hearing it, many a French sailor might repent of his ways and take up missionary work in the Congo.

Everyone stared at him, dumbfounded.

Augustus shook out of it first and glanced at Sir Russell. The policeman could have Moustafa arrested for swearing at an officer, but he looked so shocked it appeared to have slipped his mind. Dupris had gone pale, Cavell Martin was shaking with a mixture of rage and terror, and the Egyptian workmen had made themselves scarce.

Moustafa, after detailing the foulness of Dupris's heritage back for seven generations, finished off his litany with, "I will never work for such an uneducated fool as you ever again! I am too good for the likes of you!"

With that, he stormed off. Augustus followed him, leaving Dupris sputtering incoherently.

Moustafa glanced over his shoulder and saw Augustus catching up to him.

"None of that was meant for you."

"I know."

"Thank you for getting me free."

They continued over the dunes. Behind them, they could hear angry shouting in French.

"Dupris is a fool," Augustus said. "Did you really mean that part about the baboon's backside?"

"I meant every word," Moustafa said, kicking a rock out of his way.

"Why did you hide the fact that you could speak French?"

"It wasn't required for the job, and it was interesting to hear how they speak when they think I can't understand."

"Then you have shown remarkable restraint. I'm amazed you haven't called him the 'illegitimate offspring of an Alexandrian syphilitic whore and a rabid, three-legged mongoose' before today. I'm also impressed that you can read hieroglyphs."

"Better than that fool."

They passed in front of a line of tourists grinning at something. A squawk told Augustus that he and Moustafa had just gotten into someone's picture frame.

"Where did you learn?" Augustus asked.

"French I learned in Khartoum. Hieroglyphs I learned as a night watchman at the French mission there. They had a library, and since no one else was around, I could read to my heart's content. I have been refreshing my learning by sneaking looks at Dupris's books. That flatulent emission of a baboon's rectum was telling the truth about that much. I did sneak into his tent on a number of occasions, but I never carried away anything but knowledge."

"I suppose you need a job."

"You are a master of stating the obvious."

"Steady now, or I might not hire you."

Moustafa looked at him in surprise. "Hire me?"

Augustus produced a card.

"Sir Augustus Wall, dealer in antiquities, 12 Ibn al-Nafis Street," Moustafa read aloud.

"You read English too. Good. I need a guard and an appraiser. I didn't think I'd get both in one man. What did Dupris pay you?"

"Twenty-five piastres a day, and that oozing of a beggar's gangrenous toe still owes me for two weeks."

"I'll pay you double, and you will have free access to my library. An educated employee is a valuable employee. I must warn you that the job may not always be a safe one."

Moustafa waved the card. "This is not the best of neighborhoods in which to store valuable antiquities."

"I wanted to live far from Europeans."

Moustafa cocked his head. "And still sell antiquities to them?"

Augustus ignored the question. "You'll take care of some of the day-to-day contact. I won't be able to avoid dealing with them at some point, though."

"They will not buy from a black face."

"No, so I'll be out front as much as I'm needed. But you must promise not to make up stories about my customers' grandmothers performing unnatural acts on diseased donkeys."

"I will control myself if they show me the proper respect," Moustafa said with a grin.

Augustus grinned back. "That's the best I'm going to get from you, isn't it?"

Moustafa grew serious. "Yes."

The Englishman offered his hand. Moustafa looked at it with surprise for a second and then took it.

"When can I start?"

CHAPTER FOUR

It was Moustafa's first day of work, and Mr. Wall was showing him around the main floor of the house. Moustafa looked at all the artifacts and felt his heart swell at the thought of working in such a place. His new boss had mentioned a library too. He couldn't wait to look through that!

"This is quite a collection you have, Mr. Wall. It is like a room in the Cairo Museum."

"Thank you. I've spent quite a lot of time and money building it up."

The Soudanese stopped in front of the giant statue of the crocodile-headed god.

"Sobek, god of the Nile," he said.

"Yes, he's my favorite among the ancient Egyptian deities."

"Why?"

"Because he's ugly. He's the ugliest god in the ancient world. Oh, and they had some ugly ones—Bes, Anubis, and then all the Babylonian demons, but this one is the ugliest. What a foul creature to look upon. I love him."

Moustafa's gaze rested for a moment on his new boss's mask. The Englishman looked like he was about to say something more and changed his mind. Moustafa went over and examined a shelf full of statuettes. He picked up a few and put them down, nodding appreciatively and making a few comments, then stopped and pulled an ebony statuette of Horus off the shelf. He studied the inscription for a moment, frowning.

"Quite a rare piece considering the style," Augustus said. "It should fetch a fair price from a discerning collector."

"The inscription is perfect," Moustafa observed. "Whoever did this knows his work. Where did you get this?"

"From a wholesaler here in Cairo when I was visiting last year. I'll be teaching you more about the business end of things as we go along."

"Well, you must have visited in the summer or autumn of last year because you couldn't have bought it before then."

"As a matter of fact, you're right. But whatever do you mean?"

Moustafa waggled the statuette in his hand. "Monsieur Dupris uncovered this himself in the last week of the spring excavation of 1918."

"Are you sure?"

Moustafa nodded. "Quite sure. The carving and inscription are identical."

"You mean to say Dupris sold it on the black market? For all his failings, I would have never thought—"

"He did not sell it. It sits in the Institut d'Égypte storage room. This is a forgery."

"A forgery? Nonsense! How can you tell?"

"Everything is the same except for one detail. See this chip on the base? That wasn't on the original, and there was another chip on the thigh that is missing from this one."

Augustus leaned forward and peered at the statuette. "Are you certain?"

Moustafa felt insulted. "Ask Monsieur Dupris if you do not believe me."

***

Augustus decided not to ask Dupris because it would involve an entire trip out to Giza and suffering through a conversation with the archaeologist, so instead he went directly to the Institut d'Égypte. Once there, he came up against the formidable brick wall of Gallic bureaucracy. The objects hadn't yet been cataloged, the institute's director claimed, and thus it was "impossible" for him to show them to "the public." Augustus led the director to believe that Dupris had invited him to examine the artifacts. This failed to make an impression, and Augustus got the hint that he was expected to leave.

The director, of course, would never be so gauche as to say that directly. In fact, he was the very model of courtesy. Augustus enjoyed a delicious cup of coffee, two cigarettes, and half an hour of intellectually stimulating conversation on art and history, and he had achieved precisely nothing.

A casual mention of his Légion d'Honneur changed all that. The director became effusive, all doors were thrown open, and within five minutes Augustus was examining the statuette of Horus.

One look told Augustus his new assistant had been correct. The chip on the statuette's thigh was exactly where Moustafa had said it was, and there was no damage to the base like there was on his own statuette.

His next stop was the antiquities wholesaler who had sold him the ebony Horus. At the expense of a few minor purchases, he was able to get the name and address of the individual who had sold the wholesaler the statuette.

Augustus was surprised to learn it was a woman, and a Turkish woman at that. He wrote her a short note.

Dear Mrs. Zehra Hanzade,

Allow me to introduce myself. I am Sir Augustus Wall, antiquities dealer, lately of Alexandria. I recently purchased an ebony statuette of Horus from Abdul Rahman, and I must commend you on the brilliance of the forgery. It is exact in virtually all particulars to the statuette excavated by Pierre Dupris in his spring field season of 1918. I am curious as to why you would make the damage to the figure in different spots than the original. Considering that it is otherwise all but identical, such an obvious mistake must have been deliberate, and I am curious as to why it was done.

Please rest assured that I will not expose you. In fact, I might become a regular customer of your brilliantly executed knockoffs. Please contact me at your earliest convenience so that we may discuss terms.

Kindest regards,
Sir Augustus Wall

***

Madame's earliest convenience turned out to be the very next day. A liveried Circassian servant came to the house on Ibn al-Nafis Street and delivered Zehra Hanzade's business card embossed in gold. It gave her address in French, Turkish, Arabic, and English in that order. The servant informed him that he would be welcome any time after lunch. Augustus gave him a generous tip and told him to inform the lady that he would be there at five.

The Hanzade mansion stood on a leafy side street lined with French colonial homes half hidden by tall walls enclosing lush gardens. Only the upper balconies and treetops were visible above the line of gleaming brass spikes protecting the top of the wall from intruders. A Turkish servant showed him in and led him through a marble front hall adorned with Classical statues. After passing along a corridor lined with tastefully selected French and Dutch landscapes, they entered a sitting room.

Zehra Hanzade was a curvaceous Turkish beauty of middle age, dressed in a loose green caftan embroidered in gold thread. She had olive skin, a heart-shaped face framed by flowing black ringlets, and the most lustrous eyes Augustus had ever seen. Gold bangles clattered on her wrists as she rose to shake his hand. Her fingers sparkled with a small fortune in gemstones. She greeted Augustus with perfect French and did neither of the two things that new acquaintances almost invariably did to anger him—she neither avoided looking at his mask nor stared at it. Instead her soft brown eyes took it in with a mixture of regret and acceptance and then moved to meet his eye.

Sir Thomas Russell, for all his annoying traits, was the only other person he'd met in Cairo who had passed that particular test. When Russell had first met Augustus, he'd looked at his mask without trying to hide his doing so and asked, "What regiment?"

"Oxfordshire and Buckinghamshire Light Infantry," Augustus had replied.

"I was in the Royal Horse Guards myself, not that we got much riding in that war. A damned cock-up from start to finish. Hated every minute of it."

And that had been that.

His hostess offered him a gilded Louis XIV chair while she reclined opposite him on a divan inlaid with mother-of-pearl in the Ottoman style, kicking off her slippers and curling up on the divan in a manner that was shockingly casual yet completely unaffected. Augustus caught himself staring at her toes, which were perfect, and switched to staring into her eyes, which were equally perfect. Ordinary women in the East did not look a man in the eye, but it was already obvious that this was no ordinary woman.

"I'll have my servant bring some tea. Have you had Turkish-style tea?"

"Many times. I quite enjoy it."

"Cigarette?" she offered. "Most English gentlemen prefer Woodbines, isn't that correct?"

An unopened packet of the English cigarettes sat on the table between them.

Augustus thanked her and lit one, while she took a drag from a *sheesha* standing near the divan. The smell of pungent Turkish tobacco filled the room, almost blotting out the milder scent of the British blend.

Conversation lapsed into a comfortable silence until tea came. Once the servant had left again, Zehra Hanzade asked, "You are new to Cairo, yes?"

"I moved here only last month and lived at Shepheard's Hotel until I could find a house."

"Yes, the one on Ibn al-Nafis Street. A perfect example of the kind of Cairene architecture that is sadly no longer being built. If I collected buildings like I collect art, I would have bought it myself. Do your wife and children live here as well?"

"I never married."

"Surely a man of your standing must have had many interested women."

"I had a fiancée before the war. After the war, she made her excuses."

Zehra Hanzade clucked her tongue. "Then she is unworthy of you." She took a puff from her *sheesha*, and the bubbling of the water seemed to emphasize her point.

Augustus didn't reply. His hostess treated him to a warm smile. "My husband and I got a great deal of amusement from your letter. You are wonderfully direct for an Englishman. It was almost American in its directness."

"Now let's not get off on the wrong foot, Mrs. Hanzade."

She laughed in clear, bright tones that convinced Augustus that he'd like to hear that laugh as often as possible. He tried to ignore the mention of the husband.

"Oh, I don't mean to imply you are an American. You are too much a man of the world. And do call me Zehra. I will call you Augustus. That is more suitable between good friends, don't you think? And I do think we will be wonderful friends."

"Whatever you wish, Zehra," he replied, and meant it.

"Excellent. That makes me so happy. So may I ask why you wish to buy artifacts you know are forgeries when you have a steady supply of real ones?"

"To sell to the tourists who are less interested in ancient art than they are in impressing their friends back home. I see no reason why irreplaceable pieces of ancient history should end up in the hands of fools."

Zehra laughed again.

"Ah, an idealist! Only the wealthy can afford to be idealists. I, too, am wealthy, but I never took up the habit." Zehra gave Augustus a level stare. "I have enough vices."

He held her gaze for a moment, cleared his throat, and asked, "Can you make artifacts to order?"

"Of course. You need to speak with Suleiman, my husband. After you have spoken with him, we will have another tea and discuss terms."

Augustus's hostess clapped her hands to summon a servant, who led him out the back door into a spacious garden enclosed by a high stone wall. The back half of the garden was taken up by a large wooden building. The sound of a chisel on stone echoed from within.

The servant stopped at the entrance, and Augustus entered through an open sliding door a full eight feet tall.

The first thing he noticed was a strong smell of burning hemp.

The second thing he noticed was a treasure trove of Egyptian art. Within the interior, he beheld a collection to match his own—statues and sarcophagi, weapons and amulets. The shed contained every kind of artifact imaginable. Some of the statues were almost monumental in size, explaining why the shed had such a high door. Augustus peered around the dim interior, made dimmer by a haze of pungent smoke.

At the center of the room stood a thin man of middle age in a simple white jellaba and skullcap, whose features showed a mixture of Turkish and Egyptian ancestry. He was using a small chisel to finish the cartouche on a three-foot alabaster statue of Ramesses V sitting on a stone pedestal.

"Well done," Augustus said. "If I hadn't seen you carving it, I would have sworn it was genuine XX Dynasty."

Suleiman turned and fixed a pair of bloodshot eyes on him. He bowed and put his hand to his heart.

"You must be the Englishman. My wife said to expect you. She says you are a connoisseur of art? Then you are a man after my own heart, for I am an artist."

"You are indeed," Augustus replied, stepping farther into the shed and looking around.

"Welcome to my humble studio. If you see anything you like, I will give you a very good price."

"This is very nice," Wall said, running a hand along the alabaster statue of the pharaoh Suleiman was working on.

"This is not for sale yet. It's not finished."

With that, Suleiman pushed it off the pedestal. It landed on the stone floor with a crash. Augustus leaped back. Suleiman picked up a sledgehammer and started hitting it as hard as he could.

"What are you doing?" Augustus shouted.

"I am making it very old."

"Stop! Why are you destroying a work of art?" Augustus demanded as a piece of the shoulder cracked off and clattered several feet across the floor. Several smaller chips flew off too, one stinging Augustus's hand as it struck him.

"What is the purpose of art if not to make money?" Suleiman asked as he swung the sledgehammer down again. "If it is in perfect condition, no one will believe it is ancient."

Suleiman mopped his brow and dropped the sledgehammer with a thud. The statue at his feet was now marked with several cracks and chips.

"Next I need to rub it with sand for some hours to abrade the surface, especially where I broke it. That way it will look like it has been in the desert for a long time," Suleiman said with obvious pride.

Augustus shook his head. "It seems a shame."

"There is no shame in creating a perfect forgery. Everyone is happy. My family and I get our money, the dealers like you get your money, and someone thinks they have purchased a piece of history."

"Unless someone figures out you're passing fakes."

Suleiman went over to a corner where a lit hookah stood in front of a stool. He set out a second stool.

"Please join me for a smoke. No? It is better than alcohol, which the Holy Koran forbids."

"I seem to recall a passage in the Koran forbidding deception."

Suleiman shook his head and took a toke from the hookah. "I never say that something is ancient. I only say that it is a statue of Ramesses or a faience ushabti in the style of the New Kingdom. I never say it is actually old."

Augustus decided not to argue the point. "Aren't you worried that people will discover your secret like I have?"

"You are the first," Suleiman said, then took a puff of his hookah. The water pipe bubbled.

"Well, I have to admit that was sheer bad luck on your part. You imitated an artifact discovered by Pierre Dupris last year."

Suleiman nodded. "One of my assistants works as one of his laborers. I visited him, posing as his brother, and was present when the statuette was discovered. A most excellent piece."

"You slipped, though. You put the chips and cracks in the wrong place."

Suleiman took another puff of his hookah and replied, "I did nothing of the kind. I have a pattern for how I damage my work so that I can always tell if a piece was made by my own hand or if it is genuine. Otherwise I might fool even myself."

"If I hadn't seen you at work, I would have thought that a boast. But since I have seen, I can only congratulate you on your artistry," Augustus said with a laugh. The smoke was making him feel light-headed.

Suleiman beamed a smile. "Most kind of you to say so. Sir Wall, I think we shall do some wonderful business together."

***

Faisal crept along the narrow space behind the market stalls, ignoring the rotting produce that squished under his hands and knees. He was almost there. A sack of flour leaned against the wall out of sight behind a heap of others. The shopkeeper wouldn't know it was gone until he cleaned up for the night.

The boy licked his lips in anticipation. He'd keep half to make into flatbread tonight on a hot plate over an open fire, and the other half he would sell so he could buy some sugar cane.

A strong hand grabbed him and yanked him to his feet. At first he thought the shopkeeper had caught him, but then he discovered it was someone else.

Someone far worse.

Hassan hauled him into a doorway. Passersby glanced in their direction and continued on, suddenly eager to mind their own business.

The street thug gave Faisal a slap upside the head.

"You warned him, you little goat turd!"

"I didn't know it was you!"

"Liar! I should cut you open and hang you with your own entrails."

Hassan pulled out a knife and gave Faisal a wicked grin.

"You didn't think I had another knife, did you? I have lots of knives, enough to cut you into mincemeat."

Hassan moved so he blocked Faisal from view of the street and lowered the blade.

"I told him about your cousins. I saved your life!" Faisal pleaded.

Hassan's hand went up to the bandage on his shoulder. "I will kill him for insulting me, but first I want to see what's in his house. You must get me inside if you want to live."

"How?"

"Think of a way," Hassan said, shoving the boy again so he jammed his back against the doorknob. Faisal hissed in pain. "Pretend to be his friend. You warned him about the attack, after all, you stupid little bastard."

"I am not a bastard."

Hassan laughed. "Oh, you think your mother and father were married? Your father was a drunk, and your mother was a whore."

"She was not!" Faisal wailed.

"Shut up. Get inside that house somehow."

"No."

Hassan grabbed him by the neck.

"I mean, I can't!" Faisal managed to choke out. "He'll never let me in."

Hassan considered. "No, I suppose not. Why would he want you in there dirtying up his nice clean European house with your dirty little goat turd feet? You'll have to sneak in. You can do that. Despite being a stupid little bastard, you are a good housebreaker. You are good climber and can fit through places others can't. I know you've done it before, so don't pretend you haven't."

"What if there's no way in?"

"There is. When the house was still empty, we got onto the roof. I knew the day would come when the house would be occupied again, and I wanted to know how to get in. There's a window slat that you can fit through. If you go to the alley behind the house, you can climb up a drain that takes you to the roof."

"It's three stories high!"

"Climb that drainpipe or I'll slit your useless little throat. I noticed he has no womenfolk. He doesn't even have any servants. It will be easy to break in when he is out. No, wait. I have a better plan. You sneak in late at night when he is sleeping and open the door for us. Then we will enter, kill him quietly, and take whatever we find."

Faisal hesitated, looked at the keen edge of Hassan's knife, and gulped.

"When do you want me to go in?"

"Tonight, after the neighborhood watchman passes by calling midnight. We'll be waiting and watching the front door. Now get out of my sight."

Hassan shoved Faisal into the street. The boy turned around.

"My mother was not a whore! She was an honorable woman who died giving birth to me!"

Hassan laughed. "Is that what your drunkard of a father told you? What a joke! She was a whore who left you as soon as she dropped you in the dust. Everyone got a taste of her. I was smaller than you, and even I got a taste!"

"That's not true!" Faisal shouted, and started to cry.

"Aw, look at the little whore's son crying like a baby!" Hassan's words rang in Faisal's ears as he ran off. "Don't forget our appointment tonight, or I'll be selling your meat to the butcher in the morning!"

CHAPTER FIVE

The visitor came unannounced, and he came after hours. Augustus had just let Moustafa off for the night when he heard a knock on the door. Thinking his new employee had forgotten something, he answered.

Instead of the hulking Soudanese, he faced a small, slender European. The man had a deeply lined face, bright blue eyes, and full lips. He looked to be in his fifties or sixties, pale and somewhat sickly. The man wore a fine suit and cravat. A gold ring with a Roman intaglio adorned his finger, and his cuff links were of purest ebony. Augustus noticed a lump in the side pocket that looked suspiciously like a gun. The man's eyes widened at the sight of Augustus's mask. Then he remembered his manners, bowed politely, and did not look Augustus in the face again.

"How may I help you?" the antiquities dealer asked stiffly.

"Allow me to introduce myself," the man said in English with a German accent, "My name is Dieter Neumann, a collector of antiquities. I know of your reputation in Alexandria and was overjoyed to hear you have moved your business to Cairo. I am most anxious to see your collection."

"How did you find me? We aren't open for business yet."

Herr Neumann inclined his head as if he expected this question.

"The circle of reputable antiquities dealers is a small one, Sir Wall. News travels quickly. I apologize for not waiting until your grand opening, but I am a most selective collector and wanted to see your stock before the general public is allowed in."

Augustus considered for a moment, then opened the door farther and invited the German inside.

"Most kind of you. Ah!"

Neumann's eyes lit up with unaffected joy as he beheld Augustus's collection. He went first to a shelf full of various fragments of inscriptions and examined them closely. After a few minutes, he shook his head and turned away in obvious disappointment before moving to a set of well-preserved alabaster canopic jars.

"These are very fine."

"I saw you studying the inscriptions. Are you looking for anything in particular?"

"Um, no. But these canopic jars would grace any collection. How much can I offer you for them? I can pay in British pounds. To carry such an amount in Egyptian pounds would require a suitcase."

Augustus named a figure and was surprised when Neumann agreed without haggling.

"I'm glad to do business with you. I will draw the money from my bank tomorrow and return with a couple of workmen to pick up the pieces."

"I'll have them packed and ready."

The man paused and studied the room.

"This is a fine old house. Do you know the date of construction?"

"No. In fact, no one seems to. I would say that it's perhaps early Ottoman."

"Perhaps," the German mused, "perhaps much older. The carving on the doorjamb, for example, although much eroded, looks to be from the time of the Bahri Dynasty, as does the mosque down the street."

"My specialty is more ancient than medieval."

"I see. Um, may I ask to use the restroom? Ah, um, a bit of indigestion. The local cuisine doesn't agree with me."

"You'll find it through the back hall on your left."

"Most kind, thank you." The little man bowed and moved away.

Augustus watched him go, feeling slightly uneasy. There was something strange about this fellow. He had seemed fascinated by the inscriptions and barely gave anything else a glance before deciding to buy the canopic jars almost at random. Then there was his unusual interest in the house. While Augustus at first had thought nothing of the man carrying a gun—a wise move in some parts of Cairo, after all—that combined with his behavior made him think twice.

Courtesy made him hesitate. This man had just offered a considerable sum for the canopic jars. Should he really interrupt him while he was on the loo with a case of Sultan's Revenge? He seemed an odd little fellow, and perhaps it was only that which made him appear suspicious.

Augustus couldn't shake a feeling of rising unease, however, and he had long since learned to trust his instincts. He walked to the doorway through which the man had disappeared, hesitated a final time, and then made his way to the water closet at the end of the hall, right next to a narrow spiral flight of servants' stairs.

The washroom door was closed, and he could see through the crack at the bottom of the door that the light was on. Quietly he moved up to the doorway and placed an ear against it. No sound came from within. He did, however, hear a faint click come from up the stairs. Augustus paused. The sound did not repeat.

Narrowing his eyes and balling his hands into fists, Augustus tiptoed to the bottom of the stairs and peered upward. He had left a light on upstairs, but he could see no one in the narrow slice of the upstairs room visible from his vantage point. Another sound caught his ears, a faint scuff, as if of a shoe on the carpet he had placed in the room immediately above him.

Augustus crept up the spiral staircase. It was of stone, and he had to take care that the hard soles of his shoes did not make any sound that could give him away.

As he ascended and turned the corner, the room upstairs came into view through the arched doorway. This was one of his spare rooms, given over to a bookshelf of some of his lesser-used volumes and various pieces of drafting equipment. As Augustus suspected, Herr Neumann was in the room, but he seemed uninterested in any of the objects within.

Instead, he was shining a small but powerful electric torch through some cracks in the masonry.

Mystified, Augustus pulled back until he was all but hidden from view and watched as his visitor stared into the crack between two large stones, shook his head, and moved to another. At this one he seemed to find something more to his interest. His eyes widened, and his lips pulled back in a toothy grin. The man nodded and glanced at the stairway. Augustus ducked back out of sight. When he looked again, Neumann had crossed the room to a third crack between the stones and was shining his light in there. Once again he grinned.

Nodding with evident satisfaction, he turned off his torch and put it in his pocket. Augustus noted it was a different pocket than the one where he had noticed a bulge he had interpreted as a gun. That pocket remained filled with something else. He had not mistaken the torch for a pistol.

Augustus himself was unarmed. His own pistol lay in the drawer by his bed, and his other weapons were in a different room at the other end of the house. He had to take care.

Guessing that Neumann would come back downstairs since his pretense of going to the washroom would soon run out of time, Augustus tiptoed down the staircase and moved to one side of the doorway at its bottom.

An instant later, he heard Neumann walking down the steps.

As soon as his figure appeared in the doorway, Augustus grabbed his arm and twisted it behind his back.

"Ow! Help! Oh, it's you. What are you doing? Unhand me!"

Augustus pinned Neumann against the wall, slapped aside his other hand as it reached for his pocket, and put his own hand inside it. He pulled out a small automatic and pocketed it.

"Robbery! The police will hear of this!" Neumann bawled.

"The police commandant is a personal friend, and he'll be very interested to know what you were doing sneaking around my house."

"Nothing! I merely am an admirer of medieval Cairene architecture. This is quite an old house, one of the oldest private dwellings I've seen."

"If you wanted a tour, you could have asked for one. Instead you sneaked off and looked through the cracks in the masonry. Why?"

Neumann's cheek was pressed against the wall, his arm twisted painfully behind him, and yet he relaxed, his face taking on a confident air.

"Do you read German, Sir Wall?"

"I do. What of it?"

"Since you are so fond of rifling through other people's pockets, how about you take my wallet from my left pants pocket and examine its contents?"

Curious, Augustus did as the man suggested. Flipping open the wallet, he saw an identity card that named the bearer as a member of the German diplomatic corps.

THE CASE OF THE PURLOINED PYRAMID

Neumann grinned. "If you do not wish to be at the center of an international incident, I suggest you unhand me. Despite the recent misunderstanding between our two nations, my diplomatic immunity still holds, and molesting me in this fashion could get you into very deep trouble with the law, no matter how high your connections."

Augustus snarled and let the man go.

"Get out of my house," he ordered, shoving Neumann down the hallway.

Neumann chuckled and extended a hand. "My pistol, please?"

"Don't push your luck."

Neumann grinned over his shoulder at Augustus and walked into the front room. He glanced at the canopic jars.

"You really do have excellent taste, Sir Wall. A pity I won't be buying those."

"I wouldn't sell them to you for all the tea in China."

"That will be ours too one day," Neumann murmured, and strolled out the door.

Once he was gone, Augustus locked the door and paced back and forth, deep in thought.

What could he do? Should he call on Sir Russell and tell him what happened? No, that might make matters worse. Besides, what could he tell him? That an eccentric diplomat had been examining the cracks in his masonry? While that was odd and more than a little suspicious, it wasn't illegal, while his manhandling of Neumann constituted assault. Then there was the little matter of stealing his gun. No, he couldn't go to the police.

Just what was so interesting about those cracks, after all?

Augustus retrieved his own torch and peered through the same cracks Neumann had. He saw nothing but dust and white limestone. He took a ruler and poked around a bit, but could find no hidden objects.

Shrugging his shoulders, he got back to work. He'd check on Neumann and put out feelers with the people he knew.

He stopped what he was doing. What people? He had virtually no friends in this city and had refused all invitations forthcoming to a new member of the cultured set of British Cairo.

"And I thought I'd find some peace here," Augustus grumbled, and got back to work.

49

***

That night, a small shadow slipped into the alley behind Augustus Wall's home. Padding through the refuse on bare feet, the shadow moved silently to a drainpipe on the back wall. The figure looked around, cocked an ear, and began to ascend.

Faisal climbed quickly, silently, and with an experience and confidence beyond his brief years. The pipe ran up to a ledge that he could edge along to a window. It was locked, as he had suspected, but the stone frame made for a good handhold and foothold to ascend to another ledge, and then another windowsill.

Within a minute, he had climbed over the lip of the rooftop terrace wall and dropped silently onto the tile. He peered around, aided by the light of a gibbous moon. Cairo's rooftops were all more or less the same, although this was bigger than most. A few low benches stood to one side, covered by a trellis that in a normal home would have been interlaced with vines and surrounded by potted plants to give shade and cool breezes to the family. But this house had been abandoned for years, and the pots were all cracked, and the dry desert wind had blown the last shriveled vine away long ago.

On the other side of the roof stood a small shed, which no doubt held nothing of value. Anything of worth the family had left behind up here would have been stolen long ago. Next to the shed, a string still hung suspended between a pair of poles on which to hang laundry.

An open central area looked down on the courtyard. Moonlight shone on a fountain, the burbling water gleaming faintly. All the interior windows were shut and dark.

Of real interest was a raised area on the other side of the roof. It sloped up and had a row of windows facing the north, the direction of the prevailing winds. Below, Faisal knew, would be the main sitting room. These windows brought the breeze into the house.

As the night was warm but not hot, only one was open. That was all Faisal needed. He lifted himself up on the sill and peered down. The house was dark and silent within. The sitting room had a divan and a few chairs, plus some books scattered here and there.

Faisal was twelve and small for his age. Life on the street had left him skinny but with a wiry strength, yet even so, he had trouble forcing himself through that narrow opening. Gritting his teeth and trying not to make any noise, he managed to worm his way through feet first, keeping a tight grip on the windowsill.

Once through, he held there for a moment to catch his breath and then swung himself over to grab the lip of an arched doorway between the sitting room and a hallway. He was about to drop down when he noticed the stone was old and had easy holds for his fingers and toes along the side of the arch. Good. That meant he could climb up again if he wished. He could come and go through this house as he pleased.

Once at the bottom, he paused. Jinn often took up residence in abandoned houses. Had the sheikh who had cleared out the snakes also cleared out the jinn?

Faisal peered into the shadows, his eyes going wide and his heart beating fast as he imagined what might lurk in them. Jinn did not affect Europeans. Everybody knew that. The English and the French dug up the ancient places without harm and even kept the wrapped bodies of pharaohs in their houses. What if this house contained such things? It would be crawling with jinn!

He should say a prayer to keep them away, if only he knew any. Osman ibn Akbar had tried to teach him, but he had never listened to the old beggar. Faisal tried to remember what the adults had said. But they were all day-to-day things, nothing especially to keep away spirits.

No, the sheikh must have gotten rid of them, he tried to reassure himself as he walked through empty, darkened rooms, looking fretfully at every corner. Besides the sitting room, it appeared this entire floor was abandoned. The jinn liked abandoned places.

But since the sheikh knew he was working for a European, would he have bothered? Wouldn't he have left the jinn in the Englishman's house, where they could do no harm, so they wouldn't fly to another home and find some Muslims to bother?

Faisal found the staircase leading down to the next floor and stopped. What was he doing here anyway? Hassan and his cousins waited outside, and if he didn't go down to the ground floor and open the front door for them, they'd skin him alive. But he didn't want the Englishman to get killed. When Hassan's gang set upon them, the Englishman's first instinct had been to protect him. No one ever did that for him. No one ever did anything for him. How could he betray the Englishman?

No, he wouldn't betray him. He'd wake the Englishman up and tell him everything. Maybe the man could get the colonial police to arrest Hassan and his cousins. Foreigners could get anybody arrested with a few words. The Englishman hadn't done it at first because he thought Hassan would leave him alone. Now that that was obviously not going to work, the only thing to do was to go to the police. Well, the Englishman could go to the police. He wouldn't dare go himself. They'd just beat him and send him on his way.

Faisal moved down the stairs to the next floor. This one, at least, had furniture. The barren rooms upstairs had frightened him. These rooms gave him a little more confidence because they looked lived in. The Englishman was brave. Perhaps he had scared the jinn away.

A low snoring led him to the right room. A few thin rays of moonlight shone through the slats in the window to illuminate the bedroom, with an open door leading to a bathroom beyond. The Englishman was barely visible as a dark lump on the bed. Moonlight gleamed on his strange mask and a glass bottle sitting on the nightstand.

A half-forgotten scent tickled Faisal's nostrils. He padded over to the bottle and sniffed, then wrinkled his nose in disgust.

Alcohol. That was the one thing he remembered about his father—the stench of alcohol, usually followed by a slap. That had been years ago, before his father had disappeared, either dead in a gutter or in prison or simply gone. It didn't matter. Faisal didn't miss him.

Faisal put his hands on his hips and glared at the dark form in the bed. It would serve the Englishman right to get murdered by Hassan and his crew, the drunkard. All he had to do was go down and unlock the door. They had even promised him a cut of the take.

As soon as he thought it, Faisal felt guilty. He knew he couldn't do it. The Englishman had tried to protect him.

"Psst, Englishman," Faisal whispered.

He looked around nervously, worried that the jinn might hear. He noticed the cane the Englishman had used to prick Hassan leaning against one wall and grinned. That had been a good trick, pulling a sword out of a cane! Hassan had looked like a frightened monkey! That got Faisal giggling. He had giggled all day about it.

"Hey, Englishman, wake up," he said, louder this time.

The man didn't move. His snoring continued uninterrupted.

Faisal scratched his head. Frustrated, he nudged the man, taking care not to look at his face. No response. He nudged him harder.

Shaking his head in frustration, he looked back at the bottle. How much did he drink? Was he completely senseless?

The boy squinted in the dim light. Something else sat on the nightstand. He picked it up and saw it was a little tin box. Inside he found a stick of dark material like kohl. He sniffed it, and it didn't smell like anything he had ever smelled before. It was sticky and gave a little when he pressed it between his finger and thumb. With a shrug, he put it back down and picked up the bottle. To his surprise, he found it nearly full. Had the Englishman gotten so drunk on so little? His father had been able to drain a bottle twice this size, but his father had been a giant, a monster of a man. No normal man could expect to match him when it came to drinking.

Faisal moved over to the bathroom, poured the contents of the bottle down the sink, and replaced it on the nightstand.

"Drinking is a sin, you silly Englishman. Even I know that. Now wake up!"

Faisal thumped him on the shoulder. The man continued to snore.

Raising his hands in exasperation, Faisal left the room. He'd just have to hide from Hassan tonight and warn the Englishman tomorrow.

Normally he slept in a shack he and some of the other boys had made in an alley. It stank of cat's piss and garbage, but with everyone crammed in there, it kept fairly warm even on the coldest nights. The problem was that Hassan knew of it and would search for him there.

Better to go to his secret hiding place, the front entrance of the mosque of Sultan Hassan. The dead Hassan would protect him from the living one! The huge arched doorway gave shelter from the wind. Many beggars slept there, and the imam didn't mind as long as they cleared out before dawn prayer, when hundreds of students from the four schools of Sunni Islam came to make their peace with God before starting their lessons. Faisal would have to get up even earlier than that in order to lead Osman ibn Akbar to prayer at the mosque on Ibn al-Nafis Street. The blind man usually got some bread and a coin or two every morning from the other worshippers and shared some of his food with Faisal. He'd have to take care that Hassan didn't see him, but the son of a dog usually slept late. If Faisal left right after he got some bread from Osman ibn Akbar, he should be able to warn the Englishman before Hassan showed up.

Then a thought came to him, a wonderful thought. The Englishman had promised to pay him if Faisal saved his life again. Didn't leaving the house without opening it to Hassan and his cutthroats count as saving his life? He deserved a reward!

Rubbing his hands with glee, he began to search the house. The jinn were all forgotten as he rummaged around the rooms. The bedroom and another room beside it were filled with objects that might be of value. Most would be hard for him to sell, though, like books and European clothes. Everyone would know they had been stolen. Faisal saw some strange things too, like a box with a circular plate attached to the top and a big cone sticking up next to it. He opened a leather case and found two tubes connected by a metal bar. The tubes had glass on either end.

Best not to take those. He didn't even know what they were worth. Faisal needed to find something he could sell easily or use for himself.

He hadn't looked downstairs yet. Perhaps he should start there and work his way up.

Faisal went downstairs and discovered a hallway leading to a large, dark room. The size of it and the near complete darkness made him pause. The thoughts of all the jinn hiding in the shadows came back to him. His heart started beating fast again, but he summoned up his courage and tiptoed in.

Faisal shivered and looked around him. The shelves along the walls had strange shapes on them. In the middle of the room were more strange shapes. He couldn't make anything out. Faisal felt an urge to run. What if one of those shapes moved?

Some light would harden his courage. Since the Englishman obviously wouldn't wake until tomorrow, Faisal felt confident enough to pull the stub of a candle out of his pocket, strike a match, and light it.

The first thing he saw was a huge man with a crocodile head leering down at him.

Faisal screamed and fled the room, and screamed again as the candle blew out in his hand. He raced up the stairs and into the Englishman's room.

"Wake up! Wake up! The jinn are going to kill us!" he shouted as he pounded his little fists against the man's back.

The Englishman muttered something in his sleep and turned over. A shaft of moonlight illuminated the terrible wound on his face. Faisal screamed for a third time and fled the room, streaking upstairs, scrambling up the archway, and forcing himself through the narrow opening, not caring that he ripped his jellaba and scraped both knees.

Within moments, he scampered down the side of the building and ran off into the night.

CHAPTER SIX

Moustafa Ghani El Souwaim could not believe his good fortune. It had been a long journey from his village in the Soudan to this wonderful private library in an Englishman's house in Cairo. Born the third son in a respectable family, Moustafa had experienced little of the suffering growing up that so many of his countrymen had. But even so, his options had been limited and uninteresting. His eldest brother had inherited the land. With the little money left over, his father had been able to buy and stock a market stall in the village for his second brother and provide dowries to his two older sisters. That left Moustafa with nothing other than the choice of which brother to work for.

Moustafa had taken a different choice than had been expected of him—at the age of sixteen, he had broken his parents' heart, and his own, by leaving his village. It was the first of many untraditional choices, and making untraditional choices had become his habit.

When he told them of his decision, his mother wailed and covered herself in dust as if she were mourning by his grave. His brothers tried to dissuade him. His father got angry and then burst into tears. Moustafa cried too, because he knew he might never come back, and even if he did someday, so much would have changed in his absence. Despite all this grief, his resolution never faltered. He knew there was something else out there beyond the palm trees and herds of sheep and the cluster of mud and thatch huts that made up his village, and he wanted to see what it was.

For a year, he worked as a porter loading goods onto the boats heading up the Nile. Once he saved some money, he found work on a boat heading to Khartoum, where he got odd jobs and lived hand to mouth before having his first stroke of luck. A foreigner standing by the riverfront picked out the strongest of the young men from Moustafa's work team and hired them for a strange job—to go into the desert where there were some old ruins and dig them up.

Moustafa didn't understand what it was all about, but this man, who turned out to be the famous English archaeologist Somers Clarke, paid well, and so Moustafa was happy with the work. Soon they were uncovering statues and stones with strange rows of pictures carved on them. Mr. Clarke seemed very happy with the result. Mr. Clarke spoke Arabic, and one day Moustafa plucked up the courage to ask why they were digging in the ground where the pagans had once lived.

What Mr. Clarke said in reply changed his life.

"Once there was a great civilization here, the greatest in the ancient world. You have heard of the pyramids of Egypt to the north, yes?"

Moustafa nodded. He had heard of them but didn't really know anything about them.

"Well, the people here at one time ruled over the land of the pyramids."

That impressed Moustafa greatly, because in all their wars, the Soudanese had never conquered the Egyptians.

"So who were these people? Where did they go?"

Mr. Clarke laughed. "Why, they're *you*, Moustafa! They're your ancestors."

Moustafa thought Mr. Clarke was teasing him and got angry. He was careful not to show his anger, though, because his job paid well. Instead he didn't say a word and got back to work.

Two days later, they found the statue.

It was Moustafa's own shovel that clunked down on something hard in the sand. He already knew from experience that sometimes Mr. Clarke gave a bonus to men who discovered something he liked, so he eagerly brushed away the sand . . . and uncovered the face of a Nubian pharaoh.

If Moustafa lived to be a hundred, he knew he would never forget that moment.

The statue was hewn from black basalt. It lay on its back, and its powerful face looked up at him with features much like his own. Seventeen-year-old Moustafa stared down at the face of a man who could have come from his village, and yet it was the face of a king, a king from an ancient kingdom that Mr. Clarke said had once ruled over Egypt.

He later learned that the statue depicted the great Pharaoh Taharqa of the XXV Dynasty. It was this dynasty that moved northward to occupy Egypt, but it was not the first or last great dynasty of the Soudan. Other pharaohs had built great cities and pyramids of their own to rival the Egyptians. He learned all this and much more, because after he uncovered the statue, he bombarded Mr. Clarke with questions. At every opportunity, he would find an excuse to work by his boss's side and find out more about this civilization. He also began to ask about the sketches Mr. Clarke made and what he wrote in the notebooks he always carried around.

Some of the older workmen warned Moustafa that Mr. Clarke would get annoyed with all this pestering, but in fact, the Englishman found it amusing. He took on Moustafa as his personal servant.

Moustafa did everything he could to make himself invaluable to Mr. Clarke. He worked from right after the dawn prayers to well after dark, cleaning Mr. Clarke's rooms, taking care of the artifacts, making the tea, everything. Within a few months, he could carry on a conversation in English and had learned the names of all the principle types of artifacts and their uses in ancient times.

Mr. Clarke was amazed by Moustafa's ability with languages and started teaching him French as well. That, too, Moustafa picked up with startling rapidity. Mr. Clarke began to bring his friends over to show off his prize servant, betting them that Moustafa couldn't speak English, French, and discuss Egyptology all at the same time. So Moustafa would stand in the middle of Mr. Clarke's drawing room while the European men sat around and fired questions at him about Egyptology in English and French.

Mr. Clarke always won these bets. Mr. Clarke did not share his winnings with Moustafa.

Moustafa knew this was unjust, but he didn't mind so much, because Mr. Clarke shared something far more valuable than money—he shared knowledge.

It didn't last. After another year, Mr. Clarke returned to England and dismissed all his servants. Moustafa begged to go with him, but Mr. Clarke refused with a derisive chuckle. He paid Moustafa the last of his wages and left with a curt goodbye. The young Soudanese man was quite sure that the famous English archaeologist had forgotten all about him by the time he boarded the train for Cairo.

Now without a job, Moustafa went from door to door in Khartoum's European quarter, calling on the gentlemen he had so impressed at Mr. Clarke's dinner parties. The house servants turned him away. The one time he managed to catch a European on his way out the door the man claimed never to have met him before.

Then Moustafa remembered that one of Mr. Clarke's friends was director of the French Institute. Moustafa squatted in the shade of a palm tree all day waiting for the man to come out of his office.

When he did, he introduced himself in his best French and asked for a job. The man remembered him and gave him a job as a night watchman. Moustafa thought this beneath him, but at least he would eat.

And then he discovered an unexpected bonus to his work. The French Institute had a library. Once the last foreigner left at night, it was only him and his fellow watchman Mohammad until the next morning, and Mohammad always fell asleep promptly after evening prayer.

Moustafa didn't mind, because it gave him free run of the library. He devoured books on every subject, from geography to philosophy to linguistics, but always left time for his favorite subject of all—the wonders of his ancestors' civilization.

That job lasted four wonderful years, until a new manager came in and changed all the native workers for ones he had brought with him. By then, Moustafa had enough money saved for his next move, to go to the center of Egyptological research—Cairo.

There he soon got places on excavations, working for various foreigners and building up his knowledge. The researchers always ended up returning to Europe, leaving Moustafa without a job, but Moustafa got good at anticipating what foreigners wanted and never stayed out of work for long. The work was rewarding and paid enough for him to find a good wife and support two sons and three daughters.

And now he was working for his latest foreign boss. Moustafa had long since become accustomed to the strangeness of Europeans, but this one was stranger than most. That mask must hide some terrible injury, probably suffered in the war that had ripped Europe apart. The war and the injury had twisted Mr. Wall's mind. It hadn't made him brutal or a drunkard like he had seen with other Europeans who had come through that war, but it had made him shut himself away. He seemed to hate his fellow Europeans, and yet here he was opening up a store for them.

Moustafa suspected that Mr. Wall didn't really hate Europeans, but rather hated that they reminded him of the war. His hatred also had the strange effect of trying to understand and sympathize with Africans. Of course he didn't really, but he tried, and that meant that unlike with all his other bosses, Moustafa could sit down at a table in a European home with a European book open in front of him and read it without constantly looking over his shoulder in fear of getting caught.

That bought a lot of loyalty from Moustafa.

Currently he was studying a field report of a survey of Saqqara and its stepped pyramid, believed by some scholars to be the earliest pyramid of all. It made for fascinating reading.

But now it was time to stop reading and start working again. He shut the report with a sigh. This Englishman was kinder than most, but he demanded hard work like the rest of them. To be ruled by Europeans meant being ruled by their worst invention—the clock. It was time to open up the shop for its first round of guests, and he had been warned to keep a sharp eye out for anyone trying to leave the front hall and sneak into the back rooms or upstairs. Mr. Wall had told him about the German man snooping around upstairs. If he caught anyone doing that, he'd beat him within an inch of his life, European or not. No one was going to endanger the man who allowed him access to such books.

**

Augustus Wall knocked back a scotch and soda, considered having another, and decided against it. He hated these soirées, but in his business, there was no avoiding them, and if he wanted to sell a few things tonight and make good connections, he'd have to pace himself.

Besides, he was worried about the other night. He had dissolved some opium in a glass of wine as he usually did so that he could sleep without nightmares. He had only drunk the one glass, he was sure of it, but the next morning he awoke to find the entire bottle empty. He must have drunk it in that hazy period between when the opium began to take effect and when he drifted off to an untroubled sleep.

He had never done that before. It must have been the stress of moving into his new house, along with that little brat knocking his mask off. That had shaken him badly—the way those children screamed, and that pesky one's (what was his name? Farouk?) look of terror. The amusing little street fight with that band of thugs later that day hadn't eased the tension nearly enough.

So apparently he had downed an entire bottle of wine along with his daily dose of opium, all with no hangover. That truly was disturbing. He hoped he wasn't turning into a dipsomaniac.

So only one drink, and the inevitable champagne toast as everyone gathered around to cheer on his new venture, whether they gave a damn about his success or not. What a bore. At least he could rely on Heinrich Schäfer to be there, a fine old colleague and expert on Egyptian art who was the closest thing to a friend he had in Cairo. Schäfer was of limited means and so wouldn't buy anything, but he could be relied upon for excellent conversation. The German had been too old to fight, the lucky devil, and had sat out the war in Egypt working on a vast treatise on Egyptian art. It was a good thing he'd confirmed he would come because Sir Russell had pulled out at the last minute pleading urgent police work, and Zehra Hanzade had not replied to his invitation. That bothered him more than he cared to dwell upon.

He came down to his front room to find everything in preparation. The electric lights were all working (something never guaranteed in Cairo), Moustafa manned the door in a brilliant new white jellaba and skullcap, a pair of servants on loan from Schäfer had already set up the table with the snacks and drinks, and Schäfer himself sat smoking a pipe in a corner with that faraway look he always got when communing with the pharaohs.

"Hello, Heinrich, how goes the book?"

"I'm busy with hunting scenes at the moment. I've found the most fascinating details in some of the tombs excavated in Upper Egypt," the art historian replied in heavily accented English.

"Glad to hear of it. When do you think it will be finished?"

Heinrich sighed. "There are times when I think it will never be finished. The pages just keep piling up. But what can I do? The topic is vast. I notice you have quite a selection of art from the Saite Period. Quite rare."

THE CASE OF THE PURLOINED PYRAMID

"Ah yes, the last native dynasty of Egypt," Augustus declared. "I've always had a fondness for last things, especially dynasties and the fall of empires. Romulus Augustulus, the Palaiologoi, and of course our own empires in Europe are crumbling away. Most refreshing."

Heinrich Schäfer took another puff from his pipe. "But endings always lead to new beginnings. Have you turned into an optimist since we last dined?"

"You'll have finished ten books before that happens, my friend."

"Too bad. These pieces are quite nice, though. For example, that sarcophagus lid. Quite typical of the period with its wide features and somewhat squat appearance. I know of a similar one uncovered in the Delta last year."

Heinrich launched into an informative lecture of the minutest detail, needing little prompting to continue. Augustus noticed that Moustafa was listening, no doubt absorbing every word.

The guests started to arrive, and reluctantly Augustus had to cut his friend short. Soon he was mingling with various near strangers whom he'd rather avoid, but the necessities of business forced him to accept the inevitable. Just as a conversation with three members of the Imperial Cotton Exchange couldn't get more tedious, he noticed Moustafa beckoning him over to the front door.

"Boss! Look at this."

Moustafa pointed down the street, where a pair of Egyptians bearing torches walked ahead of an ornate wooden litter carried by four burly Turks. The litter was entirely enclosed except for small mashrabiya windows on the front and each side that hid whoever sat within. Intricate mother-of-pearl inlay glimmered softly in the torchlight.

One of the other guests noticed, and soon everyone crowded at the door. The Turkish bearers stopped in front of the entrance and gently laid the litter on the ground. A little door opened, and Zehra Hanzade alighted.

Unlike many high-society Turkish and Egyptian women attending functions that were predominantly European, she had made few concessions in her apparel. She dressed in a flowing peach robe tied with an Imperial waistcloth from which hung a series of tassels that swayed as her hips moved. The sides of the robe were open to reveal puffy red-and-green-striped pantaloons and white silk shoes with upturned toes. This high-class Ottoman look was broken by a delicately crafted diamond and gold Rolex on her wrist and the fact that she did not wear a headscarf. She did not even tie her hair up and inside a hat like a European woman would. Instead her black ringlets flowed free over her shoulders like a girl.

She also broke another tradition—she came unaccompanied by her husband.

As she alighted from the litter, Augustus went to greet her—a little too quickly, he had to admit, but he couldn't help himself.

"Augustus," she said, "how delightful to see you again! Suleiman sends his regrets, but he is engrossed in his work. Artists unfortunately cannot be relied upon to keep social engagements."

She hooked her arm around his, and they walked together into the house as the guests gaped.

"I'm so glad you could make it," Augustus said in all honesty.

The crowd parted for them like the Red Sea.

A servant came up with a tray of glasses, some with champagne and others with mango juice. After the slightest hesitation, Zehra took a mango juice.

"How goes our business?" she asked, gazing at him over the rim of her glass.

As if on cue, one of his guests, a Scottish engineer associated with the railways, came up to him.

"Oh, excuse me, I didn't see any statues of Isis. My wife wants one for her birthday. Is there one that I've missed?"

Augustus shrugged. "I'm sorry, but I'm afraid I haven't one at the moment."

"Oh, Augustus, don't be silly!" Zehra chimed in. "Don't you remember that lovely little statuette you have at my house?"

"Oh right, that."

Zehra turned to the railroad man. "You must forgive Augustus. He has such a large collection he can't even remember everything in it! The space he rented in the warehouse is filled to bursting, and he begged me to leave some things at my house, including the Isis. It's in wonderful condition, in the style of the New Kingdom I think, but what do I know of these things?"

"Oh, well, I've learned a thing or two while living here. It's not all railway schedules with me!"

THE CASE OF THE PURLOINED PYRAMID

At this point, the man launched into a lecture on ancient Egyptian mythology, much of it wrong and the rest superficial to the point of banality. Zehra made a brilliant show of being entranced. Augustus fled back to Heinrich.

"She's stunning," his friend said. "Are you finally climbing out of your shell?"

"She's married, and I'm hideous."

"That wasn't my question," he said with a smile. Heinrich had a way of ignoring his comments that managed to totally disarm him. The art historian turned in the direction of the collection of inscription fragments. "Did you invite him?"

Augustus studied the man his friend had indicated—a well-built Nordic-looking fellow in his early twenties. He was looking at each of the inscriptions and then checking something in a small notebook.

"Not that I can recall, but the guests were encouraged to bring friends."

"He showed up at the German Club the day before yesterday. Got quite drunk, which isn't uncommon at the club, but he was a morose drunk. I cannot stand a morose drunk. It seems to me contrary to the purpose of drinking."

"I'm cutting down myself," Augustus admitted, remembering how that wine bottle got mysteriously drained.

"I've never seen you as a morose drunk, or perhaps I cannot tell the difference from your usual mood. In any case, this fellow began grumbling about how the Jews led to Germany's defeat."

"Really? I thought the British Empire and its allies had something to do with it."

"Apparently not. 'We had the enemy worn to exhaustion, and the Jews stuck a knife in our back' was one of his lines. I remember it exactly because he repeated it so often."

"German anti-Semites are even more common than English anti-Semites. Why point him out to me?"

"Because beyond his distasteful prejudices he's an uneducated boor. I see no reason why he would be here. I doubt he's anybody's guest."

"That's two Germans interested in my inscriptions in as many days. What's going on?" Augustus murmured.

"Whatever do you mean?" Heinrich asked.

But before Augustus could explain, another visitor showed up. This one he recognized.

Cavell Martin stumbled up to the front door, obviously drunk. Moustafa blocked his way. When Cavell saw who it was, his face twisted in rage.

"Get out of my way, you ape!"

"Unless you want to get torn in half and stuffed down the privy, I suggest you leave," Moustafa growled.

This did not have the desired effect. Instead of becoming frightened or getting angrier, the Frenchman looked past Moustafa at the German standing by the inscriptions. His mouth opened in shock.

"You! I knew I'd find you here!"

The German spun around, jerked back in surprise, and whipped out a pistol from his pocket. The gun barked, and Cavell flew backward, his forehead punctured by a bullet hole. He fell flat on his back on the threshold and didn't move.

Before anyone could react, the German bolted for the door. Moustafa moved to stop him, but a near miss from a second shot sent him diving for cover behind the statue of a Middle Kingdom scribe.

The German sent another shot after him, which chipped off part of the statue's base but missed Moustafa.

Within an instant, the gunman had disappeared out the door.

CHAPTER SEVEN

Faisal felt terrible. He had acted like a coward and had left the Englishman to get killed by the jinn. The foreigner had risked his life to protect him from Hassan, and this was how he repaid him? Where was his sense of honor?

That thing with the crocodile head looked a thousand times more frightening than Hassan. Even an Englishman wouldn't be safe against such a creature. Faisal was sure that it had come up the stairs after him. He could have sworn he heard great, ponderous footsteps on the stairs as he ran out of the house and had dishonorably left the Englishman to his fate.

Despite all his troubles, despite being hungry most of the time, despite sleeping in alleyway shacks and in the doorways of mosques, despite spending much of his time stealing from market traders and avoiding the police, Faisal had always prided himself on being a good friend. If one of the other boys who shared his shack was cold on a winter night, he'd share his blanket. If someone had come back from begging and scrounging with nothing, Faisal always had a scrap of bread for him. Plus, he tried to protect the smaller ones from the human jackals that prowled these streets.

Now Faisal had to deal with his own pack of jackals. Not only had he gotten the Englishman killed, but he faced death himself. He had defied Hassan, and the gang leader and his men would be looking for him.

Faisal had been hiding all day, avoiding the neighborhood around Ibn al-Nafis Street. After the dawn prayer had forced him and the other beggars to leave the portal of the Sultan Hassan mosque, he had wandered the city, carrying his blanket with him. Begging hadn't produced anything to eat, and he hadn't been able to steal anything either. His stomach growled. Faisal ignored it. He'd dealt with hunger so often before that it was as close a companion as the lice in his hair.

And now the muezzin called for evening prayer. It looked like he wouldn't eat today. He didn't dare go back to Ibn al-Nafis Street to escort Osman ibn Akbar to the mosque and share his food. Wearily, he turned back toward the Sultan Hassan mosque when a familiar voice stopped him.

"Hey, Faisal!"

It was Yacoub, a ten-year-old who shared his shack. Faisal remembered that Yacoub sometimes begged in this district.

"You get any food?" Faisal asked.

Yacoub shook his head. "Sorry, but guess what! You have to come to Ibn al-Nafis Street. That Englishman without a face is having a big party."

"What? Are you sure?"

"Of course I'm sure. There are lots of Europeans there and some rich Ottoman woman."

Faisal's jaw dropped. Could this be true? The Englishman actually got away from that jinni with the crocodile head? That man was invincible!

But wait, could this be a trick to lure him back to the neighborhood? No, that didn't make any sense. Hassan didn't know about the jinni, so he couldn't force Yacoub to make up stories about the Englishman being alive.

So the Englishman really was alive! That made Faisal feel better. He had still run like a coward, though, and he still needed to warn him about Hassan and the others. He owed the Englishman that much. The man might be invincible, but they could still rob his house.

Faisal needed to take care. Hassan would be lurking about, attracted by all the rich people. He'd be watching, awaiting his chance.

"You coming back to the shack tonight?" Yacoub asked.

"Um, maybe later. Goodbye."

Faisal took a back route to the neighborhood, deep in thought. How best to do this? With all those foreigners coming and going the street would be crowded with servants and people standing about staring. There would be police too, like when the Englishman moved in. Faisal decided his best chance was to boldly walk down the middle of the street in plain view. Sure, Hassan would see him, but with him watching the front of the Englishman's

THE CASE OF THE PURLOINED PYRAMID

house like a hawk, Hassan would see him no matter what he did. Hassan wouldn't want to make a disturbance while the police were there. He'd be more interested in waiting for his chance to rob some rich European rather than going after Faisal. After he saw the Englishman, Faisal wasn't sure how he'd get away, but maybe it wouldn't matter. The Englishman could protect him like last time.

Faisal found Ibn al-Nafis Street in as big of an uproar as when the Englishman had first moved in. Several carriages were stopped outside the house, plus a beautiful litter for some rich woman. Two bright electric lights flanking the front door illuminated a whole section of the street. A curious crowd was kept away from the front door by a large Nubian and several servants who had obviously come with the foreign guests. Strangely, Faisal didn't see any policemen. Nevertheless, he decided to stick to his plan and go directly to the front door. With this crowd, he could probably slip away from Hassan if he needed to.

Faisal darted through the crowd, trying to keep in the thick of it to make himself less visible. His heart beat fast. He didn't see Hassan, but that didn't mean Hassan didn't see him.

Working his way to the door, he ducked under a carriage and peeked out from behind the shelter of a wheel. With such a crowd, he could barely see inside, but he caught a glimpse of the Englishman with some other foreigners. Then he noticed something that made his heart clench.

The jinni with the crocodile head stood in the corner. It had changed back into a statue like they often do when it was light. Right now it stood stiff and frozen, looming over the crowd, but Faisal knew as soon as all these people left and the Englishman went to bed, that thing would come to life.

He had to warn him!

When he saw a foreign man and woman walking to the door, he scampered out from beneath the carriage and walked in their shadow.

Just as he stepped on the threshold, he was lifted up by the scruff of his neck.

"Oh no, you don't!"

The Soudanese man unceremoniously dropped him back on the street.

"But I need to talk to the Englishman!" Faisal objected.

"Go beg somewhere else."

"You don't understand. There's a j—"

69

"Move!"

Faisal stuck out his tongue at the man and moved off into the crowd, frustrated. How could he get in? A foreign man shoved past him, talking angrily to himself and stinking of alcohol. Briefly Faisal considered trying to repeat his trick and decided against it. That big Nubian at the door would catch him for sure, and this time he'd give Faisal a beating.

Wait—the upstairs window, of course! He could sneak in that way and wait until the Englishman was alone and warn him then. It might be a long wait, but at least he'd be off the street and safe from Hassan.

Faisal was just about to make his way around to the back of the house when a sound of a gunshot rang from inside. The crowd buzzed with curiosity, and Faisal got jostled by all the adults as they pressed closer to the entrance to see what was going on.

Then came a second shot, and a third, and the crowd started running away from the entrance. A fleeing shopkeeper knocked Faisal down. The boy leaped up immediately to avoid being trampled and saw a burly foreign man run out of the house with a gun in his hand.

Like everyone else, Faisal tried to get out of his way, but the press of bigger bodies was too much, and he ended up right in the foreigner's path.

The foreigner was looking over his shoulder at the Englishman's house as he ran and didn't notice Faisal until he tripped over him.

Both fell hard on the ground.

The man snarled at Faisal, picked himself up, and ran off.

Faisal sat on the ground for a minute. The impact had knocked the wind out of him, and he hurt all over. Everyone ignored him as some shouted for someone to go catch the gunman and nobody volunteered, others called out to their friends to see if they were all right, and others acted bolder than the rest and started gathering around the entrance to the Englishman's house again to see what had happened.

Faisal peeked through all the legs, trying and failing to see what was going on inside. He soon gave up. It was time to get out of here. The police would come and perhaps search the whole house. Faisal knew he'd have to wait until later before he could help the Englishman.

Just as he was getting up to leave, he noticed a small notebook lying on the ground. It was encased in leather and had a strange symbol on it, maybe a letter. It certainly looked like something a European would have, not an

THE CASE OF THE PURLOINED PYRAMID

Egyptian. Had the gunman dropped it when he'd tripped over Faisal?

Faisal picked it up, put it in the pocket of his jellaba, and disappeared into the crowd before Hassan spotted him.

***

"He's dead."

Augustus felt silly for saying it. Cavell Martin lay on his floor, a neat bullet hole in his forehead and the back of his skull shattered from the exit wound. Of course he was dead. Back in the war such a sight wouldn't have even elicited comment, but here in his own home in the supposedly peaceful city of Cairo, he felt he owed his guests some sort of statement. A circle of them stood around him as he bent over the body.

"Why did this happen?" Zehra asked. Unlike the other women at the party, she had not allowed herself to be led away. She stood, pale and trembling, along with the men staring down at the body.

"Cavell got sacked from his excavation for selling an artifact to someone. That German must have been him," Augustus said.

"Ach, I knew that man was trouble," Heinrich Schäfer said.

One of the guests grabbed a sheet from the refreshment table and covered the body.

"Someone call the police," Augustus ordered. "Moustafa, close and lock the door. I doubt he'll come back, but we can't risk it. Sorry, everyone, but I think we'll all have to stay here until the police have taken a report."

One of the British cotton merchants ran to find an officer. He took almost half an hour before returning with a British policeman in tow. When Augustus complained about the slow response time, the officer apologized.

"We're short staffed tonight, sir. Most of the lads are guarding government buildings."

"Why?" Augustus demanded.

"Sir Russell received orders to arrest Sa'ad Zaghloul and the rest of that independence lot."

An excited murmur ran through the crowd.

"They should execute them. Prison is too good for that riffraff!" one of the cotton merchants shouted.

"There's bound to be trouble tomorrow once word gets out," the policeman said.

"I daresay there will be," Augustus replied, shaking his head.

The policeman interviewed Augustus and several other witnesses. Heinrich told him what he knew about the man, and the policeman took down the information while looking at the German with obvious distaste.

"That's what we get for letting all sorts into the colonies," the policeman muttered under his breath. "So you don't know his name?"

"I'm afraid not," Heinrich said stiffly.

"Probably an assumed one anyway. May I see your papers, sir?" the policeman said.

Augustus seethed as he watched his friend hand over his papers to a policeman like some common street thug. The policeman made a show of studying them and noting down every detail before handing them back to the scholar.

"I'll have to ask you not to leave the city without first notifying the police commandant's office, sir," the officer told him.

Heinrich turned red. Augustus intervened.

"This man has nothing to do with the murder. In fact, he warned me about the killer just before the man opened fire."

"Best to leave police work to the police, sir," the officer replied in a cool voice, snapping his notebook shut. "We'll look into this killer and track him down. We're sure to get him in the end, but it might take more time than usual. Probably be a spot of bother with the natives tomorrow once the news about their leader spreads. You know how excitable they can get. I suggest everyone go home and not make any unnecessary trips outside tomorrow until this all blows over."

The policeman got a couple of the servants to help him remove the body. Before the guests left, Moustafa did a quick search of the neighborhood and reported back.

"There's no sign of that German. I suppose he's far away by now. It does not seem that anyone has heard of the arrest of Sa'ad Zaghloul either. All the neighbors' tongues are wagging about the shooting."

"Let them wag. They'll learn about the arrest soon enough," Augustus said. "Stay here a minute, will you? Heinrich, Zehra, could you stay too?"

As the guests filed out, the Scottish railway engineer came up.

"I'm so sorry for what happened. I suppose this isn't the right time, but I did want to get that statue of Isis when you have the chance. You see, we're heading back to Edinburgh the day after tomorrow."

Zehra gave him a bright smile. "Oh, I'm so glad you've decided to buy it. I'm sure she'll love it!"

The Scotsman blushed a little and returned her smile. After he left, Augustus turned to her.

"You're quite the saleswoman. I don't think anyone has ever sold an antiquity at a murder scene before."

She smiled back at him. "Oh, I'm not so sure about that."

Augustus lowered his voice. "Can Suleiman make the statuette in time?"

"The man can work wonders. You'll see."

Once the guests had all left, the four of them sat down in the study. Heinrich's servants cleaned up in the front while Zehra's porters guarded the front door.

"There's something strange going on," Augustus said. "A German diplomat comes to inspect my inscriptions before I even open and doesn't see what he wants. He asks to use the water closet, and I discover him upstairs examining the cracks in the wall. Something about the masonry of the house seemed to have excited him. Over on the Giza Plateau, a large piece of stone with an inscription gets stolen. I uncover Cavell Martin as the thief, and he shows up tonight hunting for another German, who came uninvited and also evinced an interest in my collection of inscriptions."

"Even though he almost certainly didn't know or appreciate what he was looking at," Heinrich Schäfer interjected.

"Indeed," Augustus said, lighting a cigarette. "But perhaps he was told what to look for by that diplomat, Dieter Neumann. That fellow certainly seemed to know his business. He probably thought that I might have some new inscriptions on display for my grand opening, and I do."

"But none of them are large blocks of polished limestone with giant hieroglyphs," Moustafa pointed out. "The only thing unusual about the inscription Cavell stole was that it was of high quality and the hieroglyphs were so large, obviously from some immense monument."

Zehra brightened. "Several antiquities dealers have mentioned in recent days that customers have asked for large monumental inscriptions on polished white limestone."

"Were the customers German?" Augustus asked.

"I didn't ask. I will."

"Please do, although I think I can anticipate the answer. It's interesting that they specified the type of stone. Customers don't usually care about that."

"I thought that was strange as well," Zehra agreed.

"Perhaps they are looking for fragments from the same inscription," Heinrich said, puffing on his pipe.

"That's a pretty tall order after all this time," Augustus said. "And why would it matter so much to them?"

The art historian gave a helpless gesture. "That I do not know. You said Herr Neumann was inspecting the cracks in your masonry."

"Yes. At first I figured he might be looking for some hidden safe or room, but he seemed happy just from what he saw in the cracks. When I had him pinned to the wall and asked him about it, he clammed up and claimed diplomatic immunity. I had to let him go to avoid trouble. I couldn't even tell the police."

"Shall we go inspect these cracks?" Heinrich suggested.

"Very well. They're upstairs."

"One moment, let me call my eunuch," Zehra said. "Mehmid! Come with me!"

"Whatever do you need your eunuch for?" Augustus said.

Zehra raised her eyebrows. "Really, Augustus. A married woman can't go upstairs with three men who aren't her relations without the guardianship of her eunuch. I may be a woman of business, but I haven't lost all sense of propriety."

Mehmid stepped forward from where he had been guarding the door. He was an older Turk with a smooth face and a fair amount of flab, but beneath the fat, Augustus discerned muscles to rival those of Moustafa.

Now safely chaperoned, Zehra accompanied the men upstairs to the room Neumann had examined. Augustus produced a torch, and they shone the light in the cracks.

"Nothing but dust and stone," Moustafa said.

"He wasn't interested in this particular crack. He seemed to like this one better."

Augustus led them to the next crack. They all peered inside.

"Ah, look!" Heinrich said. "See the stone beyond the one that makes up the inner wall of the room? It's limestone. White limestone."

"And it's polished like the one stolen from Monsieur Dupris's dig,"

Moustafa added.

"Let's check this other one across the room," Augustus said. "Neumann liked that one too."

As they suspected, the inner stone was also of white limestone. They couldn't see anything except a chipped corner, but everyone suspected that it was polished on one side as well.

"Does Neumann really think that my house is partially built with ancient Egyptian stone?" Augustus asked.

"Ancient stone was often reused in later buildings," Zehra said.

"Yes, and Neumann said this house might date back to the Bahri Dynasty," Augustus mused. "That's fourteenth century, isn't it?"

"From 1250 to 1382," Zehra said.

Heinrich looked impressed. "You are quite an educated woman, Mrs. Hanzade!"

Zehra lowered her eyes modestly. "The Bahri Sultans were Mamluk Turks, Herr Schäfer. Any proud Turk knows her history."

"I wish the Soudanese did," Moustafa said. "No one in my village ever heard of Meroë or Kush and wouldn't have cared if they had."

Augustus studied the wall. "So Neumann and his henchman are searching for an Egyptian monumental inscription. But why the subterfuge? And why kill a man?"

No one had any ideas.

Augustus turned to Moustafa. "Did Dupris sketch or photograph the inscription before it was stolen?"

"He did a preliminary sketch, yes."

"We need see it," Augustus said. "Tomorrow you and I will go back to Giza. Maybe the inscription will give us a clue as to why Neumann wants the complete text so badly."

CHAPTER EIGHT

Khadija umm Mohammed was well known throughout the neighborhood for being wise in the ways of the hidden world. When a woman had trouble with childbirth, the family called on her. Before a man asked his beloved's father for the girl's hand in marriage, he called on her. If a house was haunted by jinn, the family brought in Khadija umm Mohammed.

So that's why Faisal found himself in the courtyard between four ramshackle buildings where the old woman sat sifting grain in the morning sun, the light shining off her white headscarf.

"I have nothing to give you. I can barely provide for myself," Khadija said, giving Faisal a dismissive wave as soon as he entered the courtyard.

"I'm not here to beg. I need your help."

The woman fixed her watery eyes on him. "With what?"

"How do you get rid of jinn?"

"Recite surahs from the Koran. God will protect you," she said, bending back over her work.

Faisal shifted uncomfortably. "It's not for me, it's for a friend. His house is plagued with jinn. There must be a thousand of them from the front door all the way up to the rafters!"

Khadija umm Mohammed looked at him seriously for the first time. She thought about his question for a moment and then replied, "It's very difficult to protect an entire house, but I know how to make a special amulet, engraved in precious stone with a secret spell that will make all the jinn in the house flee in terror. All you have to do is put it in the house, and the entire building will be safe as long as it is not removed."

Faisal leaped with joy. "That's what he needs! Can I get one?"

"It's a very difficult spell and takes some time to prepare. It will cost twenty piastres."

Faisal's heart sunk. Twenty piastres? Where was he going to get such a sum?

Khadija pointed a withered finger at him. "And one more thing, the money must be honest money. God knows all. If the money is stolen or earned by selling goods that are stolen, the spell will have no effect."

Faisal trudged out of the courtyard, utterly defeated. Stealing twenty piastres would be difficult enough, but how could he ever earn it?

Even if he could save the money somehow, it would take forever. He'd tried to enter the house the previous night after the police went away and the street became deserted, but the Englishman had closed the window. There was no other way in, and he was afraid to knock on the front door in case Hassan noticed him or the Soudanese giant threw him onto the street again. Now he had to risk going there by daylight.

He was in luck. As he came to the square that led to Ibn al-Nafis Street, he saw Hassan half a block away, swaggering through the crowd and heading the other direction. Faisal waited until Hassan rounded the corner and hurried to the Englishman's house.

He found the Englishman outside with the big Nubian getting into a motorcar. All the men in the café across the street were staring at the machine. Faisal couldn't remember seeing one on this street before.

Faisal waved and ran up to the Englishman.

"Go away. Nothing for you," the Soudanese barked.

"Wait! Do you remember me?" he asked the Englishman.

"Oh yes, Farouk, the little beggar boy who never seems to go away."

"Faisal."

"What?"

"My name's Faisal."

"What of it, Faisal?"

"You're in danger!"

"Yes, I did notice someone got shot at my party last night. Thank you for informing me."

THE CASE OF THE PURLOINED PYRAMID

The two men climbed into the motorcar.

"No, wait! I have to tell you. Hassan was bragging about how he will take his revenge. He wants to break into your house and kill you so he can steal everything you have."

That got their attention.

"How does he plan to break in?" the Nubian asked.

Faisal paused. What could he say? Certainly not the truth!

"Um, I don't know. He didn't say."

"Well, thank you for the warning," the Englishman said, digging into his pocket. "Here's a half piastre."

Faisal took it, and the Englishman turned back to the motorcar.

"Wait! There's more."

The Englishman sighed. "And how much will that cost me?"

"Nothing," Faisal replied while pocketing the coin. "But of course, um, if you want to give me something that would be fine."

"I'm in a hurry, Farouk."

"Faisal."

"Fine. I'm in a hurry, Faisal."

"Your house is infested with jinn!"

Both men burst out laughing.

"What's so funny?" Faisal asked.

The Soudanese wagged a finger at him. "Listen to how you talk. This is why Egypt isn't a great country anymore. People cling to silly superstition."

Faisal stamped his foot. "I'm not silly!"

"Look, I used to be just like you," the Soudanese man continued in a fatherly tone. "I grew up ignorant in a little village way down south in the Soudan. I believed in jinn and spirits and magic of all kinds. But that's in the past. We have to put those childish things aside and improve ourselves. Do you think the Europeans are so strong because they believe in jinn?"

"Jinn are real! I've seen them!"

"Thank you for your concern, Farouk," the Englishman said.

"Faisal!"

"Right, Faisal. Anyway, I'll be sure to watch out for the jinn." The Englishman tried to say this with a straight face and failed. He climbed into the driver's seat. Moustafa got in beside him. "But seriously, thank you for warning me about Hassan. I'll be on the lookout. Now we need to go."

The Englishman started the motorcar. Faisal stared at it in wonder. Just as the car moved forward, he remembered the third thing he needed to tell him.

"Wait! I almost forgot!"

The Englishman rolled his eyes and stopped the car.

"Now what?"

"That foreigner who shot one of your guests. He dropped something."

He had their attention again.

"What did he drop?" the Englishman asked, his arm on the door of the car as he looked at Faisal intently.

Faisal stared at the car. He'd never been in one before.

"Are you going to answer me?"

"Where are you going?" Faisal asked.

"Giza. What did he drop?"

"He dropped a little book. It has writing in it. And pictures."

The Englishman got out of the car. Faisal took a step back.

"Give it to me," the Englishman demanded.

"Can I ride in your motorcar?"

The Nubian stormed out of the motorcar.

"Enough of this, you little infidel! He already gave you half a piastre, and that's more than you deserve. Hand it over."

The giant lunged for him, but Faisal scampered away. Both men followed. They ran a circle around the motorcar before the two adults got smart and split up, coming around the motorcar from different directions. Faisal ran across the street to a nasty pool of stinking water. He pulled the little book from his pocket and dangled it over the water.

Both men stopped, still out of reach.

"Take me in your motorcar, or I'll drop this in the sludge."

"I'll tear you apart!" the Nubian roared.

"Not if I do it first," the Englishman said.

"Come on. What difference does it make to you? I'll ride in the back and be no trouble. If all the foreigners go to Giza, it must be like paradise! I want to go there, and I've never been in a motorcar before."

"This car is on loan from a German gentleman, a scholar!" the Nubian said. "We will not repay his hospitality by letting you infest his car with fleas!"

"No ride, no book," Faisal said with a grin. "And buy me a big lunch when we get there."

The Nubian glowered at him. "The Nile will run dry before Mr. Wall ever takes you to Giza."

***

Moustafa glared at Faisal in the rearview mirror. The boy sat in the back seat, an idiotic grin plastered on his face. Moustafa swore that if that little brat so much as left a fingerprint on Herr Schäfer's motorcar, he'd pluck the boy's fingers off his hand one by one.

At least Mr. Wall had put a blanket down for the urchin to sit on. The filthy fabric of the boy's jellaba would probably rot the seat if it came into contact with it. The blanket couldn't stop the things the wind was blowing out of the boy's hair, though.

"When do we get to Giza?" Faisal asked.

"It takes some time," Mr. Wall said.

"When do we stop for lunch?"

"When I say so," Mr. Wall said, swerving around a man leading a donkey down the middle of the street.

"I'm hungry."

"Wait."

"There's a man selling *simit*! Can you get me some *simit*?"

"No."

"Quiet back there!" Moustafa said.

"Can I have twenty piastres?" Faisal asked.

Moustafa turned around in his seat. "Twenty piastres? Mr. Wall lets you ride in the motorcar, and you ask him for twenty piastres?"

Faisal stuck out his lower lip. "It's for something important."

"Important? Bah! You'll just waste it."

Faisal was the kind of African Moustafa loathed—dirty, ignorant, and with no interest in bettering himself. Granted, he was a child, and God had given him a rough start to life, but that was no excuse for filth and no excuse for willful ignorance. Jinn? What nonsense! Faisal was an embarrassment.

The only kind of African Moustafa loathed more were the Africans who tried to be more European than the Europeans, sitting in high-class cafés wearing imitation Western suits and speaking bad French. There was much to be admired in European culture, but Africa was not Europe and should not try to be European. Take the best parts of Europe, yes, like science and technology and learning, and leave the rest. Moustafa had read the papers. He knew what the war in Europe had been like. The Europeans had everything and had almost lost it all over some pointless struggle. So the heir to the Hapsburg throne had been assassinated. What of it? They had caught the assassin, hadn't they? They should have tortured him to death in a public square, and that would have been the end to it. Instead they launched a war, and now there was no Hapsburg throne. Fools.

Sa'ad Zaghloul and the other independence leaders were the kind of Africans who thought they were more European than the Europeans. All those leaders were aristocrats, living in fine mansions in 'Abdin, thinking their French wine and English cigarettes would earn them respect in London. The fools! And now they were in prison. Served them right for forgetting their religion and thinking they were something they were not. Better to be stuck with the British than to be ruled by a cheap imitation of the British.

"So what does that notebook say, Moustafa?" Mr. Wall asked as they got onto a wide street leading to downtown Cairo. There were more motorcars here and a tram line. The crowded bazaars gave way to tidy shops with European-style facades.

"It is in German," Moustafa replied. "That is a language I haven't learned yet."

"We'll have to get you lessons with Herr Schäfer. The way you are with languages he'll have you reading Goethe in a month."

Moustafa laughed, enjoying the compliment because it was true. Languages just seem to fall into place inside his head. He never understood why some people had so much trouble with them. Too bad Mr. Wall was joking about the lessons. Europeans often made promises they never intended to keep. They didn't even realize they were doing it.

Some German lessons wouldn't be a bad idea, though. Perhaps he could convince Mr. Wall to really arrange it?

"When I flipped through it all I saw was some occult mumbo jumbo," Mr. Wall said. "I'll take a closer look at it after we speak to Dupris. First things first, though. Hey, what's this?"

They were passing through the Sayyid Zaynib neighborhood and saw a large crowd ahead. The traffic, mostly horse carriages and motorcars, began to back up as the crowd marched along a cross street. As they approached, the chants of the marchers became audible.

"Long live Sa'ad Zaghloul! Long live independence! Long live Sa'ad Zaghloul! Long live independence!"

"They didn't waste any time. I'll back up and take another way," Mr. Wall said.

"Why are they shouting?" Faisal asked as he peeked between the shoulders of the two men in front.

"They are angry the British arrested Sa'ad Zaghloul," Mr. Wall said. "Do you know who he is?"

"Of course I do! The British said he would be the next sultan of Egypt!"

"Not quite," Moustafa said, although that was probably what the fellow really wanted.

"Why did they arrest him?" the boy asked.

"Because he was causing trouble," Moustafa said.

"Because he was reminding the British that they don't keep their promises," Mr. Wall said.

They had to drive several blocks to get around the protestors, who numbered in the thousands, mostly young men, students by the look of them. There were too few policemen around, and all they could do was channel the protest down the street. The crowd seemed to be heading for the high commissioner's building. Moustafa had no doubt the main group of police would be there, waiting.

Moustafa sent up a quick prayer. "Please God let there be no bloodshed."

Once they got past the gathering crowd, they made much better time. They crossed the bridge over the Nile and sped down the long, dusty road to Giza. The three main pyramids loomed on the horizon.

Faisal gasped and pointed. "What are those?"

"Those are the pyramids," Mr. Wall said.

"I thought people were supposed to have built them."

"People did build them."

"No, those are too big. The jinn must have built them."

Moustafa clucked his tongue and turned around in his seat. "Stop talking about jinn! People built them, your ancestors and mine."

"They must have been the greatest magicians in the world," Faisal said, still staring at the pyramids as they grew larger and clearer through the haze.

"What do you mean?" Moustafa asked, frowning.

"Because they'd have to have been great magicians to get the jinn to do all that work for them."

Moustafa grunted, shook his head, and looked back toward their destination. He had better things to do than try to educate some little snot-nosed child who couldn't appreciate his heritage. He had to figure out how to get that sketch from Monsieur Dupris. The man was sure to go mad when he laid eyes on Moustafa again.

Mr. Wall must have been thinking the same thing, because as the car trundled up the road onto the Giza Plateau, passing through a little village of mud huts shaded by palm trees, he said, "Best leave Monsieur Dupris to me, Moustafa. Once we have the sketch, I'll let you read the inscription. You're far better at reading hieroglyphs than me."

"Oh, you're quite good, sir."

"Nonsense. You're better than I am, and we both know it. I hired you to help me, not give me false praise."

Moustafa looked at his boss out of the corner of his eye. Since when did a European not enjoy false praise? It was one of the cornerstones of European-African relations, although the false praise always went only one way.

They parked the motorcar near the Great Sphinx, where a flurry of men idling under its shade rushed to them offering their services.

"Hello, guide?"

"Camel ride to see pyramids? For you special price!"

"Hello, postcard?"

Moustafa recognized a man he trusted in the crowd.

"Hey, Naguib! Guard the motorcar until we come back, and my boss will give you a piastre."

"Thank you, Moustafa, but make it five piastres. He looks richer than even most Europeans."

"You'll get one and be happy with it. We're on serious business," Moustafa growled.

He glanced at his boss and saw he had a blank expression on his face, the very same Moustafa put on when he listened to conversations he pretended he couldn't understand.

"Two piastres," Naguib said.

"One and a half and not a millieme more."

THE CASE OF THE PURLOINED PYRAMID

"Oh, all right. Why is that urchin sitting in the back?"

"Because my boss is more generous than is good for him," Moustafa said pointedly.

As they walked away, Moustafa shooing away a flock of men waving souvenirs in their faces and offering camel rides, Mr. Wall said, "Too generous? I think a car ride and lunch are a small price to pay for this notebook. What do you make of the symbol on the front?"

The little leather-bound volume had a strange symbol embossed on the cover. It looked like a capital *T*, but the top curved downward and each terminal came to a point. The letter was surrounded by a floral design. Next to it was a stylized swastika, the sun symbol of the early Indo-Europeans, with curving arms that almost touched one another to make it look like a circle with crosshairs. The swastika served as the pommel for a sword.

"The swastika is famous, but I've never seen it as part of a weapon, and I have never seen a *T* like this before," Moustafa admitted.

"Nor have I," his boss said.

"Wow!" Faisal gasped from some distance behind them.

They had climbed to the top of the plateau, and the three main pyramids, surrounded by several smaller queen's pyramids, had come into full view. The boy had stopped in his tracks and stood with his mouth hanging open and eyes bugging, amazed by the scene.

A sunburned woman snapping photos nearby noticed him.

"Oh, look at this darling little urchin. So picturesque!"

This was said in a nasal American tone to her bored-looking husband, equally sunburned, who studied the pyramids with a noticeable lack of interest.

The woman walked over to Faisal.

"Now you stand right here while I take your picture, and I'll give you a shiny new coin," she said, and put her hands on his shoulders in order to keep him from walking away.

"Don't touch him, Edna," her husband warned. "You might get parasites."

Faisal didn't know what she was saying but understood what was expected of him well enough. He struck a pose, leaning on one leg with his head cocked and an innocent look in his eyes.

"Oh, aren't you a little doll? Now hold still."

Edna pulled a Kodak portable from her bag while her husband rolled his eyes and turned his back.

The woman fussed over the camera for a minute as Faisal looked increasingly impatient. Finally she took a couple of snaps, put away her camera, and opened up a coin purse. Faisal grinned and extended a grubby hand. The woman pulled out a half piastre coin and gave it to him.

"Now you go and buy some nice candy with that!" she said, obviously proud of herself.

Faisal looked at the coin in disbelief, gazed up at the woman, and burst into tears.

"Oh dear! I seem to have upset him!"

Faisal whined incoherently, pointing to his patched jellaba and his bare feet.

"Oh, the poor thing must be starving. Here you go. Um, Winston, how many piastres to a dollar? I can't remember. Oh well, take this."

Moustafa's eyebrows shot up as the woman handed over a ten piastre coin. Faisal grinned and skipped off. Mr. Wall looked equally astonished. Shaking their heads, they continued on their way.

Faisal caught up with them a minute later.

"You're too big to burst into tears just because someone didn't give you what you thought you deserved," Mr. Wall told him.

The boy looked insulted. "Me, cry? I never cry. I can fake it. Look."

Faisal fixed him with a woeful look. His lower lip trembled. His eyes filled. His face turned red, and the tears started to pour down his cheeks.

The boy grinned. "Or I can do it suddenly, like I did with her. Whichever works best."

Mr. Wall shook his head. "I'll never pity a wailing child ever again."

"If they don't feel sorry for you, they won't give you money. Then you look happy and make them feel good. But I've never received so much! Usually I get just a bit of bread or one or two milliemes. Are Europeans always this generous?"

"They aren't European. They're American."

"I don't care. I need to get in more pictures!"

He spotted another group of tourists with a camera and ran toward them.

"Hey, Faisal!" Mr. Wall called after him.

THE CASE OF THE PURLOINED PYRAMID

Faisal turned and smiled. "You remembered my name!"

"I might not remember to take you back to Cairo if you're not around when I leave. See those diggings over there? That's where we're going to be."

"After you're done, we will get lunch, right?"

"Yes, Faisal."

"As much as I want?"

"Whatever. Now leave us alone."

Faisal leaped in the air, spun around, and charged at the tourists.

"That should keep him from bothering us for a while," Mr. Wall said. "Ah! There's Dupris."

The French archaeologist was approaching them as his crew worked in the background. Dupris glared at Moustafa.

"Good morning, Monsieur Dupris," Mr. Wall said before the man could object to Moustafa's presence. "I'm afraid I have some very bad news."

"Cavell? I just heard," Dupris said, giving Mr. Wall a stiff handshake and turning his back on Moustafa.

"I'm terribly sorry. He didn't deserve that. You probably also heard that he was shot in my house by a German man nobody at the party knew. There appears to be a group of Germans looking for inscriptions to match the one stolen from you. I've already caught another fellow sneaking around my house. Might I take a look at the sketch you made of the missing fragment? It could help me piece this whole thing together."

Dupris paused for a moment, then nodded.

"Very well. I suppose the police have their hands full. My workers have been surly all morning."

Moustafa couldn't help himself. "Perhaps treating them as human beings would improve their attitude."

Dupris treated him to a sneer and turned back to Mr. Wall.

"You're more than welcome to borrow it if you think it will help. Leave your ape here, and we'll fetch it."

Moustafa resisted the urge to pop Dupris's head off his shoulders and kick it like a football over the nearest pyramid. A man had been murdered in Moustafa's workplace, and the murderer had taken two shots at him. He had more important things to do.

After a short time, Mr. Wall returned with the sketch. When Moustafa studied the inscription, he nearly fell over with shock.

CHAPTER NINE

"It's from the Great Pyramid of Cheops. It must be," Moustafa said, his voice almost stilled with wonder. "Look here. It's very fragmentary, but it says 'is one belonging.' Cheops's title in his mortuary temple here at Giza was 'Cheops is one belonging to the horizon.'"

They sat in the shade of the Sphinx, that great enigmatic face looming above them.

Augustus felt a thrill go through him. Could this be true? He pointed to the fragment of a curved line at the far left of the slab where it was broken off. "You're thinking that's the end of Cheops's cartouche?"

Moustafa nodded. "It would make sense. And remember that it was of polished white limestone. The few remaining fragments of casing from his pyramid are of the same material."

Augustus grew excited. "And look at the size of the inscription! It would be visible from the ground even if it was halfway up. Wait. So this means the original casing had an inscription. This is fantastic!"

"Pity we didn't find more of it," Moustafa said.

The antiquities dealer looked at him with renewed appreciation. His employee's eyes gleamed with interest to match what he himself felt. This was a magnificent discovery. It didn't explain their present predicament, though.

"Why do the Germans want this so much they're willing to kill for it? Why steal the inscription at all? Dupris would have published it along with the rest of his findings for all to read."

Moustafa shrugged. "That's still a mystery. I suggest we go back to Cairo and check with every antiquities dealer, and with the museum too, for any other fragments of this inscription. If we could piece the message together . . ."

A shiver went up Augustus's spine. They had stumbled upon the greatest Egyptological discovery in decades.

"We need to have another look at my house as well. Neumann seemed convinced that my house included some of the reused material that he was looking for. I find it hard to believe that the casing from the Great Pyramid would have ended up in a house in Cairo though."

A dim memory flickered at the back of his mind, something he had read long ago. He paused and chased it, but it eluded him. Never mind. It would come to him. He hoped.

"Let's go," Moustafa said, standing and brushing the sand off his jellaba. "Now where did the Little Infidel get off to?"

They looked around and saw no sign of Faisal. They did hear some shouting in the distance, however, coming from the direction of the pyramids. The two men glanced at each other. It sounded like an angry crowd, and it was drawing closer.

"Could the workmen have rioted?" Augustus wondered.

Moustafa grinned. "Perhaps they beat Monsieur Dupris with their sandals and stuffed camel dung down his pants."

"An amusing thought, but let's get to the motorcar just in case they decide to do the same to us."

Just as they made it, Faisal appeared over the brow of the hill, running as fast as he could in their direction. He was even dirtier than usual, and his jellaba had several new tears.

As he descended the slope, a crowd of children appeared behind him, all shouting in rage and brandishing sticks and whips. The bigger boys and girls made up the vanguard of the horde, with a trailing tail of smaller children, some as young as five, taking up the rear. A hail of stones flew after Faisal, who ducked and wove and managed to dodge most of them. Several tourists pointed their cameras at the scene.

"Start the motorcar!" he shouted.

"What did you do?" Augustus demanded, running for him. Moustafa followed.

"Nothing!"

Faisal shot past them. Augustus flourished his cane at the oncoming crowd, which stopped, unsure of what to do.

"Get out of here!" Augustus told them in Arabic. "Leave him alone."

A cocky boy of about fourteen shouldered his way to the front of the seething mass of angry youngsters.

"He robbed us!"

"I knew it!" Moustafa roared, shaking his fist at Faisal, who had stopped about twenty yards behind them by the car. "You're nothing but trouble."

"I didn't do anything except pose for pictures," Faisal whined.

"Only the children of the village of Nazlat al Shamman are allowed to pose for pictures," the leader shouted at Faisal. "Go back to your stinking city!"

Faisal threw a rock at him, which flew between Augustus and Moustafa and caught the boy on the temple. The boy groaned and fell to the ground.

Within a moment, he was up. Although blood trickled down his forehead, he looked undefeated.

"Get the little city bastard and his foreigner friends too!"

The crowd charged.

Moustafa turned to Augustus. "What do we do?"

"Run!" Augustus decided.

Faisal had a head start and hopped into the motorcar well ahead of them. Augustus and Moustafa fled the oncoming tide of angry village children, several rocks thumping off their backs. Their longer legs allowed them to pull ahead of the mob, and they scrambled into the motorcar. Frantically Augustus started the engine and roared away from the Sphinx. The man Moustafa had hired to guard the vehicle squawked and leaped on the hood.

"You haven't paid me yet!"

"Here," Augustus said, tossing some coins at him.

"Thank you, sir," he replied, and leaped off into the sand.

As they pulled away, Faisal stood on the back seat tossing stones at the pursuing crowd.

"Get down, Little Infidel!" Moustafa ordered. "I should get Mr. Wall to drive at top speed and then throw you out on your head!"

Faisal threw the last of his stones and bounced up and down in the back seat, laughing hysterically.

"We should come to Giza again!"

"Why? So you can get beaten up by village children a second time?" Augustus asked, swerving to avoid a line of camels.

"I made twenty-one piastres!"

"Not bad for a morning's work and what looks like is going to be a beautiful black eye," Augustus said.

"Bah, they are weaklings! I could beat them all up blindfolded."

"Yes, they were all running from you, weren't they?"

"Are we going to eat now?" Faisal asked hopefully.

"I know a place on the road to Cairo. We'll stop there if they'll take you."

"As much as I can eat?"

Moustafa turned around in his seat and shook his fist at him. "Stop being impertinent!"

"But I'm hungry!" Faisal whined. "I haven't eaten since the day before yesterday."

"You'll be lucky if Mr. Wall gives you a crust of bread. And if he gives you that much, you'll be grateful!"

***

Faisal shoveled rice and chunks of chicken into his mouth as fast as his hand could move. A stack of flat, circular *aish baladi* bread had already been consumed, a bowl of soup gulped down, a heap of vegetables demolished, and Faisal had started looking speculatively at Augustus's and Moustafa's meals.

Augustus tried not to get distracted by the street boy's atrocious manners and the horrified looks their table got from the Egyptian waiters and European diners. Instead he examined the notebook.

It was in German, a language he knew tolerably well, but much of the writing was contractions or single letters, as if the writer was familiar with the subject and didn't need to spell everything out. The few lines that were fully written out were esoteric. There was a lot of nonsense about pyramid power and the wisdom of the ancients, plus something about how the Aryan race had founded ancient Egypt at the same time as they had built a lost civilization in Germany.

"What does it say?" Moustafa asked.

"Apparently the pyramid builders were German."

"They were?" Faisal asked around a mouthful of lentils. One flew out and landed on Augustus's cuff.

"No, they weren't!" Moustafa snapped.

Faisal looked to Augustus for confirmation.

"The pyramid builders were Egyptian," Augustus said, cleaning his suit with a napkin. "The ones to the south were built by the Soudanese."

The boy shrugged. "That makes sense. Europeans don't understand anything about jinn."

The two men went back to ignoring him.

"Anyway, it appears Neumann and our pistol-wielding friend think there's some great old German magic involved in the pyramids, and they want to find its secret. They think they can do so if they get the whole inscription. There are some drawings of hieroglyphs here too. Take a look at these. This is the cartouche of Cheops, isn't it?"

"Yes." Moustafa nodded. "And this line is interesting. It says, 'Cheops leads the way to the underworld.'"

"That's an odd phrasing. It was the job of various gods with the help of the *Book of the Dead* to lead the deceased to the underworld. That line seems to imply that Cheops would act as some sort of guide to the afterlife."

"Ah, you misunderstand me. When I said 'underworld,' I didn't mean it in the usual sense. This symbol here means 'country,' and this one means 'beneath.' I've never seen that used to refer to the land of the dead. I think it may actually mean some sort of world underground."

"Perhaps some large subterranean tomb complex, like the Serapeum?" Augustus suggested.

"Perhaps," Moustafa murmured, studying the sketches.

"What do these other inscriptions say?"

Moustafa grinned. "Have you given up reading hieroglyphics altogether?"

"You're better at it."

"Many of these are fragments, single words or parts of words, and I'm afraid they don't make much sense. There's this one other lengthy fragment here, though. It says, 'Down the main corridor past the guardians who stand eternal watch to the great altar of Isis, collector of body parts.'"

"Hmm. Not sure what that's all about."

"Surely you know the legend of Isis collecting the dismembered Osiris and putting him back together."

"Of course, but I've never heard her referred to in that fashion. Egyptian inscriptions tend to be quite formulaic, and here we have two inscriptions with previously unknown turns of phrase. What could it all mean?"

"I don't know. We'll have to find that gunman and force it out of him. He took two shots at me. I'd like to get my hands on him." Moustafa balled one of his meaty hands into a fist to emphasize his point.

"If we do catch him, I'll give you free rein. I don't think he knows what this is all about, though. Schäfer said he's an oaf, not an educated man at all. I bet he was given this notebook to help him look for what the Germans want."

"But then what do we do? You said Neumann is a diplomat. We can't touch him."

"No, but perhaps it isn't just the two of them. Perhaps there are more, and not all have diplomatic immunity. Well, there's nothing more to do here except finish our meal and go back to town. I'm friends with the police commandant. Perhaps he'll have nabbed our gunman. Hello, what's this? All my bread and half of my chicken have disappeared."

"You ate it, you silly Englishman," Faisal said around a mouthful of food.

Moustafa turned to Augustus. "I will give up a week's wages if you let me kill him."

***

They headed back to town, dropping off a bloated and still living Faisal close to Ibn al-Nafis Street before driving to the main police station on Tahrir Square.

They found it in an uproar. The holding cells were packed with Egyptian students shouting slogans, and the police were hauling in fresh batches of them. Several of the officers had torn uniforms and bruises. The students looked far worse. Some had to be carried in by their comrades.

The desk sergeant informed Augustus that Sir Russell was out dealing with the protests.

"How is it going?" Augustus asked. "Is he getting the upper hand?"

The man shook his head. "No, sir. One group got a bit bold, and the troops had to open fire. Killed one of the natives, sir. That's got them even more worked up than before."

"I don't suppose there's been any further investigation of the murder at my house last night."

"I'm afraid we don't have the manpower, sir. The man's description has been sent to all railway stations and ports, but the way things are . . ." The man gave a helpless shrug.

Augustus thanked the officer and headed back to the car. Moustafa waited for him outside the entrance.

"Any luck?" Moustafa asked.

"In abundance, and all of it bad. Those idiots just gave the independence movement its first martyr."

CHAPTER TEN

"It's almost ready," Khadija umm Mohammed said.

Faisal watched as the old woman scratched lines of Arabic and mystical symbols onto the back of a little stone scarab beetle made by the ancients. The flat base had those funny picture words the ancients made, but the smooth carapace of the scarab had been left blank. Now the old woman was adding a spell onto the empty space that would banish all jinn from the Englishman's house.

How clever she was! She combined the power over the jinn that the ancient ones had with the power of the Koran. It was sure to work.

Faisal's hand gripped hard on the twenty piastres in his pocket. Khadija umm Mohammed blew the last dust away from her inscription, said a prayer over it, and held it out to him.

"Do you have the money?"

Faisal's hand gripped the coins tighter. He'd never had so much money in all his life. It was enough to eat for a couple of weeks. He could get his jellaba cleaned and patched or get the man down the street to weave him a pair of rush sandals. He could do so much with it.

But then he remembered how the Englishman had protected him from Hassan and protected him again from the village children, and he remembered that wonderful car ride and the huge meal that would keep him satisfied all day. And he'd swiped enough from the table to eat well tomorrow too.

He pulled out the money and gave it to her. He couldn't help feel a bit bad at seeing it disappear into her pocket. All that money gone for a little amulet. It had better work.

She gave him a stern look.

"You earned it?"

"Yes."

Her eyes narrowed.

"How?"

"Posing for photographs for the tourists."

"Then go with God," she said, and handed the amulet over.

Faisal turned it over in his hand. He could feel the power in it. It prickled his skin and sent shivers up and down his spine.

"So what do I do?" he asked.

"Just put it someplace in the house and say a prayer."

Faisal looked at her. "What kind of prayer?"

Khadija umm Mohammed sighed and raised her eyes heavenward. "This is what happens when a child's parents stray from the path of God and abandon their children."

"My mother didn't abandon me. She died giving birth to me."

The old woman looked at him sadly. "Of course she did."

Faisal nodded. "So what do I say?"

"Can you say, 'God is great'?"

"Yes."

"Say that then."

***

Faisal was in luck. The night was warm, and the Englishman had left the window open. He squeezed through, swung himself over to the arch, and climbed down.

Even with the amulet clutched in his hand, he watched the shadows nervously, alert for jinn. He waved the amulet in front of him.

"God is great," he whispered.

He began to go from room to room, poking the amulet in the far corners and darkest shadows, everywhere the jinn liked to hide. He repeated the prayer Khadija umm Mohammed had told him over and over again as he worked his way down to the second floor. Like the previous time, he could hear the Englishman snoring softly. Faisal crept into his room and was irritated to see another bottle by the bed next to the mask and the little tin box with the strange smelling gummy stuff. Frowning, Faisal took the bottle, emptied it down the sink, and replaced it where he had found it. Then he waved the amulet over the Englishman's sleeping form.

Now that the top two floors had been cleansed of all the lesser jinn, Faisal had to summon up the courage to face the worst jinni of them all—that giant one with the crocodile head that lived on the ground floor.

He paused at the top of the stairs, his heart racing fast.

"God is great!" he repeated, and made his way downstairs. His shivered as he crept down the dark hall leading to the main room.

His breath caught as he saw it standing in its usual corner. Faisal almost bolted, but he managed to summon enough courage to stand his ground and hold the amulet in front of him. He looked at the jinni, suspicious. Had it really turned back to stone like it did in the daytime, or was it trying to trick him?

Keeping the amulet between himself and the creature, Faisal moved around the room, clearing it of unseen spirits before returning to the crocodile-headed one. He approached it warily, until at last he was close enough to touch the amulet to the jinni's chest.

"Ha! Now you're trapped in stone forever. I've saved the Englishman's life once again!"

Faisal thought for a moment. Had he saved the Englishman more times than the Englishman had saved him? He couldn't remember. Maybe he shouldn't take anything just to be on the safe side. Well, maybe some food. The Englishman would never miss it, and he'd feed him if Faisal asked anyway. He was a generous man but a preoccupied one. He didn't like to be pestered with questions and requests. So the Englishman would prefer it if Faisal just took some food instead of bothering him by asking. Yes, that would be all right. Just some food for tonight. And tomorrow. And some to share for the other boys.

"But first I need to hide this," he whispered, "and I know just the place."

He squeezed his thin arm between the frozen jinni and the wall and pushed the amulet into the narrow space behind the stone base. No one would see it there, and it would keep the crocodile-headed jinni from turning back into a living thing again.

Satisfied he'd done something good for the Englishman, he hurried off to the kitchen to get some food. Just a little. Just enough for tonight, tomorrow, the other boys, and maybe a little extra if he felt hungrier than usual. Just a little extra. The Englishman wouldn't miss a thing.

***

"Must you leave so early?" Nur asked. "We've only just finished the dawn prayer."

Moustafa smiled at his wife. The firelight in their hut by the road to Giza illuminated her face as she bent over the hearth. His five children slept nearby. They lay on a mat all in a row, from largest to smallest, covered by a couple of blankets. It was still only half light outside, the rising sun hidden by the Mokattam Hills. It was that wonderful quiet time between making your peace with God and the start of a new day.

"I'd like to wait until they wake up and have breakfast together as usual, but the protests will make travel difficult. It's going to take time to get into the city."

"God be with them," his wife said.

"They're fools. The British have brought so much to this country, as did the French before them."

"We shouldn't be ruled by Christians. This is a Muslim country, and it should be ruled by Muslims."

"The Europeans are too smart to interfere with our religion. Plus, if they go, they will take their wealth with them, and their organization. Did we have a Suez Canal before the French built it? Did we have reliable steamer services and trams before the British made them?"

"They made those things for their own benefit," Nur said, wrapping up some falafel and bread for Moustafa's lunch.

"Of course they did. No one does anything for free in this world unless it's for family. But we benefited from those things too. The Europeans are smart enough to know that a prosperous colony is better off than one that's squeezed to the limit. Sure, they squeezed us during their war, but that's all over now, and the good times are starting again."

Nur looked at him with a knowing smile. "You're too proud to live in a colony. You want independence as much as the protestors."

Moustafa kissed her on the forehead. "Leave the politics to men."

She went back to preparing breakfast for the children. Moustafa smiled as he watched her work. It had been hard to find a wife as a stranger here with no family. It had taken him more than a year, and plenty of gifts to a matchmaker, to finally find a woman, and then he had to settle for an uneducated woman from a poor family whose father had been impressed by Moustafa's salary.

God had made sure it all turned out for the best. Nur was a wonderful woman—pious, modest, and hardworking. Most important of all, she had borne him five healthy children, including two sons who would carry on his family name.

He gazed at his children for a minute, gave Nur a final kiss, and left for work.

All during the long early morning walk through the outskirts of Cairo to the nearest tram stop, and then the second-class ride crowded in with the other Egyptians while staring through the glass partition at the Europeans and rich Egyptians riding in the first-class carriage, Nur's words haunted him.

While she was a simple woman who didn't know anything about how the world worked beyond her home, she was right in a way. It always had rubbed him wrong that he lived under the rule of foreigners, even relatively benign foreigners. He had read enough history to know that Egypt was better off under the British than it had been under the Ottomans or the Mamluks or even the glorious Muhammad Ali. And the Soudan was far better off. Before the British came there had been only the Mahdi, and before that lunatic, there had been nothing but greedy warlords until you got back to the great Nubian pharaohs. Egypt should be ruled by Egyptians and the Soudan by Soudanese, but neither people were ready. Someday, yes, but not now. The protestors were acting too hastily.

Yet he still he couldn't shake a low, simmering anger at riding in the tram standing up, packed together with a bunch of fellow Africans while Europeans who couldn't even speak his language sat on padded benches up front.

He had to watch that anger. It had nearly spelled disaster for his family. What would have become of them if Mr. Wall hadn't hired him directly after he'd quit working for that bastard Dupris?

But what could he do? There was only so much humiliation one man could take!

The tram turned a corner, running smoothly along the tracks, and jerked to a stop. The driver started ringing the bell as if he was going through a busy intersection or telling a donkey cart to get out of the way. There was a disturbed motion in the first-class carriage in front. People put their heads out the windows, then hurriedly pulled them back inside and slammed the windows shut.

Moustafa muscled his way to the side of the car and peered out a window.

A large crowd blocked the street, chanting, "No trams until independence! Long live Egypt! Long live Sa'ad Zaghloul!"

"No trams until independence?" Moustafa scoffed. "What is this nonsense? Do the fools think stopping Egyptians from getting to work is going to win them a nation?"

"Go back south if you don't like it," someone said behind him.

Moustafa whirled around. "Who said that? Who said that to me?"

No one met his eye.

Still ringing the bell, the driver slowly edged the tram forward. The chanting grew louder. The Europeans and rich Egyptians in the front carriage grew more animated. Through the glass partition, Moustafa could hear them shouting at the driver in a mixture of English, French, and Arabic, some telling him to back up and others telling him to drive full speed into the crowd.

The driver did neither. Instead he kept edging forward, slowly but resolutely advancing while giving the protestors plenty of time to get out of the way.

Suddenly the tram jerked to a stop, and he heard several loud thumps against the tram's sides. A woman in the first-class carriage screamed.

At first Moustafa thought they'd run somebody over, but then he saw that the crowd was pounding the sides of the tram with their fists.

"All Egyptians off!" some of them shouted. "We are on strike until they fulfill their promises!"

They yanked the doors to the second-class carriage open.

"Get out of the tram, you Egyptians! Stand with us. Already one of us has been martyred by British bullets, and you give our oppressors ticket money?"

Some of the Egyptians got off, while the rest bunched at the center of the car and stood stiffly, not looking at the angry faces of the protestors. Moustafa glanced inside the first-class car and saw the conductor had locked the doors.

"The rest of you, get off! Why are you still standing there?"

"I have to get to work," one of the braver commuters said. "I work in an Egyptian-owned business, making money for our nation!"

"And you pay the British to get to work. Get out!" the protestors shot back. "Get out or we'll pull you out!"

At that, several more commuters sheepishly got off the tram. The man who spoke stayed put, as did several others. Moustafa glared at the protestors and flexed his muscles. If these idiots dared come aboard, he'd throw them out on their heads.

"Why are you still standing in there?" one protestor demanded. "I was forced into the Labour Corps and spent two years slaving away in France, and when I got back, the price of food had doubled! How am I to feed my family? We need to stand together against them, brothers!"

The protestors moved forward. The ones on the front line grasped the handrail and looked about to step up into the car.

The sound of police whistles cut through the shouting. The protestors turned and looked down the street. Moustafa saw a line of colonial police, led by white officers, blowing on whistles and waving truncheons overhead. They charged the protesters at a full run.

Most of the protestors broke and fled. A brave few held their ground. Many of the passengers who had stepped off a moment before leaped back onto the tram, waving their tickets at the conductor.

The police were upon the remaining protestors the next instant, their truncheons swinging down. A chaotic, whirling melee broke out, with the protestors getting the worst of it. One policeman got punched in the face. Another got thrown to the ground, but a dozen protestors fell to the pavement to join him, heads cracked open and blood pouring down their faces.

As the tram pulled away, the driver ringing the bell furiously, Moustafa craned his head out the window and watched the scene dwindle into the distance. All the protestors who hadn't fled were on the ground now, each with a circle of policemen smacking them with their truncheons and stomping them with their booted feet.

"God protect them!" Moustafa gasped.

***

He arrived at work feeling ill. It seemed like the whole city had gone insane.

The memory of those bloody truncheons swinging down would not leave his mind.

Mr. Wall had already opened up the shop. No customers had come, and he sat at a desk in the corner studying the strange German notebook. When Moustafa entered, he snapped the notebook closed.

"I'm afraid you'll be on your own for a while. I need to see Herr Schäfer about this. Perhaps he can unravel a bit of this mystery."

"Be careful. The protestors are out in force. They're angry after losing one of their own."

Probably more than one now, Moustafa thought.

"I've handled worse," Mr. Wall said, grabbing his cane and doffing his hat before heading out the door.

Moustafa watched him go, worry plucking at his heart. That man assumed that because he spoke Arabic and showed more kindness than other Europeans that he had nothing to fear, but Moustafa knew that for some of his countrymen, that wasn't enough to make Mr. Wall safe in these streets.

***

Despite his bravado, Augustus kept a sharp eye out on the crowd as he hurried down Ibn al-Nafis Street. The loungers in the café across from his house stared at him as usual, but instead of open curiosity, he saw a mixture of guarded faces and frowns. Others in the crowd didn't seem to notice him at all. He'd already become a common sight in the neighborhood, and most Cairenes, too busy with their own affairs, had no time to waste on a strange-looking foreigner.

Augustus noticed the blind beggar who had brought Faisal to his house sitting against a wall on a tattered reed mat with his begging bowl in front of him. Augustus walked over and put a half piastre coin into his bowl. A public display of generosity couldn't hurt his standing in the neighborhood.

"Thank you, Englishman," the beggar said, not turning his face toward him.

Augustus paused. "How did you know it was me?"

"You walk like a European, and you are the only European who regularly walks down this street."

"You have sharp ears, Osman ibn Akbar ibn Mubarak al-Hajji."

The old man smiled. "Faisal said you were a strange one. Europeans generally forget our names."

"I am no longer European. Europe and I have parted ways."

The beggar's smile widened and took on an indulgent air. "Are you one of those Europeans who come here wanting to be more Arab than the Arabs? I have heard of those. There was one who led the fight against the Turks, an Englishman like you I believe, but he went home in the end."

"My home is here now."

"So you say. May God protect you."

"Thank you. Good day." Augustus turned to go.

"It was his idea," Osman ibn Akbar called after him.

Augustus stopped and turned back. "Excuse me?"

"Faisal told me what happened. It was his idea to apologize. He asked me to come with him because he was afraid."

"He seems to have overcome his fear."

"He told me that too," the beggar said, then paused. "I am old and will die soon."

"May God grant you long life."

"He already has. Now I can feel it coming to a close, and where will Faisal get his breakfast then?"

Augustus looked at him a moment, and then turned and continued on his way.

As he headed for the main streets in order to catch a tram, he sensed a growing unease in the back of his mind. Something on the edge of his perception was not right, and while it hadn't made it fully into his consciousness, his senses had picked it up.

He'd learned not to ignore that sensation. Every soldier who wants to live learns to trust his instincts.

He scanned the crowd. Everything looked normal.

No, wait. A young Egyptian man turned away when Augustus looked in his direction. Was that one of the fellows he had taught a lesson to on his first night here?

Augustus wasn't sure. The man didn't have a shaved head and a scar, so it wasn't Hassan, but it certainly could be one of his gang.

Augustus quickened his pace. He was still several minutes away from the main street with the tram line and, hopefully, some police. He turned a corner, jogged for a few yards as he wove through the crowd, then stopped and turned.

The man was just coming around the corner. Their eyes locked.

Seeing the game was up, the man met his gaze with a bold sneer. They stood several yards apart, and the passing crowd kept hiding the man from view. Augustus scanned the crowd nervously, worried that there might be more.

Yes, there was another next to that fruit seller, glaring at him. When Augustus caught the man's eye, he raised his cane.

"Do you remember this, my good fellow?" he said, even though the man was too far to hear him.

The man spat.

Augustus's eyes flicked in the direction of the first one and couldn't locate him.

That worried Augustus more than if the man had been charging him, knife in hand.

Augustus turned and hurried on his way. He shouldered through the crowd, which grew thicker as the way narrowed, and nearly bumped straight into Hassan.

The thug's hand went to his pocket. Augustus gripped his cane with both hands, ready to unsheathe the sword hidden within. A few people glanced in their direction, but mostly everyone continued to move past in both directions, intent on their own business.

"You might want to reconsider, my good man," Augustus told Hassan. "You didn't come out the winner last time, and there's no street urchin to plead your case today."

Hassan treated him to a wicked grin. "And who is here to plead yours?"

The thief pointed a finger at Augustus and shouted. "Look at this damned Englishman, coming to spy on us! He just bought the Rifaat house on Ibn al-Nafis Street, and you know why? Because he's only the first! They plan on taking over the entire neighborhood and kicking us out!"

"Stop talking nonsense!" Augustus replied in a loud voice. "Who's going to believe a common thief like you?"

Looking around at the faces now turned in his direction, Augustus spotted more than a few who looked like they did.

"You dare call me a thief? You're the thief, you and your whole evil race. You come here and take all our crops. You even take our people to go fight in your wars. You've been robbing this country for years, and now you've stolen our beloved Sa'ad Zaghloul!"

That got Augustus even more dark looks. People began to stop and gather. Hassan addressed the crowd.

"When he moved in, I overheard him speaking to that Turkish solicitor. The Turk boasted that within a year he'd sell all the houses on Ibn al-Nafis Street. He said this Englishman wouldn't be alone for long. Soon all his neighbors would be Europeans, and the mosque would be turned into a bar."

"That Turk is a Muslim!" a shopkeeper in a pale blue turban scoffed. "I've met him. He'd never do that."

"Yeah, and what do you care about the mosque, Hassan?" a water seller called out. "You haven't darkened its door in years."

A few people laughed at that, although no one who was close enough for Hassan to see. Augustus realized that Faisal wasn't the only person in the neighborhood who feared this man.

Hassan, seeing he had overstepped, changed tactics.

"So why is he here then? Tell me that! When have we ever had a foreigner living in this neighborhood? And how many foreigners have you met who speak perfect Arabic? He's a spy! The British know we are fighting for our freedom, and so they put this spy in an Egyptian neighborhood to listen in on us!"

"If the British wanted to spy on you, they'd send an Egyptian, you idiot," Augustus snapped.

"No Egyptian would betray his people that way!" Hassan declared. Augustus was impressed with his performance. The thug might even be convincing himself.

"Yes, they'd only rob them like you do," Augustus shot back.

That brought more laughter. It also brought some scowls.

"Who are you to come here and insult us?" an old man said.

"And why do you wear a mask?" another questioned.

"I was injured in the war," Augustus said, his shoulders tensing.

"It's true." A burly laborer nodded. "I heard the boys talking about it."

"That's just a lie he told them," Hassan sneered. "It's to hide his identity!"

"Then the mask would be over my entire face, you moron," Augustus replied coolly. That elicited a few laughs.

Hassan treated him to a sly smile.

"Let's see if you're telling the truth," he said, and reached for the mask.

Augustus smacked him on the hand with the cane. An instant later, he realized he'd fallen into Hassan's trap.

"He assaulted me!" Hassan said, clutching his hand like it had just been broken.

"Grab him!" someone shouted.

Several hands lunged for him. Augustus whirled in a circle, swinging his cane and knocking the crowd back, then turned to Hassan just in time to see the thief's fist flying straight for his face. Augustus managed to dodge enough that a punch that should have knocked him out cold only glanced off his cheek. Even so, he staggered back, his face singing with pain.

Someone pinioned his arms and was immediately thrown off by someone else.

"Leave him alone. He's done nothing!" a man said. Augustus recognized one of the loungers who always drank tea in the café across from his house. A couple of his companions crowded around him and tried to shield Augustus from the circle of angry men.

"But Ali! You're as much for independence as anybody. Your own son sent around the petition we all signed."

"My son is an educated boy studying at Al-Azhar University. I've raised him better than to attack a neighbor."

"He's not a neighbor. He's a spy!" Hassan said. Several others grumbled in agreement.

"I sit across from his house in the Sultan El Moyyad Café every day, and I have never seen any evidence of his spying. You, Hassan, just want an excuse to loot his house."

"And why not?" someone shouted. "All his wealth is stolen from Egyptians anyway."

"Enough of this!" one of Ali's friends said. "If we raise our hand against a neighbor because he's British, who is next? The French? The Italians? The Copts?"

"All the foreigners should be thrown out. The Copts too!"

"The Copts are Egyptian," Ali said, "and my son says they are in the front lines of the protests."

"God preserve your son from being shot by European vermin such as this!"

The crowd pressed in, but Ali and his café friends pushed them back.

Ali forced a way through the crowd and hustled Augustus out of the angry circle.

"Go!" he shouted while his friends argued with the crowd.

Augustus hurried away. He did not run, because he didn't want the mob to smell blood and give chase, but he walked as quickly as he could. He dreaded going back to his neighborhood now. Hassan was ten times as dangerous as he had been before.

CHAPTER ELEVEN

Augustus arrived at Heinrich Schäfer's home exhausted and shaken. A servant let him in and brought him to Heinrich's drawing room, a cozy little place with a few comfortable chairs, a coffee table, and floor-to-ceiling bookshelves on every wall.

When his friend saw the state he was in, he dropped the volume he was reading and leaped to his feet. "Are you all right?"

"Spot of trouble with the mob," Augustus replied, slumping into an armchair.

"There's been fighting with the police in three districts. It's a good day to stay home and write."

"I don't have that luxury," Augustus said, fishing a cigarette out of his pocket.

"You're investigating the murder in your house? I see you've kept your old habits from Alexandria."

"The police don't have time to do it themselves. Plus, there's more to it than a simple murder. Much more. That's why I'm here to speak with you."

"I'll help in any way I can, of course. You look a state." Heinrich moved over a drinks trolley. "A bit of brandy will set you right."

Augustus waved away the offer. "None for me, thank you. I think I'm going to stay off it for a while."

The scholar gave him a curious look. "Really? Why?"

"Well to be honest, I think I might be drinking a bit too much. You know how the doctor prescribed me a dose of opium in the evenings to help me sleep?"

"And do you remember what I said about that?" Heinrich said, sitting back down.

"Oh, don't be paranoid. Doctors prescribe opium all the time. It's harmless in small doses. In any case, I've been dissolving it in a small glass of wine. Better than smoking it and stinking up the place. It ruins the wine, sadly, but I find it brings on sleep more quickly—blessed, dreamless sleep. Or if I do dream, it's of beautiful things."

"So you say, but what seems to be the problem?"

"Well, it appears that once I go into a stupor I drain the entire bottle! I've done it twice now. And if that's not bad enough, last night I took to sleepwalking. I went to the kitchen and cleaned out the pantry."

Heinrich Schäfer started packing his pipe. "Perhaps you should stop taking opium."

"But my dreams. Opium is the only thing that doesn't send me straight back to the trenches in my sleep."

"There's a certain psychologist from Vienna who has been researching dreams."

"I've read a bit of his stuff. I most certainly do not harbor a secret desire to have carnal relations with my mother."

"I am not saying I agree with all his theories, but I do believe he is correct in saying that dreams are the key to the subconscious. I think you need to face your dreams, Augustus."

"Why? All I'm dreaming is what I faced in the trenches. I faced that for three bloody years."

"And you haven't made your peace with it, hence the nightmares and the need for opium."

Augustus raised a hand. "Stick with what you know, my friend. You are the world's foremost expert on Egyptian art, and that is why I'm here."

Augustus filled him in on all he and Moustafa had discovered. Once he finished, he handed the notebook to Heinrich. The art historian sat in his armchair studying it for several minutes, smoking his pipe, his brow furrowed in concentration. Augustus waited patiently. This was another thing the war had taught him—you do not rush a man doing an important job.

At last, Heinrich looked up at his friend. Awe and fear mingled in his features.

THE CASE OF THE PURLOINED PYRAMID

"This is a remarkable discovery!"

"So our hunch about the Great Pyramid inscription is correct?"

"Yes, and so much more! Your assistant read the hieroglyphs correctly, but there was something he missed because he has not had access to the latest literature."

"Moustafa complains constantly that he doesn't get enough time with books."

"He can have access to my library whenever he wishes, and I mean that. The more intelligent natives need to be encouraged. That's the best way to create a flourishing colony. My own nation has not learned this. Look at what we did in German South West Africa. We slaughtered the Herero people, and now the colony is mired in poverty and ignorance."

"Moustafa's education can wait for another day. I'm a little more concerned with what you've discovered in that notebook."

Heinrich tapped the page. "Several things. First and most importantly, I have found a few clues to this underground area Moustafa told you about."

"So it isn't a parable for the underworld?"

"Yes and no. Moustafa was correct that it referred to an actual underground chamber, or series of chambers, but the place seems to be a physical stand-in for the passage through the land of the dead that all ancient Egyptians had to make. Unfortunately, the fragments they have so far recovered do not reveal more."

"Can you theorize?"

Heinrich took another puff of his pipe. "If I were to make a guess, I would say that the underground complex to which they refer was some sort of highly sacred temple. Only a few high priests and the pharaoh himself would be allowed to enter. It would have been built by prisoners of war, who would have then been killed to keep its contents secret."

"Charming."

"There are many similar cases throughout history in many cultures. From what I can glean, the pharaoh would have been the chief priest of this temple, in charge of performing powerful magic known only to a select few. Just what they were doing with these spells remains a mystery, one which these occultists would be most eager to discover."

"Occultists? There was quite a bit of pyramid power nonsense in that notebook. And what of those symbols on the cover?"

Heinrich turned it to face him, tapping his finger on the stylized letter T. "In my line of work, I get all sorts of marginal people besieging me with questions. I try to avoid them because they distract me from important work, but they persist. One of the most persistent groups is this one, the Thule Society."

"Never heard of it."

"Nor had I until a year ago. A whole crop of occult societies have bloomed in my nation ever since the war turned against us. They're like poisonous mushrooms. This one seems more active and better funded than most. That oaf at the German Club was only one of several members I have met. Another fellow approached me just a couple of months ago asking to see my notebooks of inscriptions. I tried to brush him off, but he was most persistent."

"What was his name?"

"Klaus Baumer. At least that was the name he gave me. It didn't quite roll off his tongue the way it should. He said he was an archaeologist, and he did have some knowledge, but more that of an educated layman than a true scientist. He claimed to have a doctorate from Berlin and to have run excavations in Anatolia and Palestine. I believed that less than I believed his name."

"These pseudoscientists always take on fake credentials," Augustus scoffed. "Do you know where he is?"

Heinrich shook his head. "I have no idea."

Augustus rubbed his chin. "Then I daresay we're a bit stuck. These idiots already overplayed their hand when they shot a man in my home. I doubt they'll be in touch again. And with all the rioting, they'll have gone to ground."

They sat in silence for a time, the only sound the faint ringing of a telephone in another room. A moment later, a servant appeared with the telephone on a tray, the receiver off the hook. A long extension cord trailed behind him.

"Telephone, sir," the servant said. Augustus had always wondered why they were trained to state the obvious.

Heinrich picked up the receiver.

"Hello?" A voice on the other end made him smile. He looked at Augustus with a twinkle in his eye. "Good to hear from you, Mrs. Hanzade."

Augustus felt his insides roil with jealousy.

"Yes, we're all safe here. No trouble in my neighborhood. Most kind of you to ask. Yes, yes, he's here. Oh, that's very interesting. We'll come over right away. Thank you. Goodbye."

Heinrich turned to him as he tried and failed to suppress a smug smile.

"You gave her your telephone number?" Augustus asked.

"I suppose she found my lecture on depictions of New Kingdom nude dancers invigorating," the art historian said, taking a puff from his pipe.

"Balderdash. What did she say? She asked about me, didn't she?"

"Well, she did mention you in relation to the case. Which are you more interested in?"

"Heinrich, I'm warning you . . ."

Heinrich laughed. "Oh, all right. Apparently our friends, having not found satisfaction with the retailers in town, are now hunting down antiquities wholesalers. Mrs. Hanzade was contacted yesterday and, being the bright woman she is, told them that she did, indeed, have an inscription of the kind that interested them. She wants us to come and listen in on the conversation. Perhaps we can find out more."

"Excellent idea! Let's go," Augustus said, checking his coat pocket to make sure his automatic was still there.

They went out to Heinrich's automobile. As the German drove them down the narrow residential street, Augustus noticed it was almost deserted. The houses were shut up tight, all windows closed. He suspected all the European neighborhoods looked like this.

"One thing worries me," Heinrich said. "What's going to happen when the members of the Thule Society come to her house and Mrs. Hanzade can't produce a monumental inscription on polished white limestone?"

"Oh, I'm sure one has already been produced."

"Whatever do you mean?"

"You'll see," Augustus replied.

***

Augustus and Heinrich hid behind a thick tapestry adorning the wall of one of Zehra's sitting rooms. A small tear in the old fabric allowed them to peek out while they remained hidden from view in the deep shadow between the tapestry and the wall.

They had been waiting for several minutes before Zehra made her appearance. Giving the tapestry a smile, she sat down on a divan on one side of the room and faced the doorway to the tapestry's right. A moment later, two muscular servants entered, struggling under the weight of a large block of polished limestone that they set down on a pile of cushions in the center of the room. They then took up position on either side of their mistress's divan, crossing their arms and becoming as still as statues.

Augustus and Heinrich took turns peering through the rent in the fabric. Heinrich's eyes went wide when he beheld the carving.

Augustus smiled. Suleiman had done his work well. It looked perfect. In style and dimension, the inscription was the exact match of the one found at Giza, although it was turned too far away for them to read. When they had arrived, Suleiman had pulled him aside and promised extra creativity in the contents of the inscription, something to lure even the most skeptical occultist.

Zehra glanced at her Rolex with obvious impatience and then opened up a ledger, picked up a pen, and began to work on a balance sheet.

Augustus watched in surprise as the open, flirtatious expression she usually wore vanished and was replaced by a hard, determined focus that almost startled him. This was a different side to her, one she didn't show to associates. With her business work in front of her and her guests out of sight behind the tapestry, she had momentarily forgotten herself and shown her other face.

Suleiman may have been the artist, but it was obvious that Zehra was the businesswoman in the Hanzade household.

At last, the doorman announced the guests. Zehra snapped the ledger shut, and her demeanor warmed. The servant ushered in a pair of Europeans. Augustus immediately recognized Dieter Neumann, the diminutive diplomat who had searched his house. The other man was a stranger to him. He was powerfully built, with thick arms and broad shoulders, but with the beer belly and florid features of a German in comfortable middle age. A nudge from Heinrich hinted that this was Klaus Baumer.

The two shook hands with Zehra, obviously enchanted, and gazed at the inscription.

"This is one of them, isn't it?" Neumann asked his companion in German.

"Yes, and look at this inscription!" Baumer replied. "'. . . the fourteen keys of wisdom unlock the doors of wisdom found beneath . . .'"

"Beneath what?" Neumann asked breathlessly.

"I don't know. It breaks off there."

"Blast! We're so close! But it makes sense. Ah, yes, the fourteen keys. I'll wager those are for the portals."

"But where? Where are those damn portals?"

"Be patient. We'll find it. There's still that other one to look at."

"Do you find this interesting?" Zehra asked in English. Augustus wasn't sure if she knew German or not. At least she was acting like she didn't.

"Oh yes, most interesting, Mrs. Hanzade," the diplomat said. "May I ask where it was found?"

"It was found ten years ago on the Giza Plateau by an, um, amateur excavation. It's not recorded in any archive."

The two Germans looked at each other and nodded, obviously pleased.

Tea came, and they chatted for a time. Dieter asked her repeatedly if she knew of any other inscription fragments, and Zehra hinted that she did and would track them down. Finally they got down to business and quickly agreed on a price. Augustus had to fight to suppress a chuckle at hearing the high price she asked. Dieter barely tried to haggle.

"Thank you most kindly, Mrs. Hanzade," Dieter said, handing over the money in British pounds.

Klaus Baumer went out and returned with four husky Germans. One had a livid facial scar that Augustus recognized as a poorly healed shrapnel wound. All four had the air of hardened veterans about them. They lifted up the inscription fragment with little effort and hauled it away.

A few minutes later, the Germans were gone, and Zehra, Augustus, and Heinrich sat having tea.

"I must compliment you, Mrs. Hanzade, on an excellent forgery," Heinrich said.

"Oh, please call me Zehra, and it was my husband's work."

Augustus turned to him. "How did you know it was a forgery?"

Heinrich took a sip from his tea. "Not from the work—that was perfect—but from the fact that it was exactly what our friends were looking for. By the way, I didn't recognize the four toughs. I think they're new in the city. I wonder how many more men they've assembled."

"What's this other fragment they're talking about?" Augustus asked.

"I don't know," Zehra replied. "I'll make enquiries."

They were waiting for one of Zehra's trusted servants to return from tailing the Germans. Both Augustus and Heinrich would have been recognized, and while Augustus was chafing at the bit, he had to force himself to sit calmly and await the servant's return.

"So are all your antiquities fakes?" Heinrich asked.

"Yes. Suleiman prides himself on the accuracy of his work."

"I hope he isn't getting too creative with form and content. Otherwise it will greatly complicate the study of Egyptology."

Augustus laughed. "Here we are investigating a murder by a sinister cult, and you're worried about your *magnum opus*!"

Heinrich looked offended. "I merely wish to preserve the knowledge of the past and hope that our charming host isn't muddying the waters."

"Have no fear, Heinrich," Zehra said with a smile. "Suleiman takes care to make his works as accurate as they can be. Mostly he works from genuine pieces, as he did with a certain statuette of Horus that Augustus ended up purchasing. It just so happened that his assistant had seen the original of that very same statuette come out of the ground and was able to identify it as an imitation."

"A bit of bad luck for you," Heinrich said, tamping some tobacco into his pipe.

"Oh, I don't know about that," Zehra said, smiling at Augustus.

Augustus hid himself behind his tea cup, which he hoped Zehra wouldn't notice was empty. Moments later, he was saved by the return of the servant.

"I followed the Germans to a house in Zamelek," he told his mistress.

"That's an odd neighborhood for some foreigners to live in," Augustus commented.

"Says the Englishman who lives on Ibn al-Nafis Street," Zehra replied. "They must want privacy as much as you do."

"Tell me about this house. What does it look like?" Augustus asked the servant.

"It is set apart from the other houses and is built in the old French style. It is not very well kept, and I believe the Germans only moved in recently after the house stood for a long time empty. The front door looks stout, and the windows are barred. There is a back garden I did not get to see because it is surrounded by a high wall. The top of the wall is set with broken glass."

Augustus nodded and turned to Zehra. "Your man is a quick one. He divined the purpose of my question immediately."

"You mean you're going to sneak into their house?" Zehra asked. "That's very dangerous."

"The police are too busy, and I can't just stand by while someone gets murdered in my own home. Besides, I've always liked a good mystery."

"Like when the khedive's jewels went missing in Alexandria," Zehra said.

Augustus's jaw dropped. "How did you hear about that? That was a private police matter!"

"I'm a businesswoman. It's in my interest to know all about my associates. And as for how I heard, surely you must know by now that Egyptians are the greatest gossips God ever made. Nothing stays a private affair for long. So when are you going to risk your life for the sake of an unwelcome guest?"

"Tonight."

CHAPTER TWELVE

Faisal was worried. When he had shown up on Ibn al-Nafis Street to take Osman ibn Akbar to morning prayers, he found the blind old beggar too sick to stand. Osman slept in the doorway of a ruined building, having set up some old boards and stones as a rough wall in front of the doorway to make a tiny room that contained a frayed old blanket, a reed mat, and a begging bowl, his only possessions beside his staff and the clothes on his back.

Usually Osman was sitting outside in the sun when Faisal came, ready to be led to the mosque so they could beg together. This morning, though, he still lay in his little cubbyhole.

Faisal peeked in, biting his lip when he heard the ragged breathing and saw how the old man's features appeared more sunken than usual.

"Osman ibn Akbar, are you all right?" Faisal asked after a moment.

The beggar didn't seem to hear him, and Faisal had to repeat the question in a louder voice before he got an answer.

"I think God is calling me."

The words came out so soft and weak that Faisal barely caught them. A coldness spread through the boy's chest.

"Nonsense!" Faisal said, rallying. "You just need to get out in the sun where it's warm and get something in your stomach."

"I am too weak to go to the mosque today. May God forgive me."

Faisal removed the splintered board that served as the beggar's front door and climbed inside. With a struggle, he got Osman to his feet and, fetching his stick and begging bowl, led him outside. Life on the street had made Faisal stronger than his years, and Osman felt like a bundle of papyrus reeds in his hands. It wasn't long before he got him to his usual morning spot, where the sun could warm Osman's aged bones before it got so hot he moved to a shady spot on the opposite side of the street for the rest of the day.

The beggar groaned as Faisal set him down. The passersby barely noticed the two.

"I'm sorry, Faisal, but you'll have to get your breakfast elsewhere today. I can't make it another step. God will provide for you."

Faisal felt inside his pocket for the last of the bread he had swiped from the Englishman. It was a bit stale, but neither of them were so high and mighty as to make a fuss about that.

"He's already provided!" Faisal said, trying to sound cheerful. He put the bread into Osman's hands.

The old man frowned. "Is this stolen?"

"No, I earned it!"

"Bah! You've never worked a day in your life."

"I did! I'm working for the Englishman now. He's trying to find the man who shot one of his guests. I'm helping him. I found a book the killer dropped, and the Englishman took me all the way to Giza in his motorcar!"

Osman ibn Akbar managed a weak smile. "If you're not telling tales, you are a lucky boy."

"I'm not telling tales. I got to see the pyramids the jinn built and everything. And a tourist took my picture! Eat up."

Osman extended his hand, offering him a crust. "You have some too."

Faisal paused, staring at the bread and licking his lips. His grubby hand reached for the bread, and then he pulled back.

"I've already eaten today," Faisal said, turning away.

He looked nervously up and down the street for Hassan. The bully usually slept late, so he should be safe for the moment, but he didn't like sitting here exposed like this.

The two sat in the morning sun as the old man ate, and the boy held out the begging bowl hoping someone would drop a coin or a bit of food in it. No one did.

***

It was early afternoon, and Moustafa was stuck doing all the work himself while Mr. Wall visited Herr Schäfer. Moustafa hadn't heard from him since he had confidently walked off into the riotous city alone. He hoped he hadn't run afoul of the protestors.

But Moustafa was too busy to dwell on his worries. Some workers had come to install a telephone and then demanded extra pay for coming out during the general strike. Moustafa almost had to knock their heads together to get them to do their job. And while he was keeping an eye on them, a customer had shown up, some picky little Englishman who kept asking when Mr. Wall would come back because he so obviously didn't want to deal with Moustafa. That didn't stop the fellow from asking Moustafa all sorts of technical questions about the artifacts. Moustafa got the impression that the Englishman was trying to prove he knew more than him, and he kept failing. Still, the fellow was looking at some ushabtis with interest, so perhaps he'd make a purchase after all.

Between the foot-dragging Egyptian workers and the needy customer who just couldn't make up his mind, he barely had time to perform the noon prayer. To his irritation, when the muezzin made the call to prayer, the telephone workers took the opportunity to sit in the courtyard and smoke cigarettes, but they didn't bother to make their peace with God. Once Moustafa finished his prayers, he found the Englishman waiting for him impatiently with yet another pointless question designed to show off his knowledge and Moustafa's ignorance.

Moustafa ignored him for the moment and shouted at the telephone workers to stop shirking, then went to deal with the customer again.

Shortly thereafter, the electric doorbell rang. Moustafa detached himself from another one-sided battle of wits with the Englishman and answered it.

That little monster who had found the German's notebook stood outside.

"What do you want?" Moustafa demanded.

"Do you have any food?" the boy asked.

"This is antiquities shop, not a soup kitchen. Go away!" Moustafa started to close the door. The impertinence!

"Osman ibn Akbar is sick!"

Moustafa paused. The boy pointed across the street where that blind old beggar sat. The old man looked paler and weaker than usual. In fact, he looked half-dead. He slumped against the wall, his jaw slack, lips barely moving in what Moustafa guessed was a prayer.

"Please," Faisal said. "We haven't had breakfast, not a bite to eat all day, not even a crust of bread. Can't you give us something?"

Moustafa sighed and grudgingly pulled a half piastre coin out of his pocket.

"God said to give to the poor, but that doesn't mean you can come around here any time you like. This is not a bank."

Faisal snatched the coin without so much as a thank-you and peered around Moustafa.

"Is the Englishman here?"

"No, and he doesn't want to see you anyway," Moustafa said, trying to close the door again. Unfortunately, Faisal had managed to take a step inside and blocked the way.

Faisal grinned up at him. "That notebook helped, didn't it? He's going to find the killer!"

"The notebook helped," Moustafa conceded. "But you've already been paid for that and quite well too. Now go get your beggar friend some food."

A deep rumble emanated from Faisal's stomach at the mention of food. Despite this, he stayed put.

"Does he pay you well?" Faisal asked.

"That's none of your business. If you want to know how jobs pay, why don't you find work?"

Faisal plucked up. "Maybe I could work for him! He needs a scout in this neighborhood, someone to watch out for him. Those foreigners might come back, and there's still Hassan. He needs someone like me. I can guard the house."

"Ha! And steal everything in it? Get out of here. Mr. Wall moved here because he wants to be alone."

"I know why he wants to be alone," Faisal said, going pale. "Have you seen what's under his mask? Half his face was torn away by a German cannon!"

Moustafa shook his head. "Poor fellow."

Faisal stamped his bare foot against the tile. "Poor fellow? Bah! He's not a poor fellow. A poor fellow is someone who has no place to live and has to beg for scraps to eat. A poor fellow has to run away from bullies and dogs. That's a poor fellow! A poor fellow doesn't drive a motorcar and live in a big house with lots of food."

"All right, Little Infidel, all right," Moustafa said, putting a hand on his shoulder. "But would you want to switch places with him?"

Faisal looked doubtful. Moustafa nodded.

"That's what I thought. God gives each of us a share of blessings and a share of hardships. Mr. Wall is rich and European, but he suffered terribly in the war and will carry that scar for life. He will never marry because of it and never have children to carry on his name. Even the poorest fellah gets to see his name continue. And look at me. I was blessed with a gift for languages and fascinating work, but I had to leave my village and all my relations to get these blessings."

"Well, what about me? Where are my blessings?"

"How old are you?"

"Twelve, I think."

"Eleven, twelve, thirteen, whatever you are, you have an entire life ahead of you. Only God knows what is written for you. Perhaps your blessings will come later."

Faisal brightened. "I got to ride in a car! Maybe the Englishman is my blessing."

Moustafa shook his head. "Foreigners bring wealth and opportunity sometimes, but it never lasts. They are filled with their own affairs. They all go back home in the end, and when they do, they forget us."

Sadly it was true. How many times had Egyptologists hired him and promised him the skies, only to finish the dig season and pack off back to London or Paris, never to write him or find him those jobs in Europe they always spoke about? Mr. Clarke down in the Soudan had been only the first of many disappointments. Moustafa had learned not to trust the promises of foreigners. Only God knew when each man would be called to his reckoning, and thus it was best to enjoy a good situation while it lasted.

Mr. Wall paid well and let him read books, so this was the best job he'd ever had. But Mr. Wall courted danger. He would leave Moustafa one day, but it might be in a coffin instead of a ship.

"Excuse me," came a nasal drone from the front room. "Are you quite sure this ushabti is XXI Dynasty? The writing appears to be more of the style of the Late Period."

Trying to control his anger at the idiotic customer, he told Faisal, "I need to go. Take that money and buy your friend something."

To avoid any further argument, he picked Faisal up and plopped him down outside the door, quickly closing it in his face.

After more verbal sparring, and an inordinately long haggle over price, the Englishman finally bought two of the cheapest ushabtis. Moustafa wrapped the little figurines in newspaper and tied the package up with string. As he let the customer out and resisted the urge to boot him in the rear, he glanced across the street and saw Faisal helping the blind beggar eat some falafel. The man ate slowly, without enthusiasm and with many protests, but the boy insisted, practically shoving the food into the old man's mouth. Moustafa noticed that for every three bites the old man took, Faisal took only one.

"There might be a bit of hope for that Little Infidel after all," Moustafa mumbled, and went to keep an eye on the telephone workers.

***

Mr. Wall didn't come back until early evening, looking weary and yet hurried. After what Faisal had told him, Moustafa couldn't help but look at the mask that hid half his face. A flicker of annoyance passed over his boss's features, and Moustafa looked away.

"Did you have any trouble with the protests, Mr. Wall?"

"Our friend Hassan tried to start a protest of his own. Said I planned to turn the mosque down the street into a bar."

"Shall I take care of him?"

"I'm not sure that's wise. I've heard he has a family who are even more violent than him. In any case, we have more important matters at hand. Are you up for some night work? I'll pay you extra."

"If it's against the Germans, I'll work for free, Mr. Wall. I don't like being shot at."

"Nor do I, but you'll get your danger pay in any case."

Mr. Wall led him up the stairs to a room Moustafa had never been inside before. The door was always locked, and even the cleaning lady, an old woman who came twice a week, had never been in there.

Mr. Wall produced a key, unlocked the door, and switched on the light.

Moustafa gasped. The room was filled with weapons. A rack of rifles stood against one wall, and on a table were a couple of crates, one marked ".303 rounds" and the other "No. 23 Mills grenades." On a groundsheet laid on the floor were a couple of large objects hidden under a tarpaulin.

"What are you doing with all this?"

"You never know when you need to arm a group of men for some serious work," his boss answered.

"But . . . but how did you get it all?"

Mr. Wall gave him a crooked smile. "Europe is awash with weapons. And where I'm from, no one checks the luggage of a man with a title."

Moustafa looked dubiously at the arsenal. Mr. Wall always seemed to come up with new surprises. This was not a good one.

They walked over to the rack of rifles.

"Have you fired a gun before?" Mr. Wall asked.

Moustafa nodded. "My uncle had an old Remington breechloader. He taught me to shoot."

"A fine gun, if a bit outdated. One of the favorites of the Mahdist army. Your uncle was in that, was he?"

"My uncle fought at Omdurman," Moustafa said, feeling that old swell of pride he felt anytime he thought of that great battle. The Mahdi had been a madman, slaughtering other tribes and falsely putting himself up as the final prophet, but he had stirred the Soudanese people to great things. As misguided as the war had been, Moustafa couldn't help but feel proud of the thought of the Mahdist warriors charging the red British lines, braving rifle and machine-gun fire when most of the Soudanese had carried only old rifles and swords.

"Well, I don't have a Remington," Mr. Wall said, "but I do have several Short Magazine Lee-Enfields. These were standard issue for our chaps in the war. Accurate up to two thousand yards and packs a nice punch with .303 bullets. And here's a Mauser if you want to fire at the Bosche with one of their own weapons. Its bullet doesn't have as much stopping power as a Lee-Enfield, but it's certainly accurate. Or perhaps you'd prefer this."

Mr. Wall picked up something that looked like a rifle, but with a shorter barrel perforated with holes and a bulky round magazine that he snapped into its side.

"This is an MP 18, a German submachine gun from one of their Storm Battalions. It can empty its entire fifty-round magazine in ten seconds. It fires standard 9mm pistol ammunition, but it's quite deadly at close range, believe me. I was on the wrong end of one of these more often than I care to remember."

"I'm not sure I'd know how to use one," Moustafa said, feeling increasingly awkward.

"Then it's a rifle for you, and perhaps a pistol to back it up?"

Mr. Wall opened a drawer in the table, and Moustafa saw four pistols inside.

"Here are two Webleys and two Lugers. The Webleys have more stopping power but only six rounds. The Lugers, on the other hand, have a seven-round magazine and are more accurate, but you're strong enough that the kick of a Webley won't affect you at all."

"I'll take one of the revolvers I think. Although I have never fired a revolver, only a rifle."

"Revolvers aren't too good for hunting gazelle I suppose," Mr. Wall said, making a strange little laugh. It came out too high, almost hysterical. He handed Moustafa a revolver and a box of bullets and opened one of the crates. Inside were two different types of grenades, some that looked like large dates and others that had a small can on the end of a stick.

"Are we starting another war with the Germans, Mr. Wall?" Moustafa said in a quiet voice.

"Not all Germans, just these particular ones," Mr. Wall said, making that high laugh again. Moustafa suppressed a shudder.

Against his better judgment, Moustafa indicated the two covered lumps on the floor.

"What's under the tarpaulin?"

"Ah! A man of discerning taste! Well, here are the twin prizes of my collection. I value them almost as much as that statue of my good friend Sobek downstairs."

With a flourish, Mr. Wall whipped off the tarpaulin to reveal a machine gun on a tripod and a strange device Moustafa didn't recognize. It was a short tube with a second shorter cylinder attached to the top, both of which were mounted on a squat tripod.

"May I present you with a Lewis machine gun, complete with two boxes of ammunition, and a lovely German trench mortar. I'm afraid I'm a bit short on shells for the trench mortar, but I have enough to level the Germans' hideout if need be."

Moustafa had read about trench mortars in the newspaper. They were positioned in the front trenches and lobbed bombs at the enemy. Many men had been torn apart by them. Had one of these injured Mr. Wall? Could it have been this very one?

His boss laid a hand on the smooth barrel of the trench mortar. Moustafa noticed it trembled slightly.

"So what do you say, Moustafa? Want to bring one of these along?"

"We are in the middle of a city, Mr. Wall. To use something like this would attract too much attention. It would be best if we do not shoot at all," Moustafa replied in a tone that he used when one of his children was having a tantrum.

"I suppose you're right," Mr. Wall said with a slight slump of his shoulders, pulling his hand away and leaving an outline of sweat on the barrel. "Ah! We need blades!"

Mr. Wall went over to another shelf at the far end of the room and showed him an array of bayonets and knives.

"Take your pick, my man. A pity I don't have one of those lovely broadswords the Mahdi's troops used. Straight out of the Middle Ages. I think you could do some wonderful damage with one of those. I know a dealer who specializes in African weapons, though. Perhaps as a Christmas bonus, eh?"

"Why do you have all these things, Mr. Wall? The war is over!"

His boss turned to him, his eyes ablaze. Immediately, Moustafa regretted his outburst. Europeans didn't like being confronted with their foolishness unless by one of their own, and usually not even then.

"The war is never over, Moustafa. There's always another war right around the corner. And you know why? Because mankind is stupid and selfish. It was the stupid and selfish Serbs who plotted to assassinate the stupid and selfish Archduke, and the stupid and selfish Austro-Hungarians who insisted on making a war out of it, and the stupid and selfish Germans who let them do it, and the stupid and selfish Russians who had to jump in to join the fight, and the stupid and selfish French who wanted in on the game too, and the stupid and selfish British who decided it might be fun to play as well, and then a whole crowd of other stupid and selfish countries decided the war was too good a thing to miss, and so they threw their hats in the ring as well. That will not change, Moustafa. That will never change, no matter how many millions die. So you ask why I have enough weapons to equip a heavily armed platoon in my spare bedroom? Because if mankind is going to be stupid and selfish, I'm going to be the stupidest and most selfish of them all!"

Moustafa sighed. This was going to be a long night.

CHAPTER THIRTEEN

The house was set apart from the street and the other houses by a broad lawn and driveway in the front and a walled garden in the back. It emanated an air of silent, aloof decay. It was an old-fashioned mansion built during the French occupation a hundred years before and was now somewhat dilapidated. The fine old plasterwork that decorated the façade was cracked, bits of the floral design having fallen away. Moustafa suspected that in the daytime he'd see the paint was faded and flaked. He saw no telephone line, which reassured him somewhat, and the lights that shone through the ground-floor windows were candlelight, not electric. No lights shone in the upper floor.

Moustafa carried a Lee-Enfield with a bayonet and had a Webley revolver in a holster in his belt. To placate his boss, he also had a long knife in a sheath on the other hip. Mr. Wall had tried to get him to take a couple of grenades as well, but Moustafa had held firm on that.

Even so, he felt ridiculous. It wasn't like they were going to war.

Mr. Wall himself had the German submachine gun and his small automatic pistol. Looped around his shoulder was a rolled up canvas tarpaulin and a coil of rope with knots regularly placed along its length. He had to leave his sword cane behind since he needed both hands to carry the submachine gun. He'd complained about that for the entire drive over.

"A man should look his best when going into battle, don't you think, Moustafa?"

They'd encountered little traffic and many police roadblocks on their drive across the city. The police had waved them through once they saw an Englishman at the wheel and did not even bother to look under the seats where their arsenal lay hidden.

They had parked Herr Schäfer's motorcar a block away in the shadows of some palm trees and walked the rest of the way, encountering no one. Moustafa had heard of this neighborhood but had never visited. It was mostly old French houses, taken over by rich Egyptians or divided up into several apartments for those with less means. Other houses lay abandoned, having fallen into decay.

Moustafa's heart beat fast. His boss gripped the submachine gun tight and had a sick grin on his face. He looked like he wanted a battle.

The neighborhood was quiet. The British had imposed a curfew and they saw no one. From a distance, they studied the front of the house. The lights remained on throughout the front rooms of the ground floor, glowing through the white blinds from behind the thick bars that protected the windows. A shadow passed behind one of them.

They crept around the back, to where the shadows lay deepest, and pressed themselves against the wall that encircled the garden. The tops of a few trees were visible above it. The nearest house lay fifty yards away, beyond a scraggly line of bushes and its own encircling wall. They would not be seen from here.

Mr. Wall slung his submachine gun and turned to Moustafa.

"Boost me up. I can just about reach. Once I get over, I'll toss one end of the rope to you and secure you while you climb up and over."

"Take care they don't see you and remember that we are here to find information, not shoot the place up," Moustafa replied.

They examined the wall. As was typical in Cairo, the top was covered with broken glass, set into the cement while it was still wet. Mr. Wall pulled the tarpaulin off from around his shoulder and folded it several times into a thick rectangle.

"This should do the trick," he whispered. "Here, give me a boost."

Moustafa interlaced his fingers to make a step with his hands. Mr. Wall stepped onto it and clambered onto Moustafa's shoulders. Moustafa got a good grip on his boss's legs and steadied him as he laid the canvas over the glass and hauled himself up and over, dropping to the other side.

All this had been done in virtual silence. Moustafa was impressed that he could move so silently. He moved like a thief. How often had this man crept through No Man's Land like that, looking for Germans to kill? Moustafa felt a chill go through him.

He was woken up from his thoughts by the end of the knotted rope whipping through the air close to his face. He grabbed it before it could slap the wall and make a sound.

Moustafa gripped the rope and began to climb. The rope did not slip an inch. He was half again as heavy as Mr. Wall, but the man was able to keep his weight secure as he ascended.

Moustafa got to the top of the wall, the glass jabbing at his rear but not cutting through the several layers of canvas, and dropped to the other side as quietly as he could.

The half-moon illuminated an untended garden. A few palm trees stood here and there, as well as some bushes that had obviously not been pruned in years. A dry, cracked stone fountain stood in the center of garden. Nearby was a wooden bench that had almost fallen apart with decay. The Germans were obviously only using this as a hideout, not a home.

Of more immediate interest was the back door, reached by a broad set of steps. The rear of the house was most likely given over to servants' rooms such as the kitchen and scullery, and all the back windows were dark. The front rooms, where Moustafa had seen candlelight, would have the study, dining, and reception rooms.

Mr. Wall retrieved the rope and hid it under a bush. The tarpaulin he left where it was on top of the wall. Being in shadow it was not immediately visible to anyone in the garden, and Moustafa doubted the Germans came out here much anyway.

Together they readied their weapons and crept up the back stairs.

They found the back door locked, and all the windows had bars. Moustafa smiled ruefully. He should have known. Cairo was infamous for its thieves and housebreakers. No one, not even foreigners, left a window unbarred or a door unlocked.

They stopped and stared at the house, unsure what to do.

"We could use a bayonet to pry open the door," Moustafa suggested in a low voice.

"That would make too much noise," his boss whispered. "Perhaps we could find a wire to pick the lock?"

"I don't know how to do that. Do you?"

"No."

They stared for a while more.

"Psst."

They both swung around, guns at the ready. Faisal stood a few feet behind them, instantly recognizable in the half-light by his tangle of unruly hair. Seeing the guns trained on him, he leaped in the air in shock, but he didn't let out a scream. He made no sound at all.

"What the blazes are you doing here?" Mr. Wall hissed.

"I followed you."

"How?"

"I hid in the back of your motorcar. I saw you leaving at night and knew you were going to do something fun, so I put a blanket over myself and tucked myself in the back seat when you weren't looking. When the soldiers at the checkpoint saw me, they thought I was just a pile of rags."

"You are a pile of rags," Moustafa whispered, annoyed. "Get out of here. This is man's work!"

"I am a man," Faisal said, puffing his chest out and flexing his arms. The result was far from impressive.

"How did you get inside the garden?" Mr. Wall asked.

"Bah! That was easy. This wall has lots of handholds and toeholds. You two looked funny climbing over each other, like a couple of overweight baboons."

Moustafa raised his hand and stepped forward. "Get out of here before I knock your head off your shoulders."

"Wait." Mr. Wall restrained him. He looked up at the upper windows, the moonlight gleaming off his mask. Then he turned to Faisal.

"Could you climb this wall?"

"With one hand tied behind my back."

"Do you think you can squeeze through those bars? Perhaps those shutters are unfastened."

"It doesn't matter if they are. Twenty dirhams."

"Ten," Mr. Wall grumbled.

"Twenty or you can climb it yourself."

Moustafa clipped him on the back of the head. "You'll take ten and be happy about it."

THE CASE OF THE PURLOINED PYRAMID

Faisal stuck his tongue out at Moustafa, who resisted the urge to throttle him, and turned back to Mr. Wall.

"Twenty. Osman ibn Akbar is sick, and I have to buy food for the both of us."

Moustafa softened a little.

"That's true," he told his boss.

"Fine, twenty," Mr. Wall said with an impatient gesture. "Get a move on. We can't stand about all night."

With that, the boy scampered up the wall as quickly and quietly as a spider. Once he got to the bars, he hung from them using one hand and both feet while he tried to open the shutters. He found them locked, and with a contemptuous shrug he pulled a flat piece of metal from his pocket, inserted it into the gap between the shutters, and popped them open.

He peered into the darkness for a moment, then spent a minute's tough squeezing to work his way through the bars. With a final wave to the men below, he disappeared into the darkened upper floor.

They waited in silence for a minute. Then another.

"What's taking him so long?" Mr. Wall whispered.

"He's probably looting the place." Moustafa couldn't believe they had put themselves into this little grub's hands.

"I should have told him to make his way down directly. I assumed that he would. I see my mistake now."

"I'll give him a good thrashing once he reappears."

"That will make too much noise. Wait until we get home."

They waited a few more minutes.

"Do you think they caught him?" Mr. Wall asked.

Moustafa put his ear against the door. His boss did the same. They could hear no sound from within.

Suddenly, the bolt slid back on the door and it opened. They barely had enough time to get on opposite sides of the door and level their guns.

Faisal poked his head out, looked at Mr. Wall and Moustafa, and grinned.

"You two are way too nervous to be burglars. Come on," Faisal whispered.

He brought a fat piece of chocolate cake up to his mouth and shoved it in, consuming it in nearly one bite.

"So that's what took you so long," Moustafa growled. "Have you found anything more useful than the kitchen?"

"I found a room filled with old stones covered in that funny picture writing." Faisal's voice was barely audible around the mass of chocolate cake in his mouth. "That's what you're looking for, isn't it?"

"Lead the way," Mr. Wall said.

Faisal stuck out his hand. Moustafa grabbed him by the collar.

"Fine, you can pay me later," Faisal squeaked. "Now put me down."

Faisal led the way down a darkened corridor, with Mr. Wall just behind and Moustafa taking up the rear. Barely any moonlight filtered in, and they moved slowly. Muffled voices came from another part of the house. They turned a corner and it grew even darker.

Moustafa hadn't taken three steps beyond the corner when his hip bumped into a small table set against the wall.

He looked down, and with sickening clarity he saw a vase tip over and fall to the marble floor.

Faisal dove for it and caught it with barely an inch to spare. The boy ended up sprawled on the floor, but his fall hadn't made any noise.

Faisal got up, set the vase back in its place, gave Moustafa a scowl, and continued down the hallway. Moustafa followed, mortified.

They came to a spot where a door stood open on one wall. Faisal motioned for them to stop and wait, then ducked inside. He returned a moment later with another slice of cake.

Moustafa rolled his eyes. The Germans were going to wonder why someone had broken into their home and only stolen their dessert. After another turn, they came to a doorway. Light shone from the keyhole and the crack underneath. They still heard the voices, but they sounded distant, as if in another room. Just to be sure, Mr. Wall and Moustafa took turns peering through the keyhole.

Moustafa saw part of what appeared to be a large room, bare of furnishings but with several slabs of polished white limestone lying on the floor.

An elbow jabbed his ribs. He frowned down at the beggar boy, who motioned for him to get out of the way. A tug on the sleeve from Mr. Wall convinced him to do as the boy asked rather than smack him across the face. The brat was getting above himself.

Faisal eased the door open, and Moustafa gasped at what they saw.

CHAPTER FOURTEEN

Augustus couldn't believe his eyes. They stood at the entrance to a large room that looked like it had once been a ballroom. The ceiling was ornately decorated with painted plaster reliefs in the old French Imperial style. A large glass chandelier fitted with two dozen candles illuminated the room, the crystals of the chandelier making the candles spark and pattern the walls and floor with multicolored spots.

There was no furniture. Instead, spread out on the hardwood floor, were about a hundred fragments of polished white limestone, each with a hieroglyphic inscription. They had been arranged in some sort of order. Some of them stood in tidy rows. A few were set against one another to join up fragments of inscription. Many more lay in a jumble, their part in the puzzle not yet determined.

The puzzle remained far from complete, but Augustus felt a prickle of awe at seeing what hardly anyone had seen for centuries—the inscription that once covered the surface of the Great Pyramid at Giza.

Set in a place of honor in the center of the room was the largest piece—the one Suleiman had carved himself. Augustus smiled.

Just then a side door opened, and someone entered.

Augustus raised his submachine gun and trained it on the newcomer. Out of the corner of his eye, he saw Moustafa do the same.

It was the German with the shrapnel scar across his face. He wore a cheap suit and the soft cap of a working man. He froze, half in and half out of the doorway. His eyes met Augustus's. Calmly, he closed the door behind him, raised his hands, and walked toward them.

He's a cool one, isn't he? Augustus thought. *He's seen the front. I'll wager he's seen some night raids too. Yes, he's seen everything.*

The man walked close by an inscription fragment, his foot about to "accidentally" knock it and create some noise. Augustus gave a little shake of his head. The German veteran gave him a tight smile in return and made a show of avoiding it before walking the remaining space between them. He stopped a few feet away, just out of reach.

"Faisal, listen at the door. Moustafa, see what you can learn from these fragments," Augustus whispered.

As the two went about their tasks, Augustus stepped forward, glared at the German when he made a sudden move that might have turned into an attack, and pressed the muzzle of the submachine gun against his belly. Then he used his free hand to pat him down. He found a compact automatic in his suit pocket and a knife tucked in his boot. With a tug of sympathy, he noted that those boots were German army issue, worn but still serviceable. This man still wore the boots that had been on his feet when he had been demobilized.

Augustus tucked the weapons in his own pocket and backed out of reach. The man lowered one hand slowly and traced the livid scar that marred his cheek and jaw.

"I miss women," he whispered.

"I miss many things," Augustus whispered back. "What's your name?"

"Otto. A pity that two great Aryan nations should go to war to enrich the Jews."

"Do be quiet."

Augustus glanced at his companions. Faisal had his ear pressed against the door. Now that they were in proper light, Augustus could see the boy's mouth was ringed with chocolate. Augustus hoped the little thief didn't get sick. The last thing he needed right now was a vomiting child. Moustafa stared at inscription after inscription, his finger tracing the lines, his mouth working silently. Augustus had to force himself to keep an eye on the German and not watch in wonder at Moustafa as he read the four-thousand-year-old inscriptions as easily as he himself could read the *Egyptian Gazette*. That man had a true gift for languages.

The scene didn't change for several minutes. Faisal listened, Moustafa went from stone to stone, and Augustus kept his gun held unwaveringly at the chest of a man he would have killed on sight a year ago. Every now and then, they heard snatches of conversation from the other rooms. It was in German, but the voices were too muffled and distant for Augustus to make any sense of it.

Otto looked back at him with a mixture of respect and sympathy, but it was the kind of respect and sympathy you might expect from someone about to engage in a duel. Augustus had no doubt this fellow would try to kill him at the first opportunity.

Moustafa was about halfway through the inscriptions when Faisal's eyes widened and he waved his hand urgently at the others. He scampered without a sound behind the largest stone fragment in the center of the room and ducked down. Moustafa readied his rifle and knelt behind another fragment.

The side door opened and in walked another of the workers who had been at Zehra Hanzade's house. His eyes took in the scene and he leaped back.

"Intruders!"

Augustus let him have it.

A burst of 9mm rounds tore through him and the wooden frame of the doorway, sending out a spray of splinters and blood. Otto batted the submachine gun to one side and drove a fist into Augustus's stomach.

Augustus grunted and doubled over. Otto yanked on the gun, but Augustus held on, squeezing off a few rounds that shattered the boards beneath Otto's feet and made him do a little dance. The German slugged him again. Augustus staggered to one side, and Otto dove through the open doorway into the darkened hall through which they had entered.

Augustus sent some rounds after him, then stepped into the hallway and fired another burst at the dark form hurrying away in the shadows.

The report of a rifle in the inscription room made him turn back.

Moustafa fired again, aiming for a target Augustus couldn't see beyond the side door. The first German lay in a crumpled heap, half in and half out of the room.

Moustafa ducked as a Luger made its distinctive bark. The bullet took a chip off the limestone block behind which his employee knelt, marring the inscription.

Augustus flattened himself against the left-hand wall and hurried along the side of the room until he got right next to the door. Moustafa covered him as he approached, daring another shot from the Luger to keep the German from entering the room and seeing the approaching threat.

Once to the side of the door, Augustus dropped low and swung around the corner, his gun leading the way, already firing. By the time he even saw his target, the enemy was pirouetting backward, his guts splayed open. The man behind was just raising a rifle to fire. Augustus made a quick squeeze of the trigger to save ammunition and took him out with a single shot to the forehead.

"Follow me!" Augustus shouted to his companions.

He leaped over the bodies and into a short corridor with doors on both sides and ahead. A quick look to either side showed no enemies. A slight scuff of a shoe on the floor around the corner of the far doorway made him fall to one knee, sighting down the barrel of the MP 18. His mind raced. How many bullets did he have left?

Silence.

A hand gripping a Luger darted around the corner, its owner not daring to show his face.

He had shown enough. Augustus drilled a long burst through the enemy's wrist, almost severing the hand, blood tracing an arch on the far wall and the Luger clattering to the floor.

Augustus was already leaping through the doorway. Ignoring the man right in front of him, who gripped his wrist and stared in horrified fascination at his hand hanging from a single thread of tissue, Augustus poured fire into the two men standing behind him. Both flew backward, crashing into a dining room table and scattering a half-eaten meal.

Augustus kept running. A quick glance over his shoulder showed Moustafa and Faisal right behind him. Where was the rest of his unit? He stopped at another doorway, made a quick glance to make sure no one was around, and gestured toward the front door that stood right ahead. Faisal ran for it and slid the bolt.

Just as he was opening it, he threw himself to the floor as an enemy submachine gun stitched a line of holes through the wood. Augustus looked to the left and saw a member of a German trench raiding party charging down the stairs, firing a gun identical to his own. Augustus emptied the last of his magazine in him, and the man tumbled down the steps.

Steps? Was he in a dugout?

No time to wonder. An enemy assault was in progress, and he was alone and isolated with the remnants of some colonial unit. They needed to withdraw. Now.

He turned to the native boy. (A boy? Here on the front?) and saw he'd already flung open the door. The big colonial soldier fired at someone down the hallway, covering their retreat.

Augustus looked around, confused. This didn't look like a dugout. It looked like the inside of a house. He'd seen some pretty cushy dugouts, and the Germans built the best, but this appeared far bigger than any he'd ever taken.

Was he in a command center? Was this an actual house, perhaps a general's headquarters? There had been so many missions, so many assaults, they all had blended together. Was he on another one? What was the objective this time?

Someone tugged on his arm. The boy had come back inside.

He shouted something in a strange language, trying to drag him to the front door. Augustus didn't understand a word, but he understood the meaning well enough. Meanwhile the hulking colonial soldier, who for some reason wasn't in uniform, was shouting in the same language as he fired first down the hallway, and then up the stairs. A bullet cracked off the marble floor at Augustus's feet.

The colonial soldier glanced over his shoulder at Augustus and stared for a moment. He switched to English.

"We have to run! There are too many!"

Instinct snapped through his confusion. Augustus grabbed the boy and, holding him like a rugby ball, sprinted out the door, down a flight of steps, and across a front lawn.

He found himself on a nighttime street lined with mansions in the French style. So he was behind the lines in occupied France then. That made sense. But why was it so bloody hot, and where had those palm trees come from?

He turned right, but the boy pounded on his shoulder and pointed left, repeating something over and over. Augustus turned left. This boy must be some sort of local guide. Was this even France? Perhaps he'd been transferred to the Mesopotamian Front.

Why couldn't he remember?

They ran. Dimly he was aware of gunshots behind him and the big colonial soldier catching up.

"All you all right, Mr. Wall?"

Mr. Wall? Was that some sort of cover name he was using?

"We have to get back to our lines," Augustus replied.

"Lines? You mean the house?"

"Headquarters," Augustus mumbled.

The neighborhood darkened, the houses fading. Spreading palm trees were replaced with shattered stumps, the paved road with a mud track. The moon flickered and disappeared, replaced with the intermittent flash of distant artillery fire. Shell holes and barbed wire and bits of bodies. No Man's Land.

He hit the ground. The boy let out a cry as Augustus fell on him.

"Not much farther, Mr. Wall!"

"Keep down or the snipers will spot you!"

The colonial soldier hauled him to his feet. They staggered forward and came to a car. The boy got in the back, the colonial soldier in the passenger's seat. Augustus blinked and stared at the vehicle. Was he supposed to drive? Where to? And how could a civilian car make it through the mud and wire and craters?

He rummaged through his pockets and found a set of keys. He held them impotently in his hand.

"This car will never make it through the mud. Plus the German snipers will spot us for sure. They'll call in artillery support."

The colonial soldier stared for a moment. Then he glanced down the street in the direction from which they came, got out of the car, and walked up to Augustus.

"Where are you?" he asked.

"I—I don't know."

The native slapped him across the face. The blow was so hard Augustus nearly fell over.

Augustus blinked, reeling. What were those shapes he saw behind the dead landscape of No Man's Land? They looked like houses and trees.

The colonial soldier slapped him again. Things became clearer.

"I'm . . . not there. I'm . . ."

The native levy slapped him a third time. That brought more clarity, but a gunshot from down the street added a sense of urgency to his struggle for the truth.

"Fucking hell, Moustafa, stop hitting me, or I'll sack you!"

Moustafa blinked in shock. "Such language, Mr. Wall!"

"Sorry, only halfway back. Get in the car before we get shot," Augustus said, adjusting his mask. Moustafa had nearly slapped it off.

Augustus revved the engine and sped out, turning in a tight circle when a muzzle flashed a block down the street. The gun fired again as they sped away, a bullet smashing the windshield.

"The bastard damaged my motorcar!" Augustus complained.

"Herr Schäfer's motorcar," Moustafa corrected.

"We stole it from a German? Oh no, right."

Moustafa studied him. "Are you able to drive, Mr. Wall?"

"Do you think you can do better? Were you a taxi driver back in Morocco? Um, no, the Soudan, isn't it?"

Moustafa said something else, but Augustus didn't hear. Images and sounds roiled through his brain. He had to squint at the clear path the headlights shone through the gloom, trying to see the road for a road and not a moonscape of destruction. He had to remind himself the sound of the engine was that of his own, not that of an approaching tank. The shots he heard in the distance he couldn't place. Were they real or not? Were they being pursued? He didn't dare look back. He might get lost in another world.

The drive seemed to last forever. At times, a dark hand grabbed the wheel and turned it to keep him from hitting a lamppost or a building, and he vaguely remembered a strange conversation with some soldiers at a roadblock where he tried to give them orders to repel the German counterattack, and they stared back at him in utter confusion. There were moments of relative clarity, when Augustus wanted to curl up and die rather than see Moustafa and Faisal staring at him like he was some lunatic. And then he would fall into the other world, and the barrages and machine-gun fire brought a strange comfort.

And then he was in his room, barring his door and ignoring Moustafa's shouts from the other side. He grabbed his opium and hurriedly packed a pipe. He didn't have time to dissolve it in wine.

Within a few minutes, he plunged into blessed oblivion.

Hours later, the sounds of wailing tore him out of unconsciousness.

CHAPTER FIFTEEN

Augustus peeked through the wooden latticework that screened his bedroom window and couldn't see anything amiss, only the usual crowds in the street below. The angle of the sun told him he had been unconscious for at least ten hours. It was already approaching midday. Some of the stalls in the market had already shut to escape the sun, although a melon seller was doing a brisk trade as his neighbors bought the best food with which to endure the heat.

As the wailing grew louder outside, he put on his mask, uncovered his mirror, and made himself presentable as quickly as possible. Hurrying downstairs, he found a weary-eyed Moustafa still standing sentinel at the front door, the Lee-Enfield in his hands.

"What's going on outside?" Augustus asked.

"I don't know. Um, Mr. Wall, how are you fee—"

"I'm fine," Augustus snapped.

He took up the MP 18 where it lay on a table in the front hallway, saw that in his delirium he hadn't neglected to reload it, and cautiously opened the door.

At first he couldn't see anything from this angle either, but then the crowd parted for a small procession. Four men in worn clothing and bare feet carried a board on which lay someone covered in a shroud. They were shouting and calling to God. Behind came a ragged little group of men and women, some hobbling along with the aid of canes, others bent over and coughing from various diseases. Trailing at the end was Faisal, tears pouring down his cheeks.

"It is Osman ibn Akbar who has died," Moustafa said. "God grant him eternal paradise."

"A pity. He seemed a decent sort. I hope he got to eat some of that tip Faisal earned for him last night. Speaking of, I'm famished. Have you eaten?"

"No, Mr. Wall. But—"

"I'll fry us up some eggs," he said, closing the front door and heading for the kitchen before Moustafa could say any more.

Over a breakfast of eggs and toast and a strong pot of coffee, Moustafa tried once again to broach the subject.

"Mr. Wall, what happened last night? It was like you weren't with us."

Augustus put his fork down, annoyed.

"Do you like working here, Moustafa?"

"Of course, but—"

"The pay is good enough? You like having access to my books?"

"Yes, but—"

"Then honor my privacy."

Moustafa's face hardened. "No, Mr. Wall. That will not do. We were in danger last night, and we will be in danger again soon enough. I suspect that you are often in danger. If I am to work for you, I need to know what is happening with you."

Augustus almost sacked him then. He was just opening his mouth to say the words when he stopped himself. What Moustafa said was only the truth, and where would he find someone else like him? Linguists of Moustafa's caliber were rare. Plus, he hadn't shied away from that fight.

But talking about this made Augustus squirm.

He paused, trying to find the right words.

"I . . . get confused sometimes. It's gunfire that usually sets it off."

Moustafa looked grave. "Is there a good way to bring you back?"

"Well, those slaps certainly did the trick, but I don't suggest you repeat that without disarming me first."

"And that smell coming from your bedroom last night? You were burning something."

"Medicine."

Moustafa looked doubtful.

The ringing of his newly installed telephone saved Augustus from having to say more. He hurried to answer it.

Zehra's soft voice came over the line.

"Heinrich gave me your new number. I have some news for you."

"What is it?" he asked, feeling a stab of jealousy that Zehra and Heinrich had a conversation without him. He glanced over his shoulder and was annoyed to see Moustafa standing there. Didn't this fellow know when to step back? Zehra went on.

"I made enquiries with the other antiquities dealers and discovered that one has a large monumental inscription of polished limestone. It was found during the demolition of an old house. The dealer's name is Ibrahim Shalaby, and he lives at number 28 Rue Josephine. He has an appointment with Herr Baumer this morning at eleven-thirty."

Augustus glanced at his watch.

"That's only half an hour from now. Even without the protests, getting there in time would be difficult."

"I know. I only just heard. I told him to delay Baumer as much as possible."

"You didn't tell him our business, did you?"

Zehra's musical laugh came over the line. "Of course not, you silly man! But Shalaby Bey knows not to upset a good supplier. Go get that inscription before Baumer does, and try to catch him too."

She hung up. Augustus's heart raced. He turned to Moustafa, the awkwardness of their previous conversation forgotten in the excitement. In a few words, he told him what they needed to do.

Five minutes later, they left the house. Both men carried pistols in their pockets, and Augustus also carried his sword cane. He wished he could bring better weaponry, but in broad daylight it was impossible. They hurried to Heinrich's motorcar. Augustus looked ruefully at the smashed windshield and the various bumps and scratches.

"Oh dear, that wasn't all the Germans' fault, was it?"

"No, Mr. Wall."

"Driving like a maniac, was I?"

"Faisal enjoyed it very much. I not so much."

"Poor little chap, losing his guardian like that. Remind me to give him some money the next time I see him."

"I am sure he will remind you, Mr. Wall. Oh, I got a good look at many of the inscription fragments last night. Do you remember the room of inscriptions?"

"My memory is just fine, Moustafa," Augustus replied, irritation lacing his voice. "Tell me all about it on the drive over."

The motor started and then seized up a second later. Augustus tried again, but the motor didn't respond. Augustus got out and examined the front end.

"Blast! Whatever I hit last night started a slow leak in the radiator. See this crack? It must have been leaking water all the way home. A good thing we made it. But now we're stuck."

"What do we do?"

"We'll have to take the tram."

Moustafa paused. "There have been attacks on the tram."

"Come on. We'll have to risk it."

They hurried a few blocks to get on a main street with a tram line. The neighborhood was unusually quiet, with few Egyptians and fewer Europeans about. Soldiers stood at every public building. A troop of cavalry clopped down the road. They were an Indian regiment, armed with lances as well as rifles. Augustus smiled. Such troops had been useless in the war, although a few idiot generals had tried sending them against machine-guns. Against a civilian protest, however, he supposed horses and lances would still do the trick.

"So tell me about this inscription," Augustus asked as they waited at the stop.

"Firstly, it is definitely from the Great Pyramid of Cheops. Two different fragments bore his cartouche. As you no doubt saw, there were many little fragments, single words or parts of words. I ignored those. The Germans had managed to restore a section of the writing, however. It said, 'Cheops leads the way to the underworld. Beyond his eternal house in the direction of the pole star stride . . .' And here the inscription breaks off but appears to be associated with another inscription. 'The underworld honors all gods, all goddesses, and Isis above all, the collector of body parts.'"

Augustus nodded. "That sounds related to that other fragment in the German's notebook: 'down the main corridor past the guardians who stand eternal watch to the great altar of Isis, collector of body parts.'"

"I saw that fragment in the house," Moustafa replied eagerly. "It was right next to the main inscription. Obviously the Germans believe it is associated too. But there's more. Another fragment sitting nearby said, 'Isis gives power to the limbs, power to the eye, power to the ears and mouth. Isis gives life to the living.'"

"Hm, sounds a bit like the ceremony for the opening of the mouth, except that was done on a mummy to give it eternal life, not on a living being. I wonder what that is all about? Did you find any fragments with numbers?"

"I think I anticipate your meaning, Mr. Wall. You are hoping there was a measure of distance for how far north the seeker must stride from the Great Pyramid to find the entrance to this underground chamber. When I saw that fragment, I did a quick look around the room and saw no inscriptions bearing numbers."

"Considering the size of the pyramid, we probably don't have even one-tenth of the inscription—or should I say the Germans don't," Augustus grumbled.

The tram arrived, flanked by a pair of armored cars. Augustus recognized the model—a Rolls-Royce chassis with armor plating and a cylindrical turret on top equipped with a Lewis machine-gun. In the mud of the Western Front they had been as useless as the cavalry, but they had proven vital in the desert campaigns of Mesopotamia, Sinai, and Palestine.

The tram had been given a bit of armor too, in the form of boards to cover the glass windows, with only a few thin slits for the driver and passengers to see out.

The tram pulled to a stop and the conductor opened the door. Augustus could see no one inside except a few policemen.

"First class or second, sir?" the conductor asked, pretending as if nothing unusual was going on.

"Which has thicker armor?" Augustus asked.

"I would suggest first class, sir."

"Very good. A ticket for me and my assistant, please."

Moustafa took a step back, looking at the tram uncertainly.

"What's the matter?" Augustus asked him.

Moustafa shook his head. "I cannot ride on the tram, Mr. Wall. There is a boycott."

"Oh, come now! No one will see you."

Moustafa looked him in the eye. "I cannot ride on the tram, Mr. Wall.

I'll go on foot. Don't worry. I'll be all right."

Augustus was about to object and thought better of it. He didn't have time for an argument he sensed he would lose. "Very well. See you there."

He paid for his ticket, and the tram started. Inside it was dark and stuffy. Augustus peered through the boards at the nearly abandoned streets. The police checked and rechecked their pistols and said nothing.

***

Moustafa watched the tram pull away for a moment before walking quickly down a side street. He knew a shortcut that would get him there without going on the main streets, where the protests would surely be the thickest. He sent up a quick prayer to God that Mr. Wall would make it safely and that no one would try and stop the tram.

Why had he not ridden with his employer? He had intended to, but at the last moment, he found that he couldn't. The sight of those empty cars, with not a single dark face in them, had made him pause. The authorities weren't even using the colonial police, his fellow Nubians, to guard it. The soldiers had all been white. Even the conductor had been white. None of the usual conductors were white. Was he a manager from the central office?

So he couldn't make himself get on board, and in the instant that he paused, he had made a decision. Being the only African on an African tram in an African city would have made him feel out of place. Why should all these Europeans make him feel out of place in his own land? What right did they have to make him feel like the foreigner?

Did that mean he was for the protests? He wasn't quite sure.

No. No, he wasn't. Those fools carrying placards and chanting slogans didn't know how to run a country, and if they got in power they would only run it for their own benefit. Of course the English were only running it for their own benefit too, but at least they had the experience and money to run it correctly. But was that enough to justify foreign rule?

Still mulling this over, he made his way down a narrow residential street. Few people were out, only a scattering of street vendors and some old women doing their shopping with a hurried air, stuffing their purchases into their bags of woven palm leaves and scurrying off back home. The rest of the people were either at the protests or hiding inside. Chanting echoed down the valley of tall buildings to him from far ahead.

As he continued, he saw a crowd passing along a cross street. Cursing under his breath, he took another route to try and avoid them. Here he was trying to solve a murder, and these fools were blocking the way!

He hurried down an alleyway, jogging now despite the blazing sun, and came to a street he knew would get him to where he was supposed to meet Mr. Wall. He'd probably be late now thanks to the protestors, but Mr. Wall was smart and would find some safe refuge until he showed up. Perhaps the tram would stay with him, seeing as he was the only passenger.

On second thought, the tram would not stay with him. The tram would keep to its rigid schedule. Whenever things went wrong, the English always pretended life went on as normal.

As he reached the end of the alley, Moustafa saw there was no avoiding the protest. It was huge. He'd gone far out of his way in an attempt to get around it, and the crowd was just as thick as before.

He came to the end of the alley where it opened onto a wide boulevard. People thronged the street as far as he could see in both directions. The chants for independence shook the walls of the buildings. It seemed like every window flew an Egyptian flag.

The crowd was moving in the direction he needed to go, so he stepped out of the alley and was carried along by the crowd like a reed thrown in the Nile.

Moustafa looked around him in wonder. He saw people of all descriptions here, from Nubians as dark as him to light-skinned Circassians. There were fellahin from the countryside and students from the university. Moustafa did a double take when he saw a Coptic priest chanting, "Long live Sa'ad Zaghloul! Long live independence!" as he held a cross up high. He saw other Christians in the crowd too, some with their arms linked with Muslims.

A loud cheer came from up ahead, like the roar of a desert wind. Craning his neck, Moustafa could see that they were coming to the intersection he had first avoided, where another large street connected with the one he was on. The crowd parted for a procession of some sort. All he could see was a mass of black cloth behind the whites and greens of the jellabas.

Curious, Moustafa pushed his way ahead. After a few minutes, he got close enough to see what was going on . . . and stopped in wonder.

Women were marching too! A whole procession of upper-class women, their bodies swaddled in loose black-hooded gowns, their faces covered by white veils, marched carrying banners proclaiming their support for independence. The men gave them a wide berth, parting like the Red Sea for Moses. And all around the women, the men cheered them on.

"Our mothers fight for us! Our sisters stand with us! We will drive the British out of Egypt!"

These were not working-class women. Every one of them was dressed in fine silk. Some even carried European purses, and from beneath the robe of one of the leaders poked a pair of French shoes of the latest fashion.

Moustafa shook his head in disbelief. The leading families of Cairo were letting their women march? This movement had spread everywhere.

How could he have missed it? Of course he had heard the talk in cafés, had read the articles about the Wafd Party, but he had never imagined that the fever for independence had risen to such a high temperature. Was he really so lost in his studies that he could have been so blind?

He followed the crowd once more. The road forked, and the women and some of the men went one way, probably headed for the high court. He took the other street as it would lead him to the tram stop.

He moved with the crowd, having given up trying to push through it, the press being so tight.

"Where are we going?" he asked a man next to him.

"The high commissioner's office," the man said with an air of pride. "We're handing him a list of our grievances."

Moustafa nodded. He had suspected as much. The office was just down the street from where he needed to go.

That would be a problem. The English would have the road cordoned off for sure.

After another couple of blocks, the crowd slowed. Making a series of little hops so he could see beyond the ocean of heads, Moustafa saw what he had feared—a line of mounted police forming a solid wall across the avenue. In front of them, he saw Egyptians raising their fists in the air. A chant started at the front of the crowd, rippling back to those behind.

"Egypt for Egyptians! Egypt for Egyptians!"

Moustafa made his way through the crowd to a side street that angled away from the confrontation and would lead him in the general direction he needed to go. If this one was sealed, he'd go find another. The English didn't have enough men to block all the roads.

Some others had the same idea, and Moustafa found himself near the

THE CASE OF THE PURLOINED PYRAMID

front of a group of about a hundred men hurrying down the street. No one else ventured out of their homes. All the shops, even the cafés, were shut tight.

The road angled right, and from around the corner, he heard a shout and the sound of breaking glass. Picking up speed, Moustafa and the others rounded the corner.

A British army truck was parked in the center of the road, its front window smashed. Moustafa arrived just in time to see the culprit, a young man in the trousers and collared shirt of a student, get thrown to the ground by a pair of sunburned English soldiers. Once he was down, they started pummeling him with their fists. More soldiers poured out of the back of the truck, gripping rifles.

"They're beating our comrade!" a man next to him shouted.

"Let him go!" another shouted.

The two soldiers beating the student looked up, startled by the sudden appearance of the crowd. They stepped back and unslung their rifles.

Too late. The crowd hadn't slowed at the sight of the troops. It had sped up, enraged at seeing one of its own being mistreated.

The soldiers glanced behind them and saw their comrades wouldn't be able to form a line in time. One bolted. The other, a young man barely more than a boy with red hair and freckles on his sunburned cheeks, stood his ground, pointing his rifle uncertainly at the mass of angry faces.

The crowd washed around him, enveloping him like a wave crashing over a mound of sand and leaving it isolated. The boy turned this way and that, gripping his rifle and shouting something Moustafa couldn't hear.

Moustafa got jostled as more men moved in, sensing weakness. The lone soldier still held them off, but just barely. The crowd edged closer and closer in on him, tightening the noose, while only a few yards away, the other soldiers, now having formed a line, tried to push their way forward and save him.

The troops didn't dare fire for fear of hitting their comrade, and they hadn't time to fix bayonets before the shoving match started, so now they tried to push back the crowd by jabbing at the protestors with their rifle butts. One Egyptian took a hit to the head and fell to the ground with a groan. That got the crowd angrier, and they pushed back harder, punching the soldiers and trying to wrest their weapons from them. The crowd heaved forward, then got pushed back. Moustafa, big as he was, couldn't help but get carried along.

The swirl pushed him until he ended up right next to the isolated soldier. In the few seconds Moustafa had lost sight of him, he'd lost his cap and his shirt had been torn. He swung his rifle in a big arc, trying to keep the Egyptians at bay, his eyes wide with terror.

The crowd pulled back a little, not wanting to get hit, and the soldier took the chance to pull out his bayonet and fix it on the end of his rifle.

That gave him confidence, and he jabbed at the men encircling him, not really trying to hit anyone, only to keep them back.

Then the English boy made a break for it. Holding his rifle level in front of him, he charged in the direction of the English line. The crowd parted for him.

All except for one man, a lanky fellow with the darkened skin and stained jellaba of a farmer. Whether he had decided to stand his ground or simply didn't react quickly enough Moustafa couldn't tell, but he stood right in the path of the Englishman.

The farmer raised his hands to protect himself, and the Englishman rammed his bayonet right through one of his hands, the blade jamming down to the hilt and emerging from the other side.

The Englishman yanked the blade free and dodged to the side to run past the farmer, who stood there in shock. The Englishman ducked past him and, face twisted with rage, slashed at the farmer again, the bayonet cutting deep into his side.

This time the farmer did fall.

Before he knew what he was doing, Moustafa leaped forward with a roar and grabbed the Englishman by the belt and the scruff of his neck. He heaved him off his feet and slammed him down on the ground.

A cheer went up around him. With another roar, Moustafa brought his fist down on the English boy's face, breaking his nose and bringing forth a spurt of blood from both nostrils.

Moustafa punched him again and then got pushed aside as several other men eagerly descended on the soldier to get their turn. Soon it was all Moustafa could do to stay on his feet as men scrambled to get at the soldier. His rifle was held aloft as a trophy and carried away. Moustafa caught glimpses of the boy through the tangle of limbs. He wasn't screaming, wasn't fighting back. He had curled himself into a tight ball to protect his face and groin and cowered under a shower of blows. Men kicked him or pulled off their sandals and smacked him with them. Another stomped on his head. Even through all the shouting, Moustafa could hear the sickly thud as it struck the cobblestones.

That sound was like the snap of fingers in front of a man hypnotized. Moustafa's rage vanished, and all he saw was a frightened boy who had about two minutes of misery to live.

"That's enough! He's had enough!" Moustafa shouted, plowing through the crowd.

Moustafa struggled to reach him, shoving men out of the way. Someone clutched his arm, but he tore himself free. Another got in his path, his back turned to Moustafa as he held a cobblestone aloft, ready to smash the soldier's skull. Moustafa tossed him aside.

He got to the soldier and picked him up. All around people cursed him for ruining their fun, while others egged him on, thinking he was going to treat the soldier to some fresh indignity.

Throwing him over his shoulder like a sack of grain, Moustafa shoved his way through the mass of struggling bodies toward the British line. People smacked the soldier as he passed. Moustafa tried to shield him, but the blows came from all sides. He concentrated on pushing forward as fast as possible.

Then he broke free. The line of British and Egyptians had parted, with a few feet between them. As he staggered into this open space, the soldiers looked at him with surprise. He pulled the Englishman off his shoulder and, tearing him out of the grip of a couple of men behind him, tossed him at the soldiers' feet.

The boy lay there, not moving, his face covered in blood and one arm bent in an unnatural angle.

And then very clearly, as if in slow motion, Moustafa saw the officer standing behind the line raise his sword and shout in English, "Ready!"

Moustafa ducked back into the crowd.

"Aim!"

Moustafa never heard the order to fire. Suddenly the air was rent with the sound of a score of rifles firing at point-blank range.

People fell all around him. The crowd panicked and ran. Moustafa ran with them. The shouts and screams almost drowned out the sound of the second volley.

A heavy weight hit him in the back, making him stumble. At first Moustafa thought he had been shot, but when he turned around he saw a man lying just behind him, a patch of red staining his jellaba. The poor fellow had been shot in the back and the force of the bullet had slammed him into Moustafa.

Moustafa scooped him up before he could get trampled by the others, threw him over his shoulder like he had with the young Englishman, and ran for all he was worth. The street turned not far ahead. Everyone made for the safety of the corner, people shouting to friends they couldn't find, others tripping and getting run over by the crowd. One young man who wore the robes of a religious student stopped, turned to face the line of troops, and raised his hands in prayer.

The third volley killed the student and several others. Moustafa flinched as a bullet chewed up the ground next to his feet. He sped around the corner and didn't stop running, none of them stopped running, passing through side streets and alleys, getting as far away from the neighborhood as possible. The crowd slowly dispersed, taking various routes to rejoin the main protest or go home or simply get away.

Moustafa slowed and stopped, soaked with sweat and the other man's blood. He eased his burden down on the ground. It was only then that he realized he had been carrying a corpse.

CHAPTER SIXTEEN

Augustus couldn't wait for Moustafa any longer. He'd spent a good quarter of an hour cooling his heels at the tram stop while several Egyptians gave him baleful looks from across the street. If it had not been for the pair of police officers posted at the stop, Augustus felt sure those fellows would have started trouble.

What was keeping that man, anyway? It must be the crowds. Blast him for insisting on walking instead of taking the tram! Didn't Moustafa know he was needed?

Augustus checked his watch for the tenth time. Five minutes to noon. If the Germans had lived up to their famous punctuality, they were already there, protests or no protests. Hopefully that Ibrahim Shalaby fellow was delaying them.

Well, there was no helping it. Augustus would have to go it alone. The Rue Josephine wasn't far. Checking the small automatic in his pocket and keeping a tight grip on his cane, he made his way there.

The antiquities shop was on the ground floor of a French colonial building between a bank and an Italian tailor's, both closed as were most foreign businesses in the city. The antiquities shop looked closed too, its windows shuttered, the lights off, but the slightly ajar front door told him otherwise.

Gut instinct made Augustus pause. Something was amiss.

He glanced around. The street was mostly deserted and there was no one nearby. Putting his hand in his pocket to grip his pistol without showing it, he moved to the storefront and edged along it until he got to the door. The light in the front room was off, but he could see some dim illumination, perhaps from a back room.

He paused and listened. A slight sound came to his ears, like a sigh or a choked off cough, quiet and not close to the front door. In the distance, the artillery rattled like a thousand distant snare drums.

No, not now. Get a hold of yourself.

He forced himself to focus. The artillery faded.

Augustus pushed open the door and ducked low into the room, drawing his automatic at the same time. Instinctively, he found shelter behind the nearest large object, an engraved New Kingdom pyramidion set next to the door.

Silence.

He scanned the half-lit room. It was filled with statuary, slabs of inscriptions, and glass cases displaying smaller artifacts. His skin prickled. There were a thousand places to hide in this room.

But no, the Germans were veterans. They would have covered the door and tried for him as soon as he entered.

A soft groan emanated from the back room, which Augustus could just see through an open doorway at the end of a short corridor. An oil lamp burned in there, the only illumination in the shop.

Creeping low, Augustus wove his way through the labyrinth of artifacts to the corridor. He kept his gun trained on the far door as he approached.

He saw a small office, with an antique mahogany desk and a few shelves of books. A middle-aged Egyptian lay on the carpet, which was soaked with blood from a knife wound to his gut. The Egyptian looked pale. His eyes bugged out and he had trouble breathing.

Augustus bent down, took his handkerchief from his jacket pocket, and pressed it against the wound even though he could already tell it was too late. He'd seen enough death to recognize it instantly.

Ibrahim Shalaby's eyes widened when he saw the mask.

"I'm here to help," Augustus said in a soothing voice, trying to staunch the blood.

"A-are you Mrs. Hanzade's friend?" the man choked out.

"I am. What happened?"

"The Germans came. Two older men and a young man, a tough man with a big scar on his face."

Damn, I knew I missed him. I spotted him for a survivor the moment I laid eyes on him.

Shalaby continued.

"I tried to delay them as Mrs. Hanzade asked, but they were in a hurry. They seemed worried and kept looking at the door."

Shalaby cut off and groaned. He was fading quickly.

"Why did they stab you?" Augustus asked.

"My notebook. I forgot to hide it. I copied the inscription so I could show it to you. They tore the page out."

Shalaby gestured at a notebook lying open on the floor nearby. One of the pages had been ripped out.

"Do you read hieroglyphs? Do you remember what it said?"

At first Shalaby didn't seem to have heard, but then he spoke, his voice barely a whisper.

"Something about 'the Temple of the Eternal Dawn.' I can't remember the rest. I . . ."

The antiquities dealer coughed up blood. He struggled to say more and finally whispered.

"They were very excited, talking to themselves in German. Then they saw the notebook, and the man with the scar stabbed me. As I lay here, one of the older ones used my telephone. This time he spoke in English and said, 'We have what we want. Meet me at the church in the mosque tonight at ten.' Then he hung up."

"The church in the mosque? What does that mean?"

"I think it must be . . ."

Shalaby's voice faded away and his eyes became glassy. He let out a final, slow breath and did not take another. Augustus laid him back down on the carpet and shut his eyes.

***

Faisal was going to miss the old man. Sure, Osman ibn Akbar had beaten him sometimes and his feet smelled like a pair of decomposing cats, but he had always shared his bread. Sure, to get that bread Faisal had to lead him to the mosque and endure boring lectures about not stealing, but Osman ibn Akbar was the only person in the world who gave him something for almost free. Now what was he going to do?

He should leave the neighborhood. Hassan was still looking for him. The other boys had warned him. It had been a miracle that Hassan hadn't caught him when he was stuck taking care of the old man on his final day. Faisal knew that someone like him didn't get many miracles.

So Faisal went to the shack in the alley that he shared with the other boys, wrapped up his begging bowl in his blanket, tucked them under his arm, and headed down Ibn al-Nafis Street for the last time. His feet were already tired from following the funeral procession all the way to the foot of the Mokattam Hills and standing with the other beggars as Osman ibn Akbar was laid in the grave and the ulema recited some verses of the Koran over his body. Then Faisal had to walk all the way back in the heat. But there was no time for rest. He had a lot more walking to do this day.

Where would he go? He supposed he'd sleep in the doorway of the mosque of Sultan Hassan from now on. Sometimes tourists went there. Perhaps he could get his picture taken again.

Or why not leave Cairo altogether? Besides that trip to Giza, he had never been outside the city in his whole life. There were lots of ancient places up the Nile. Maybe he could go there and beg and have his picture taken. He'd have to find a place that didn't have a village next to it. He didn't want rocks thrown at him again.

He still had the twenty piastres the Englishman had given him for breaking into the foreigners' house. He hadn't had a chance to buy Osman ibn Akbar any food, for when the Englishman screeched the car to a stop on Ibn al-Nafis Street, and Faisal had fled in terror at the look on the Englishman's face, he had gone straight back to see how Osman ibn Akbar was doing. He had found him in his niche, the blankets flung aside, his mouth and eyes wide open with a look of shock, stone dead.

Faisal shuddered at the memory and wiped away a tear.

As he trudged down the street, he approached the Englishman's house. It had been fun to meet him, although that gunfight had been scary. Faisal had been beaten, slapped, kicked, chased by dogs, and threatened with knives, but he had never been shot at before. No wonder the Englishman was a bit crazy if he had spent years getting shot at like that.

Faisal noticed the motorcar sitting outside. It was all banged up from that wild ride the night before, when the Englishman reeled in his seat and kept seeing things that weren't there and not seeing things that were.

THE CASE OF THE PURLOINED PYRAMID

Faisal walked over to it. He wouldn't mind another ride. Perhaps he should knock on the Englishman's door and say goodbye? He had frightened Faisal the night before, but he was probably fine now. The way he slept, any demons that had gotten inside his head would have gotten bored and left.

"You! Get away from there!"

It was Karim, the neighborhood watchman. Shopkeepers and property owners paid him to keep an eye on their things, although he was pretty easy to fool.

The man sauntered over, a short club in his hand.

"Get away! The Englishman wants me to watch his motorcar."

"It's not his. It's his friend's motorcar."

"Oh, you pretend to know him?" Karim said, poking Faisal in the belly with the end of the club and making the boy flinch.

"He's my friend."

Karim let out a deep laugh. "Friends with you? He'd never even speak with a little nobody like you. Get out of my sight."

Faisal hung his head and walked away, Karim's mocking laughter following him. *A little nobody.* That's what everyone thought of him. But he wasn't a little nobody. He had helped the Englishman and Moustafa with their adventures. They would have never made it into that house without him. And he led them right to the inscriptions! Everyone always looked up to people like the Englishman and Moustafa and ignored the people who did the real work.

Faisal flew sideways. By the time he was halfway into the alley, an instant before his head slammed against the wall and all he saw was stars, he knew Hassan had finally caught him.

Hassan didn't kill him outright. In fact, besides a few slaps, he didn't hurt him at all. That worried Faisal. It meant Hassan had something worse in store for him. Hassan gripped him by the hair and led him down a series of alleys to a grubby little courtyard half filled with rubble from one of the adjoining buildings that had fallen down a few years before.

Hassan's two cousins were waiting for them. They were older, with broad shoulders and arms as thick as cannons. They looked at Faisal like a pair of crocodiles that had cornered a kitten. Qamar had done five years hard labor in the Sinai for beating a man so badly he'd never walk again. Zaki had killed a man in front of one of Faisal's friends late one night. The boy had fled Cairo rather than risk being silenced forever.

Both of them moved forward, studying the boy.

"I've heard you're a good climber. Is that true?" Qamar asked.

Faisal tried to answer, but his throat was so dry he only managed a croak. He nodded instead.

Zaki drew a knife and tested its edge with his calloused thumb. He bent down and started rubbing the edge quickly against a piece of masonry. The screeching of the knife grated on Faisal's ears.

"You know what I'm doing?" Zaki asked.

Faisal shook his head.

"I'm dulling it. You know why?"

Faisal tried to run. Hassan's hand shot out as fast as a cobra striking, lifted him off his feet, and tossed him down in front of his cousins.

Zaki stood up, testing the knife again.

"Nice and dull now, but not so dull it won't cut through you. It will just take some time. A long time because I won't put much effort into it. It might take all night for me to remove your fingers and toes one by one. Then your ears and nose and eyes. You want me to do that?"

"N-no."

"Then you're getting us into the Englishman's house tonight."

***

Augustus was stumped. He had no idea what "the Temple of the Eternal Dawn" or "the church in the mosque" meant. He'd been puzzling over those phrases since he had gotten home. Moustafa was equally mystified. Augustus had called Zehra and Heinrich, and they didn't know either. He had failed to mention to his friend the state of his motorcar.

At least the radiator was getting fixed. For an exorbitant sum, he had tracked down an English mechanic, a cockney lad who had spent the war fixing lorries and had enough pluck to cross the city during a riot to fix a fellow veteran's motorcar. Augustus decided not to tell him the vehicle was owned by a German. No need to complicate matters any more than they already were.

Now the fellow lay under the motorcar in front of Augustus's house, watched by a circle of idlers, mostly old men with nothing better to do and young boys whose parents were too poor to send them to school. Augustus was surprised not to see Faisal among them.

THE CASE OF THE PURLOINED PYRAMID

Augustus and Moustafa stood watching by the front door. Moustafa wore the formal jellaba he kept at the house to receive important clients. Augustus had not asked about the bloodstains on the other one. He hoped his silence might teach his assistant the virtues of honoring another's privacy.

"Sorry for almost shooting you," Augustus said.

"I shouldn't have charged into the antiquities shop like that."

"I'm easily startled in those situations."

"Any man would be, Mr. Wall."

"I wasn't seeing things!" Augustus snapped. He hated being talked down to.

"I didn't say you were, Mr. Wall," Moustafa said in a soothing voice. That annoyed Augustus even more. He hated being placated. "Have you tried calling the police again?"

"Yes. Still busy. All their telephone lines are flooded. You can't even report a murder with all these rioters about."

"Protestors."

Augustus grunted. "Seem like rioters to me."

Moustafa didn't respond. After a while, Augustus spoke again.

"I think it would be best if you stay here tonight in case we get any more clues. We might have to move at a moment's notice."

"I already sent a message to my wife so she wouldn't worry."

Augustus turned in surprise. "Oh, I didn't know you were married. Do you have children?"

"Five, Mr. Wall." His voice came out a bit strained, and Augustus wondered why. A moment later he realized Moustafa had mentioned his family several times. No matter. He had more important things to think about.

"I don't know what our next move should be. We're stymied. I'm sure after our little visit the Germans will have abandoned their hideout. If we only knew where they were meeting tonight!"

Moustafa shook his head. "I don't know what we should do, Mr. Wall."

The mechanic crawled out from under the vehicle.

"I've patched the radiator, sir. It should hold for a time, but what you really need is a new one. That would require a visit to the shop."

"And all the shops are closed thanks to the riots," Augustus said.

"The police will knock their fuzzy heads into shape quick enough, sir.

In the meantime, just don't drive over any rough roads or go at high speed."

"I'll try not to."

Augustus paid the man and he left. By now the sun was setting. Within a few hours, the Germans would meet somewhere and he would miss it. Augustus cursed his luck. He hated being helpless like this. Shrugging his shoulders in defeat, he and Moustafa went back inside, locked and bolted the door, and ate a quick meal.

"Get some sleep," he told his employee. "You're dead on your feet. I'll puzzle through this notebook for a time and see if I can come up with some more ideas."

As Moustafa made himself comfortable on a sofa in the upstairs reading room, Augustus went to the study and looked at the notebook that the member of the Thule Society had dropped after killing Cavell Martin. Augustus felt dead tired. The stress of that firefight had wearied him more than he cared to admit. He'd had some bad episodes before, but this had been one of the worst. To take his mind off it, he stared at the esoteric symbols and the fragments of translated hieroglyphs over and over, trying to tease some more meaning out of them. He read until they swam in front of his eyes. Slowly his head sank to his chest, the notebook slipped from his hands, and the weight of the last few days pressed him into sleep as the sun sank below the horizon outside his shuttered window.

***

As soon as it was dark, Hassan and his cousins led Faisal to the alley behind the Englishman's house. As Qamar kept watch at the entrance to the alley, Hassan and Zaki dragged him over the heaps of trash until they got to the spot where he had climbed up before. Zaki had a bag over his shoulder. He opened it and took out a coil of thin but strong rope. He tied one end around Faisal's waist and played out the rope.

"Start climbing," Zaki ordered. "If you try to raise the alarm or remove the rope, I'll pull you right off the wall. If the fall doesn't kill you, I will. Once you get near the top, stand on the top of that window frame and loop the rope around the edge of the roof and through that drainage hole and tie it. Then and only then can you untie yourself from the rope."

"I'll need both hands to do that! How am I supposed to keep my balance?"

Hassan cuffed him on the back of the head. "That's your problem, you son of a whore. Now get climbing."

"It's early. The Englishman will still be awake," Faisal said.

"I can take care of the Englishman," Zaki scoffed, tapping his pocket where he kept a knife. Unlike the one he'd threatened Faisal with, this one was razor sharp. Zaki had shown it to him.

"Where's the rest of your gang?" Faisal asked.

"Why share? We don't need them. Now stop delaying and get up there," Hassan said.

Faisal started to climb, wrapping his hands and bare feet around the drainpipe on the back wall and clambering up to a ledge where he could edge along to a window whose bars and jutting stone windowsill allowed him a more stable hold than the drainpipe. He clambered up to the top of the windowsill so he could grip another ledge farther up.

Sweat beaded his brow and his limbs trembled. A long day of fear had exhausted him. Knowing he'd need his strength for the climb, Hassan had given him food and water, but in his terror Faisal had thrown the meal up. Hassan and his cousins had laughed.

What should have been an easy climb grew harder and harder. He already felt tired, and the increasing weight of the rope that Zaki played out behind him pulled at his waist.

He hauled himself up to the next ledge and was just about to straighten and reach for the bottom of the next windowsill when the rope tugged at him.

Faisal jerked, wobbled for a sickening moment, and steadied himself. The two thieves below snorted and chuckled. He looked down at them, terrified. Although the alley lay swathed in shadow, Faisal's sharp eyes spotted Zaki grinning up at him. The bully gave the rope another tug. Faisal gripped the ledge in terror. Hassan, laughing, put a retraining hand on his cousin's, then motioned for Faisal to continue.

It took a moment for Faisal to regain the strength and courage to stand up on the edge, and then he went on with the longest climb of his life.

CHAPTER SEVENTEEN

Faisal was under no illusions. Once Zaki got to the Englishman's roof, he'd be killed. They had no intention of letting him go. No one who crossed Hassan and his cousins ever got away with it. Within a minute, Zaki would be up here with him, his knife would slice across Faisal's throat in one swift motion, and that would be the end of it. No one could save him. Tonight he would die.

He stood on top of the second-floor windowsill, one hand gripping a tiny crack in the masonry as the other pulled up the slack of the rope that Zaki, far below, was giving him.

Faisal tossed the slack over the parapet and reached his free arm through the drainage hole over the pipe. His fingertips barely brushed the rope where it lay on the rooftop. He was soaked in sweat now, worn out from the long day and lack of food and the frightening climb. The hand that gripped the crack in the masonry trembled, and one of his legs kept shaking up and down like the needle in one of those modern sewing machines.

He strained to reach the rope, standing on tiptoe and extending his body as far as he could. His searching hand wrapped around the rope.

Just then, his hand gripping the wall slipped. With a gasp, Faisal fell backward, his feet slipping from the ledge.

Frantically he grasped the rope with both hands as it whipped out from the drainage hole. He plunged several feet before the friction of the rope around the parapet slowed him and he finally jerked to a stop, practically yanking his arms from their sockets. Zaki had seen him fall and had braced himself.

Faisal swung back and forth, his feet desperately seeking purchase as his tormentors guffawed below. Finally he managed to wrap the toes of one foot around the bars of a window, steady himself, and get a proper foothold with the other. He wrapped his arms and legs through the bars and rested for a moment.

Not long enough. A low whistle from below commanded him to continue.

He studied his situation. The rope was now looped over the parapet and through the hole, but if he hadn't gripped the end coming through the hole, the loop would have whipped out of the hole and over the parapet, and his being tied to the rope would have meant nothing because the rope would no longer have had contact with the wall. Good thing he had kept his head. He climbed hand over hand up the rope until he got to the hole again and got himself into a better position.

Zaki played out the rope. Once Faisal got more rope looped through the hole, he tied it, looping the rope around itself and securing it. Then he wearily climbed onto the parapet and lay there close to the edge, panting.

A creak of the rope told Faisal that Zaki was already climbing up. Faisal had only a minute or two left to live.

He had to get out of here! His fingers clawed at the knot securing the rope around his waist, but they were numb with fatigue, and the knot had tightened when Zaki had playfully tugged the rope to scare him.

The creaking of the rope as Zaki steadily climbed made Faisal desperate. Scraping the skin off his fingers, he finally managed to jam a fingertip inside the knot and tugged at the rope, loosening it.

Within another minute, he was free. He looked over the precipice and saw Zaki had made it more than halfway up.

Faisal had only a few moments. He looked around the moonlit rooftop. Could he hide? No, Zaki would find him. Get through the window into the sitting room? It was a tight fit, and Zaki would catch him before he got through. Call out to the Englishman? Before the Englishman heard him, Zaki would kill him.

He looked at the rope. Could he untie it? No, the rope was knotted beyond his reach.

Then he saw an old ceramic flowerpot sitting nearby, filled with cracked

THE CASE OF THE PURLOINED PYRAMID

and dried earth, whatever plant it had once held long since dried up and blown away. Faisal hurried over, picked up the flowerpot, and smashed it against the floor. He grabbed the biggest fragment and hurried over to the rope.

Faisal glanced down. Zaki was about two-thirds of the way up now. Wow, he sure was a slow climber! Maybe he wasn't so tough after all. Faisal started sawing at the rope with the edge of the potsherd where the rope lay flush against the edge.

While the fragment of pottery was sharp, the rope was tough and Faisal made slow progress. With strength born of desperation, Faisal sawed away at it. The potsherd snapped in his hand and he rushed to get another.

As he returned and started sawing at it again, Hassan gave out a warning cry. Zaki looked up, his eyes going wide as he saw what Faisal was doing. He stopped, uncertain. Faisal kept sawing. He'd cut halfway through.

Zaki started descending, almost losing his grip in his haste. Faisal cut more and more strands of the rope until it was thinner than his little finger. He took a breath and steadied himself for one final effort.

Then the rope snapped. Zaki fell from halfway up the wall to hit the ground with a sickening thud.

Faisal's heart went cold. He ducked behind the parapet and curled in on himself, shaking. Had he killed him?

Finally he plucked up the courage to look over. Zaki lay there, his leg bent at an unnatural angle, Hassan crouched next to him.

Zaki groaned and moved a little. Faisal felt a flush of relief wash through him, followed quickly by confusion. Why should he be relieved? Didn't Zaki deserve to die?

Maybe, but Faisal didn't want to be a killer like so many street boys grew up to be. He didn't even want to kill someone like Zaki.

Hassan looked up. Their eyes met, and Faisal trembled as he saw the fate in store for him. If he had been dead before, he was ten times as dead now.

He ducked back behind the parapet, heart pounding.

What could he do now? They couldn't get up, but he couldn't get down. He was trapped on the rooftop unless he went inside the house, but once the Englishman caught him in there, what could he tell him? He supposed he could tell the truth, but what if he didn't believe him and kicked him out?

Then he'd be dead.

Plus Faisal was already thinking of the future. Now that he wasn't going to die in the next two minutes, he was already allowing himself the possibility of being alive next week. If he was alive next week, he sure didn't want the Englishman to know he could get onto his roof so easily. No, he had to find another way.

He went over to the windows that provided ventilation for the sitting room and peered down into the unlit interior. He could just make out Moustafa's bulk stretched out on the sofa, fast asleep. Faisal studied every corner of the room as well as he could but did not see the Englishman. Perhaps he was asleep in his bedroom. Good. If he handled this right, he could get away from Hassan and still keep the Englishman's home as his personal playground. How else was he going to get all that food he had earned?

With care, he squeezed through the open window and glanced down. Moustafa lay on the sofa just a few feet away. In total silence, Faisal climbed down the wall, using the cracks in the old masonry as fingerholds and toeholds.

At last he was on the floor. He thumbed his nose at the sleeping Nubian and moved into the hallway.

To his surprise, all the lights were off and he heard no sounds of life. Was the Englishman even here? Or maybe he was asleep too? It seemed early to be asleep. Faisal tiptoed down to the second floor and found the Englishman's bedroom empty. He continued to the ground floor and found him asleep in a chair in a room filled with books.

Faisal's eyes strayed in the direction of the pantry. No, he was too nervous to eat right now. He'd eat once this was all over.

As with most Cairene houses, there were no windows on the ground floor except for a tiny ventilation window in the kitchen that even he couldn't fit through, so he went back up to the first floor, opened the latch on some shutters, and peeked out.

He could see out over the alley leading from Ibn al-Nafis Street around to the back of the house. Qamar was no longer at his post at the head of the alley. Hassan must have called him to help with Zaki. Faisal got up on the windowsill and started squeezing through the bars. He wished he could go out the front door, but someone was bound to see him. He'd be beaten for breaking into the house and probably thrown in prison, where he knew he wouldn't survive a night and a day.

After getting out through the bars that were supposed to keep the house safe from prowlers, he hung from them and prepared to drop.

Just as he let go, he saw Hassan and Qamar come around the corner, carrying their injured relative.

As soon as Faisal hit the ground, he rolled to absorb the impact, sprang to his feet, and bolted for the street, Hassan's and Qamar's footsteps right behind him.

He burst out onto Ibn al-Nafis Street and into the early evening crowd. The café across the street was full and many of the market stalls remained open. They wouldn't dare kill him right in front of all these people, would they?

Just to be on the safe side, he ran for the motorcar.

He leaped into the front seat, grabbed the horn where it sat atop the hood on the driver's side, and gave it a good squeeze. It made a nice loud noise and everyone on the street nearby turned and looked at him. He'd seen the Englishman use it on their drive to Giza and marveled at it. He'd been tempted to ask to use it, but he knew what the answer would have been so he hadn't. Now he got to.

Now he needed to.

He squeezed it again and again and made a loud honking like a hundred geese being startled by a felucca on the Nile. People began to gather, shouting at him to get out of the motorcar. He looked over his shoulder and saw Hassan and Qamar standing unsure of themselves a few yards away, fearful of all those eyes. He grinned at them.

His grin stopped when someone smacked him across the face.

Karim the watchman.

"Get out of there, you little runt!"

Karim hauled him out as the crowd shouted.

"Smack him again!"

"These brats are always stealing. Teach him a lesson!"

Karim did smack him again. Faisal only shrugged. He'd been smacked so many times in his life it didn't even really hurt much anymore, and this was much better than having his fingers and toes cut off one by one with a dull knife.

***

Augustus awoke to the sound of a horn honking frantically outside his house. Still half-asleep, he stumbled to his feet wondering what it could mean. Visions of Heinrich blaring on his own horn to express his anger at the state of his motorcar passed through his mind. That brought a spike of embarrassment that he quickly quashed. *Heinrich would never behave in such a manner*, he thought as he hurried down the hall. He could already hear Moustafa thumping down the stairs.

When he opened his front door, all he could see was a mob around Heinrich's motorcar.

"What's going on here?" he demanded.

Karim pushed through the crowd, gripping Faisal by the hair.

"Oh, not you again," Augustus grumbled.

"I need to talk to you!" the boy said, all wide-eyed.

"Why not knock like anyone else?"

"I didn't have time. Could you let me in?"

Moustafa stormed up. "What trouble are you causing now? Why can't you just leave Mr. Wall alone?"

"I seem to have picked up a street boy like some people pick up malaria," Augustus said dryly. "But he claims he has something to tell us. Let him go, Karim, I'll handle it from here. Faisal, get in the house before you cause a riot."

"Don't let him in the house. It will cause talk in the neighborhood," Moustafa whispered.

"I'm sure they're already talking about me nonstop. This won't change a thing."

They entered the house and closed the door. Augustus sighed with relief, glad to be away from all those staring faces.

"So why did you wake us by getting your filthy fingers on Herr Schäfer's motorcar?" Moustafa said, glaring down at the boy.

"I was being chased by Hassan and his cousins! They were going to skin me alive!"

"Oh, that lot." Augustus sighed. "They're like a bad penny."

"How can a coin be bad?" Faisal asked.

"It's a figure of speech. Well, you can stay here for a bit until the coast is clear. In the meantime, don't bother us. We're trying to imagine where there could be a church in a mosque. The Germans are supposed to be meeting there tonight, but we can't for the life of us figure out what the devil that could mean."

Faisal scratched his head, thinking. Augustus turned to Moustafa. "Any ideas now that you've slept on it?"

"There are many churches built next to mosques," Moustafa replied. "One is not far from here. It's an Armenian church, right beside a mosque."

Faisal brightened. "I know where it is!"

Augustus ignored him. "No, that couldn't be it. Shalaby said the exact words were 'the church in the mosque.'"

Moustafa thought for a moment.

"I know where it is," Faisal said again.

"Be silent, Little Infidel. I'm thinking. Ah, could it be one of the ancient churches that were destroyed in the seventh century when the first Muslims invaded?"

Augustus scratched his chin, noticing that he needed a shave. "One of the old Byzantine churches? That's possible, but I don't know of any example still surviving."

"I KNOW WHERE IT IS!" Faisal shouted.

The two men turned to him.

"Where?" Augustus asked.

Faisal cocked his head and looked at him slyly. "If I tell you, will you do something for me?"

"Bah! He just wants money," Moustafa growled. "Sit in the corner and keep your mouth shut."

"I don't want money," Faisal whined. "I just want you to get Hassan and his cousins arrested."

"Oh, I'll gladly do that for free," Augustus said.

"Great!" Faisal said, jumping in the air and spinning around. Then he thought for a moment. "Well, if you'd do that for free anyway, perhaps you could give me ten piastres?"

"Tell me where the damn church in the mosque is or I'll let Moustafa squash you into a pancake."

"What's a pancake?" Faisal asked.

"Want to find out?" Augustus asked.

"Um, no. Well, sometimes I sleep at the entrance to the Sultan Hassan mosque, near the Citadel. The entrance has a big arch so it makes good shelter. The ulema don't mind as long as we clear out before the students come to the madrasa."

"Get to the point, Faisal," Augustus said with a frustrated sigh. Why was he cursed with someone so annoying? It would be all right if the brat was useless because then he could ignore him, but Faisal had proven his worth on more than one occasion, which was the only reason he hadn't been thrown out on his ear.

"Oh, right! Sometimes I hang around there after we've had to move. I sit across the street and beg. Every now and then, one of the donkey boys brings tourists there because it's so big, one of the biggest mosques in Cairo, they say. The tourists stop on their way to the Citadel. Anyway, parts of the mosque are carved with pictures, and one of them is a little building that looks like a church. The tourists like that. The donkey boys tell a story that Sultan Hassan hired the best architect in Egypt to build his mosque, and that architect was a Copt. The Copt carved a little church by the door to show off his religion. Sultan Hassan cut off his hand so he couldn't design a better mosque. The tourists like that part of the story too."

"Nonsense. Sultan Hassan's mosque wasn't finished until after his death," Moustafa scoffed. "That's just a tale people are telling the tourists."

Augustus scratched his chin again. "Perhaps so, but the story doesn't need to be true for the Germans to reference it. It sounds like a good place to try. So where exactly is this carving?"

Faisal smiled. "I'll show you."

"And get another ride in the motorcar." Augustus sighed. "Fine. I don't have time to argue. Let's go. I want to be set up well before the Germans arrive."

"Can we eat first?" Faisal asked.

"No. We need to go," Augustus said, already heading for his personal armory.

"But I'm hungry!" Faisal's whine followed him down the hallway.

"Enough!" Moustafa bellowed. "Mr. Wall already said he's going to get rid of those bullies for you. Why do you always ask for more?"

Augustus fetched a large burlap sack and put the MP 18 inside, along with a Lee-Enfield and bayonet for Moustafa, plus a few grenades. He tucked the sack in the back seat, giving Faisal strict instructions not to touch it.

THE CASE OF THE PURLOINED PYRAMID

Augustus also gave Moustafa a Webley to put in his pocket and brought along his own small automatic and sword cane. At the edges of his hearing, the big guns behind the front were already starting a barrage. Augustus tried to shake it off and focus on something else.

Faisal's whining helped. The boy kept asking for food and sulked when he didn't get anything. He only brightened when they drove off in the motorcar, waving to a couple of his filthy little friends as they stood at a corner and gaped back at him.

"Will we get dinner once we capture the Germans?" Faisal asked.

"Maybe," Augustus replied, keeping his eyes on the road. The streets had more traffic than previous nights. Were the protests losing steam?

"A big dinner?"

"Maybe."

"What's in this bag?"

"I told you not to touch it."

"I just want to look."

In the rearview mirror, Augustus saw Faisal bend down to look at it. He slammed on the brakes, screeching to a halt in the middle of the road and startling a camel carrying a load of hay. Its owner shouted something at Augustus, but he didn't pay attention.

He turned in his seat and jabbed a finger at Faisal.

"Do. Not. Touch. That."

Faisal wilted. "Sorry."

The boy kept mercifully quiet for the rest of the way. Unfortunately, that meant Augustus could hear the distant sound of artillery more clearly.

The neighborhood at the foot of the Citadel appeared free of rioters. Augustus guessed this was because like all previous rulers of Egypt, the British army had taken over the fortified hill and turned it into a military base. From atop the massive stone walls strengthened by Mohammad Ali almost a hundred years before, British soldiers now stood sentinel where French and Ottoman soldiers had once stood before them. The muzzles of modern artillery poked through openings in the circular towers, ready to shell the city if things got out of control.

A few hundred yards before the foot of the Citadel lay a warren of little streets dating to medieval times. Breaking this maze was a wide, gently sloping avenue flanked by two massive mosques with high walls that created a sort of man-made canyon. On the left stood the Mosque of al-Rifa'i, a blocky edifice finished by the khedive only eight years ago, which Augustus found unlovely for its ostentation and obvious inferiority to its neighbor, the mosque of Sultan Hassan, a jewel of Islamic architecture. Completed in 1360, it was the kind of building that made Augustus forget the misery of the world and think of better things. Rising far above its imposing and somewhat spare walls were a series of Mamluk-style minarets, gracefully carved with arabesques and punctuated by a series of walkways in tiers up its length, each one like a bulb on the stem of a plant.

Both mosques had deep entryways covered by soaring arches. The two dark gaps, shaded from the moonlight, stared at each other like a pair of empty sockets in the night. Within these, Augustus spied a crowd of dark figures huddled up on the marble floor. More sat on the stairs rising between the two mosques in the direction of the Citadel.

"It's all beggars here," Faisal told him as they walked down the avenue and approached the entrance to Sultan Hassan's mosque. "Don't worry. There aren't many thieves about. Everyone here is too poor to be worth robbing."

Augustus flourished his cane. "I've come well equipped."

Faisal skipped beside him. "You certainly made Hassan and his gang look like a band of baboons!"

They grinned at each other.

Augustus wished they could have brought the heavier weapons instead of locking them in the trunk. After the last encounter with the Germans, he felt almost naked facing them with only a pistol and a sword cane, but they were under the eye of the British army, and gunfire might make them trigger happy. He'd try to get this done quietly if possible.

As soon as they started ascending the steps to the mosque, that stopped being possible.

"A piastre, sir, for the love of God!"

"Some bread, sir, for a crippled man!"

"A piastre? Cigarette? Please, sir."

The beggars crowded around, reaching out gnarled and dirty hands. All were dressed in tatters. One man had no legs and pushed himself forward on his hands as he sat on a little cart. Augustus looked around uncertainly. Faisal drew close to him while Moustafa tried to shoo them away.

THE CASE OF THE PURLOINED PYRAMID

"Don't give them anything, Mr. Wall," Moustafa said in English. "Otherwise you'll start a riot." He switched back to Arabic. "Begone, all of you! We are here on police business!"

That did the trick. Most of the beggars backed off, returning to where they had been and watching them in silence. They were replaced by new beggars, and Moustafa had to repeat his warning again and again.

"You said you sleep here?" Augustus asked Faisal, shocked.

"Not everyone in the world has a comfortable bed. Lots of people sleep like this. I have a better place off Ibn al-Nafis Street, but Hassan knows about it. So the dead Hassan protects me from the living Hassan."

"Clever boy. Where is this carving?"

"Here."

Faisal led them to the east jamb of the archway. Leaning over a pile of rags that Augustus barely recognized as a human being, Faisal pointed to a carving.

Augustus flicked on his electric torch and examined it. The corner of the archway had been fashioned to look like a square pillar. Three buildings were carved on it in low relief. The top one was too worn away to make out much detail, while the middle one had a soaring dome that resembled the Mosque of Omar in Jerusalem. The bottom one, however, showed something like a basilica topped by a pair of colonnaded towers that looked more at home in Venice than Cairo.

"Well, well, you might have found something here, Faisal. You could make a good tour guide someday."

"Do tour guides get paid well?"

"They certainly earn a big dinner."

"Let's go!"

"We have to wait for the Germans."

"But I'm hungry now," Faisal whined.

"We don't have long to wait," Augustus said, glancing at his watch and seeing it was already 9:30 p.m. "The Germans are a punctual people."

"It is something my own people should learn," Moustafa said with a nod.

Augustus didn't reply. Moustafa was always singing the praises of Europe, and Augustus never knew how much of it was heartfelt and how much of it was simply Moustafa buttering him up. The natives were experts at flattery.

The beggars started crowding around again. Moustafa shooed them away and told them if they didn't settle down they would all be arrested, beaten, and sent into the desert. The beggars moved away, sullen.

Augustus, Moustafa, and Faisal moved to the far recesses of the entranceway and sat down with their backs against the huge wooden door, now locked for the night. They curled up and tried to look like the beggars who were going back to sleep all around them. Augustus realized they didn't make very good imitations, but with the deep shadow in this part of the entrance, the Germans might be fooled if they didn't look directly at them.

"Mr. Wall," Moustafa whispered. "This is a holy place. We should not draw blood here."

"I hope not to," Augustus whispered back.

The thought soothed him. His breakdown in the house had shaken him badly. He didn't want to repeat that if he could at all avoid it.

Within a few minutes, they saw a slight figure tiptoe up the steps. He wore a tarboosh and carried himself like an Egyptian, although they could not see his features in the gloom. When some of the beggars pleaded for alms, he dismissed them in Arabic with the usual phrase, "I leave you in God's hands." Augustus had heard the natives use this many times. It seemed a rather dishonest way of saying "no."

The newcomer stood by the pillar, holding a sheaf of papers in his hand. Augustus and his companions watched him in silence.

A few minutes later, the heavy figure of Klaus Baumer ascended the steps, shooing away beggars who clutched at his legs and pleaded for alms.

"Do you have it?" he asked the Egyptian in German.

"Yes, let's go inside where we can talk without being seen," the man replied in the same language.

Augustus tensed. Were they going to come to the door where he and his companions were sitting? He relaxed a moment later when the two began to descend the steps.

"Let's follow them," he whispered to Moustafa. "I want to hear what they say to each other. Faisal, you stay here."

Baumer and the Egyptian made it to the bottom of the stairs and turned left, away from the Citadel and back toward the medieval city. Augustus and Moustafa peeked out from the arched entrance and saw them go around the far end of the mosque. They hurried to follow. Faisal tagged along, eager eyes wide in the moonlight. Augustus shook his head with annoyance. There was no time to argue with the boy.

Once they got to the corner of the mosque, Augustus crouched low and looked around the corner. He saw the Egyptian unlocking a small door that faced a garden by the side of the mosque. The two entered. Augustus and his companions hurried up to the door.

They were in luck. Whether out of carelessness or because he didn't anticipate staying long, the Egyptian had left the door slightly ajar. Augustus heard the sound of receding footsteps and low voices. He caught a snippet of conversation.

"You have the money?" the Egyptian asked.

"Of course. With this we have all we need," Baumer replied. "A remarkable discovery!"

Once the footsteps and voices faded into the distance, Augustus eased the door open, gritting his teeth as it made a loud creak. Faisal shook his head.

"You should have let me do that, you silly Englishman."

"Quiet," Augustus muttered.

The door opened onto a short hallway with smooth paving stones. At the top of a flight of three steps there was a long shelf for putting one's shoes. Beyond it, the floor was carpeted, marking the area of the mosque where people prayed.

Augustus noticed that Baumer and the Egyptian had not bothered to take off their shoes. As Augustus ascended the steps, Moustafa pulled off his own. He said nothing when Augustus didn't follow suit. There was no time for such formalities. Besides, his shoes were no dirtier than Faisal's bare feet.

They came to a side room of the mosque, a good hundred feet long and thirty wide, with a vaulted ceiling that reached for the sky. A few lamps made of glass with verses from the Koran painted in colorful calligraphy illuminated the interior. The thick carpet muffled their footsteps. From an arched doorway on the opposite wall they could hear voices.

They crept to the doorway. Augustus dared to look, his hand gripping the automatic in his pocket. Faisal squeezed between him and the wall and peeked too.

Baumer and the Egyptian stood by the *minbar*, the pulpit from which the preacher spoke during the Friday noon prayer. It was a high wooden platform reached by a narrow and steep flight of stairs, the sides and the railing intricately carved in a complex interweaving pattern.

The Egyptian handed Baumer the papers and the heavyset German handed over a wad of banknotes.

"Take care with the entrance," the Egyptian said. "As far as we know, the temple was never looted in antiquity and any traps might still be there."

"Excellent," Baumer said, leafing through the papers. "According to this, it's just north of the Great Pyramid and—"

Just then Faisal's stomach growled. Baumer spun around, pulling out a Luger from inside his jacket.

CHAPTER EIGHTEEN

Moustafa would have liked to have slapped Faisal silly for giving them away, but he was too busy dodging bullets. For a corpulent man in his late middle years, Klaus Baumer certainly had quick reflexes and a frighteningly good aim. His first shot cracked the stone doorway inches from Mr. Wall's head. His second shot buzzed by Moustafa's ear. Everyone ducked behind the doorway for protection, but Baumer ran across the room to get a better angle, and they had to beat a hasty retreat to get out of sight. Two more bullets followed them.

Mr. Wall reached around the doorway and fired three shots in rapid succession in different directions. He was shooting blind, but Moustafa guessed it was just to make Baumer and the Egyptian put their heads down. He then looked around the corner, ducked back as another bullet winged past him, and returned fire.

Moustafa hesitated. He did not want to defile this holy place by shedding blood, but it appeared he held the minority opinion.

Mr. Wall ducked around the corner, his cane in one hand and his pistol in the other, firing away. Moustafa followed, rounding the corner just in time to see Baumer disappear into a side room. The Egyptian was running off in the other direction, heading for a darkened doorway.

Moustafa snarled and chased after him. The Egyptian was older and not fit, and before he could reach the doorway, Moustafa tackled him.

The two men ended up on the carpet together, Moustafa's considerable weight pressing down on him. Moustafa punched him in the stomach to stop him from struggling and rifled through his pockets, finding no weapons.

"You call yourself a Muslim and you defile the sultan's mosque with gunfire? You walk with your shoes on carpets where men prostrate themselves before God?"

Moustafa tore off the Egyptian's European-style shoes and smacked him with them.

A couple of shots rang out from the far end of the mosque. Moustafa hauled the Egyptian to his feet and ran in the direction of the sound, practically having to drag his unwilling companion behind him.

Mr. Wall came back into the main room.

"I lost him. He opened the front door and ran out to the main street. There was a motorcar waiting there. I took a couple of shots at him but he got away. We have to report to headquarters. I mean . . ." He rubbed the eye on the unmasked half of his face with the heel of his palm. "I mean . . ."

Moustafa grabbed him by the lapel with his free hand and gave him a little shake. Mr. Wall shuddered.

"Who am I?" Moustafa demanded.

"You're a colonial . . . I mean you're Moustafa."

Faisal poked his head around the corner. "Have you stopped shooting now?"

"And who is he?" Moustafa asked, inclining his head in the direction of the street urchin.

Mr. Wall smiled. "Faisal. You call him the Little Infidel, and I think I might just start doing the same."

Moustafa smiled back. "Good to have you with us, Mr. Wall."

"And who is this?" Mr. Wall gestured toward the captive.

Moustafa gave the Egyptian another smack with the man's own shoe. "I was about to ask that myself."

Mr. Wall looked at the frightened man more closely. "Wait a moment. I think I recognize you. Don't you work at the German Egyptological Institute?"

The man trembled and shook his head. "I—I don't know what you're talking about."

Moustafa rummaged through the man's pockets. "Where are your identity papers?"

"Here they are," Faisal said, handing them to him.

Moustafa glared at the boy. "Give him back his wallet."

Faisal tried to look innocent. "What wallet?"

"I know you took it because his pockets are completely empty. You'd steal in a mosque? Give it back!"

"He shot at me," Faisal whined.

A look from Moustafa made him surrender the wallet.

As Faisal sulked, Moustafa gave the man back his wallet and inspected the identity papers.

"Talat Salih," he read. "And yes, it says here he does work for the German Egyptological Institute."

"What were those papers you handed Baumer?" Mr. Wall asked.

Salih paused a moment and then slumped, defeated. "An unpublished excavation report. He offered me money to steal it from the archives. Please, sir, I have a family to support. During the war, the institute stopped receiving funding. I haven't been paid in years. I couldn't find other work and kept my post in the hope that things would get better once the fighting stopped, but they still don't have any funding. If it wasn't for the support of my brothers, my family would be out on the street! Please don't report me to the police!"

Mr. Wall gripped him by the collar, gave him a little shake, and peered into his face. "Listen to me. You are going to tell me everything you know about the report and what Baumer and his friends are planning. And from now on, you will be my tool. Anything goes on in the German Egyptological Institute, I want to know about it. If I want anything from the archive, you're going to fetch it for me. If the director decides to have bacon instead of bratwurst for breakfast, I want you to tell me. Are we quite clear?"

Salih nodded eagerly. "Anything!"

Moustafa dragged him toward the door while the others followed. It was time to get out of here before the soldiers in the Citadel came down to investigate the gunfight.

"Start talking," he told Salih.

"Baumer has been frequenting the institute for some time, talking about all sorts of outlandish theories to anyone who would listen. He thinks the pharaohs were German. No one takes him seriously, but he donates money to the institute to keep the lights on. He's spent much time in the archive looking at reports. I run the archive and so I had to listen to his nonsense. He would sometimes give me tips so I endured them. A few days ago, he asked for access to any unpublished reports on Giza. I'm not allowed to hand those over because they are the property of the archaeologists. He had somehow learned that a dig at Giza in 1913 had uncovered an inscription mentioning the Temple of the Eternal Dawn. This is the report I gave him. He offered me enough money to support my family for six months."

They exited into the garden. Moustafa looked nervously around, but except for a few beggars staring at them, there was no sign of any response to the gunfire. He suspected it would come soon enough.

"So get to the point," Moustafa said. "What are they planning?"

Salih shook his head. "I don't know. I didn't even know Baumer was working with others until you told me."

"Did he mention the Thule Society?"

"He did, but he didn't say much. Only that it would make Germany great again and would purify the race. He said the new Germany would be free of Jews and socialists. He said the old Aryan magic was the key to Germany's renewal. He seems like such an ordinary man, and then he says such bizarre things."

Mr. Wall leaned in close to him. "Tell us more about this report. Have you read it?"

Salih nodded. "It was an excavation by Herbert Steinert during the 1912–1913 winter field season. He surveyed the area a hundred meters to the north of the Great Pyramid, digging test trenches hoping to find some of the outlying mortuary complex. It turned out he found very little, just stray finds and the remains of an obelisk that mentioned Temple of the Eternal Dawn. He also found some steps, but he didn't have time that season to dig down farther. In his report, he theorized that they were stairs into the burial chamber of a mastaba and that all the masonry had been stolen in antiquity, which is why nothing remained above ground. Herr Steinert returned to Germany with the inscriptions and wasn't able to return to resume digging because the war started. He died in 1916 of a heart attack."

"Does anyone else know of his finds?" Moustafa asked.

"I suppose the director and perhaps a few other archaeologists. I don't understand why it is so important."

Moustafa and Mr. Wall looked at each other. To all appearances, Herr Steinert had found very little. He had obviously not seen fit to publish a preliminary report until he had pursued those steps down to where they led.

But the two of them knew that those stairs didn't lead to an old tomb of some ancient nobleman. They led to something far more important.

"What did the inscription say?" Mr. Wall asked.

"I can't remember exactly. Something about Cheops being able to raise up the purest of men to the level of gods."

Moustafa nodded. That was something the fools in the Thule Society would lap right up.

"We need to go," Mr. Wall told Moustafa. "The Germans know we're onto them and they'll want to excavate that site as quickly as possible, probably tonight." He turned to Salih and jabbed a finger close to his face. "Keep your mouth shut about this. If you see Baumer, tell him you got away. If you say so much as a word about us, I'll have you up on charges, and I'm friends with the police commandant."

Salih nodded vigorously. "Not a word!"

Moustafa gave the wretch a final slap and let him go. He ran off into the darkness, forgetting to ask for his shoes. Moustafa tossed them to a nearby beggar.

"Thank you, sir!" the man cried, prostrating himself before him.

"Go away," Moustafa snapped at him. "So, Mr. Wall, what do we do now?"

"We're going to Giza, of course."

They hurried back to the motorcar. Faisal leaped into the back seat.

"Can we stop for dinner?"

"No time," Mr. Wall said, starting the engine.

"But you promised!" Faisal whined.

He continued to whine for several blocks until they passed a *molokheya* stand that was still open. The rich scent of the soup wafted over to them as they stopped nearby, making the boy's stomach grumble. Mr. Wall handed him a couple of piastres.

"Get yourself something to eat."

Grinning, Faisal bounced up and down on the back seat and leaped out of the motorcar. As soon as his feet touched the ground, Mr. Wall drove off.

"Hey! Where are you going?" Faisal shouted, running after them.

"Into danger, and you can't come," Augustus called back.

Moustafa burst out laughing. "Well done, boss!"

A rock pinked off the back of the car. They could see Faisal giving them a crude gesture as they drove off.

"That little louse!" Moustafa said, infuriated. "Turn back around and I'll wring his neck so badly he'll have to walk backward to see where he is going!"

But Mr. Wall kept on driving, a smile spreading across his face.

***

The Giza Plateau stood quiet and abandoned under a moonlit sky. The tourists always left at sundown, and those who lived off them left immediately thereafter. Few watchmen stood vigil to take care of the antiquities, and he had no doubt that Otto and his fellow veterans would take care of them easily enough. Augustus knew that they would be alone with the Germans.

Alone, but not isolated. The Mena House Hotel, a travesty of modernism, stood only a few hundred yards north of the Great Pyramid. Built in the 1880s, it offered peace and quiet away from Cairo and matchless views of the pyramids from its covered porch. The porch was decorated in a faux Islamic style, with stalactite fretwork on the canopies in imitation of medieval Cairene architecture and pillars that looked like a cross between something designed by a mosque architect later beheaded for public drunkenness and the imaginations of a *Boy's Own* hack illustrator who had never been anywhere more tropical than Brighton Beach on a bank holiday weekend. Would the horror never cease?

At this hour, that porch was filled with tourists lounging in white wicker chairs, drinking champagne and martinis and babbling about anything but Egyptology. Augustus would have been willing to bet his entire collection of antiquities that not a single one of them could accurately point out which pyramids were those of Cheops, Chephren, and Mycerinus, or indeed that those names were the Greek forms of the original names Khufu, Khafre, and Menkaure. He felt his stomach turn when he lifted his gaze from the porch up to the first floor, where the balconies of the most expensive rooms allowed guests to have a private view of the pyramids "far from the madding crowd" as the advertisement plagiarized. Some young woman was gazing dreamily out into the desert as if communing with the spirits of the ancients.

Bah! To let a swarm of silly socialites infect such a place of ancient wonder with their superficialities boiled his blood, but at least he could console himself with the knowledge that the proximity of the hotel might make the Germans think twice about starting another gunfight.

THE CASE OF THE PURLOINED PYRAMID

The hotel also gave him a convenient place to park. He noticed a pair of soldiers standing vigil at the foot of the stairs leading up to the porch. Good. He hoped Baumer and his crew had noticed them too.

Then Augustus realized that these men could not be relied upon to serve as reinforcements. Their duty was to guard the hotel. If things got ugly near the Great Pyramid, they would not leave their post. Instead they would get the guests inside and lock the place up. And on second thought, he didn't want to involve the authorities at all. There was a German diplomat lurking out there in the night, and he had no doubt Neumann would use all his power to make life difficult.

As he and Moustafa unloaded the large burlap bag of weapons from the back seat, taking care that the muzzles didn't stick out the end and give the game away, one of the young soldiers looked meaningfully at Augustus, made eye contact, and nodded.

Augustus ground his teeth.

Just because you're in uniform doesn't mean you get to have a heart-to-heart with me about my injury! Augustus railed silently at him.

Augustus thought for a moment. How would the soldiers react if they saw him and a Soudanese carrying a heavy bundle into the darkness in the direction of the pyramids? They'd probably think they were off to some grave robbing and question them before they got out of sight.

Handing the bundle to Moustafa, he walked up to the two soldiers.

"Hello, chaps. I saw a group of sullen-looking natives having a palaver on the other side of the hotel," he said, pointing away from the pyramids with his cane.

"We'll go have a look, sir," said the man who had made eye contact with him before. The two soldiers readied their rifles and went out of sight around the corner.

"Let's go," he told Moustafa, hurrying in the other direction. Within moments, they made it out of sight into the shadows. The guests hadn't so much as glanced in their direction, being too occupied with drinking and gossiping. Once he and Moustafa were in the safety of the darkness and invisible to those in the well-lit hotel grounds, they headed in a wide half circle to come at the Great Pyramid of Cheops from the west, well away from the location of the hidden temple.

"We'll have to sneak up on them unawares," Augustus said, keeping his voice low. He felt calm. The sand was staying sand and not changing into mud. The crescent moon gave the dunes a dull shine that helped keep his mind clear. The clean sand, a faint white in the moonlight, looked so different than the stinking dark mud of Flanders. And the sky was clear and filled with stars instead of pouring rain or shrouded in mist. He gripped his cane, something he would have never carried at the front, to give himself reassurance.

But he could still hear the distant artillery. Any time he held a gun in his hand, especially a lovely weapon such as his captured submachine gun, he got pulled back to 1917.

Augustus discovered he was smiling.

Try not to crack up while on the job, old chap.

They crouched low, moving to the foot of the pyramid before turning north, back toward the road and the Mena House Hotel, now just a bright rectangle in the distance. The wind carried a slight buzz of conversation from the patio, then shifted and all fell silent. Augustus peered through the night, but it was too dim to spot the Germans.

"Are you sure they are here?" Moustafa asked.

"I doubt they would have wasted time now that they have the exact location of the temple. Keep low."

Augustus got on his belly and Moustafa followed suit. They crawled forward, alert for any sign of life in the desert. Moustafa's movements were awkward and he made far too much noise. To crawl properly with a rifle in your hand took a bit of training. Augustus reminded himself to show Moustafa how, assuming they lived through the night.

A slight glow came from up ahead, the barest extra brightness against the pale glow of the moonlit sand.

Augustus turned to Moustafa and whispered in his ear, "Give me your gun. You can't crawl silently with it. This is going to take some stealth."

Moustafa didn't look too happy about giving up his weapon but saw the sense in the request and handed it over. Augustus nodded in approval. These colonial troops were reliable.

Employee, damn it! he reminded himself. *The war is over!*

The wind shifted and he caught a faint snatch of conversation that sounded German.

It's not over for tonight.

THE CASE OF THE PURLOINED PYRAMID

After another fifty yards, they could see more clearly. The first thing they noticed was a rectangular shadow against the sand. It confused them for a minute until they realized it was a tarpaulin pegged into the sand like a wall, to keep the light from being visible from the hotel or road. The glow was clearer now, although they still couldn't directly see its source. Augustus suspected it was a lantern hidden in the pit the Germans were excavating. The sound of shovels rasping against sand could clearly be heard.

"All right," Augustus whispered, trying to focus on the world around him instead of the one trying to press into all five of his senses. "There are some veterans in that crowd so they'll have a sentinel out—"

He stopped midsentence as he felt the cold muzzle of a gun press against his temple.

CHAPTER NINETEEN

"This did not go according to plan," Mr. Wall said.

"No, it did not," Moustafa agreed, although he could recall no mention of a plan.

They sat on the sand with their hands on their heads as the scarred German veteran named Otto covered them with Mr. Wall's own submachine gun. A few feet away yawned a pit in the sand about five feet wide and deeper than the height of a man. Moustafa hadn't been allowed to go to the edge and look down to the bottom, but he could see the Germans had uncovered a flight of stone steps leading down. They were following it with their spades and had already dug out of sight. One regularly came up with buckets of sand and dumped them a few yards away. A tarpaulin tied to several tall stakes screened the work from view of the distant hotel.

Moustafa marveled at the Germans' industry. They had half a dozen strong men working hard at it, rotating in groups with some taking a break while others dug or hauled sand. He supposed Neumann and Baumer were down there too, although he doubted they would much help in this hard work. He wondered how many other guards they had out hidden in the night.

It didn't matter. They had already been caught and now their fate was in God's hands. Moustafa regretted that he wouldn't see his sons grow into manhood or get to dance at the weddings of his daughters. Ah well, it was written.

"A pity we left Faisal behind in the city," Mr. Wall said.

"You wouldn't want him to get shot too? The brat isn't that bad!"

"No, no, no. I merely wish I had left him behind here in Giza. He would have followed us and figured out a way to get us free."

Moustafa chuckled at the ridiculous idea, and then stopped and gave it some thought.

"You don't suppose he might have made it here somehow?" Moustafa asked.

"I doubt it," Mr. Wall said, looking hopefully around at the shadows. "No, I suppose we are on our own."

"Quiet over there!" Otto barked in heavily accented English.

Herr Neumann emerged from the entrance, his narrow face sliced with a mocking grin as he brushed the sand off his pants.

"Good to see you again, Mr. Wall!"

"Pity I can't say the same about you," Mr. Wall replied.

"Ah, but you should be happy at this reunion. You'll get to witness the greatest discovery in the history of Egyptology! And because of this discovery, Germany will take its proper place as the leader of all nations."

Moustafa saw Otto's eyes light up with excitement as he listened.

"The master race will finally be the master," the veteran said.

Neumann nodded in agreement, then snarled and took another step toward Mr. Wall. "And you arrogant Englishmen will finally learn your place. Oh, you think you're so special with your empire, ruling over inferior peoples. Yes, we have been laggards. You became a nation in the Middle Ages, while we didn't unite until 1870, thanks to the divisive machinations of the Jews. But we will make up for lost time. Oh yes. And you"—at this he slapped Mr. Wall across the face—"you will learn some humility."

Neumann made a lunge for Mr. Wall's mask as if to rip it off. Mr. Wall knocked him down.

Neumann scampered back, spitting with rage. He got to his feet and drew a pistol.

Otto slapped him in the back of the head, and he ended up on the ground for a second time.

"You'll treat him with honor, swine!" Otto said. "He may have fought for the international bankers, but at least he fought. What did you do in the war? Pimp honorable German women while real men went to the front? Touch him again and I'll put a bullet through you."

Neumann went pale and scampered down the pit. Mr. Wall faced Otto.

"*Danke, Kamerad,*" his boss said. Moustafa didn't understand German, but he could guess at the meaning of that.

"You are a warrior and deserve to be treated with honor. But I'll kill you like a warrior if you try anything, so sit back down and put your hands on your head."

"I have the distinct impression that you are going to kill me anyway, old chap," Mr. Wall said, sitting back down. "Like I suppose you killed the night watchmen who patrol the area."

"I did it quickly and quietly. They felt no unnecessary pain."

"How charitable of you."

"What's all this noise up here?" Baumer said as he lifted his heavy frame up the ancient steps. "Ah, Mr. Wall. I had been told of your arrival, and I can't say I am much surprised. You have caused us quite a bit of trouble. Nevertheless I'd like to show you something remarkable that a man of your education will appreciate. Come."

Mr. Wall stood up and stepped forward. Moustafa, unsure what to do, joined him. Baumer gave him a contemptuous look.

"Leave the servant here."

"I am his employee," Moustafa said.

Baumer chuckled. "Of course you are."

"He's also an expert in hieroglyphics," Mr. Wall informed him.

Baumer chuckled again, but when he saw Moustafa's employer was serious, he gave them both a searching look and shrugged. "I'd be interested to see proof of that."

Otto didn't take his eyes off them for an instant as they approached the pit. The submachine gun didn't waver.

As Moustafa had guessed, the Germans had followed the staircase and had made it more than six feet down, uncovering the top lintel of a doorway. The Germans dug furiously. Neumann stood by doing nothing except gesturing at them and urging them on in German, no doubt giving useless advice. In the heap of spoil they made, Moustafa saw several potsherds and other small artifacts. These did not seem to interest the Germans at all. Moustafa sneered. These weren't archaeologists, just tomb robbers.

The lintel was inscribed with hieroglyphs, well preserved by the desert sands. Instinctively, Moustafa started to trace the lines, puzzling out the writing. His heart raced as he saw the cartouche of Khufu, the one known to the Greeks and the modern world as Cheops, builder of the Great Pyramid.

The inscription started with his praenomen, official name, his Horus name, followed by the title associated with his pyramid. "Khnum Khufu, the one who strikes. Khufu is one belonging to the horizon, who opens to doors to the Temple of Eternal Dawn. At the altar of Isis he renews his limbs, his heart, and his mouth. At the place of honoring the guardian of the pyramids he makes himself a god. At the portal to power he gives this blessing to the chosen among his people. Any but the most pure who pass this portal will die a thousand deaths."

Baumer was reading this with rapt attention, his lips moving silently. His eyes glittered in the lamplight with a feverish enthusiasm.

"Take care." Moustafa chuckled. "If Cheops considers you unjust, you'll die a thousand deaths."

Baumer raised an eyebrow. "Oh, so you really do read Old Kingdom hieratic."

"Better than I," Mr. Wall said.

"I also speak Arabic, French, and English, although I have not yet had a chance to learn your ugly language."

Baumer sneered. "No true German would teach his sacred tongue to one such as you."

One of the workmen snapped something in German in Baumer's direction, who replied with a curt command. Moustafa guessed that the workman was probably telling him to help instead of wasting time arguing with the captives.

Even without the fake archaeologist's help, the doorway was cleared within another quarter of an hour. The workmen sat down, exhausted, as Baumer and Neumann examined the door.

It was of thick Lebanese cedar, an expensive import in ancient times, and well preserved by being buried in the sand except for a couple of fresh marks from the Germans' shovels. A clay seal covered it and part of the doorjamb. This, at least, had been left unscathed by the workmen in their mad dig to uncover the door. The seal bore a cartouche and a small inscription, lettered in gold foil. Neumann shone his torchlight on it as Baumer peered at the inscription.

The two muttered in their own language for a minute before Baumer turned to Mr. Wall.

"This is tricky. It appears to be a late, corrupt version of hieratic. Would you care to examine it?"

"I see no reason to help you," Moustafa's employer replied.

"Are you not curious?"

Mr. Wall hesitated for a second and glanced at Moustafa. After a moment they both smiled, and Moustafa understood something about this strange man whose fate he was so soon to share. Like him, Mr. Wall had an insatiable curiosity, and even facing imminent death they both wanted to see what was beyond this door as much as any of their captors.

They peered at the seal. It was, indeed, a tricky text, not helped by the fact that some of the gold foil had dropped away, leaving some of the words missing or illegible.

After puzzling it over for a couple of minutes, Moustafa read aloud, "Sealed in the first regnal—here a word is missing, although no doubt it is 'year'—of Psamtik III by—another missing word, probably a name—chief—more missing words where his title should be. Isis give him strength!"

"Isis give us all strength!" Baumer intoned. Neumann bowed his head and touched his chest, then looked up. "Do you agree with this translation, Mr. Wall?"

"I do."

Moustafa glared at the Germans. For once he wasn't angered by being passed over by arrogant Europeans. He had far more serious things to be angry about. "Did you just call out to a pagan deity?"

Baumer gave him a haughty look. "The old gods gave our people strength. We only began to lose our vigor when we embraced the cringing faith of the Jews."

"You don't strike me as a Jew," Mr. Wall said.

"Of course not!" Neumann said. "We are pure Aryans who have understood that the Christian faith in which we were raised was created by the Jews to undermine our true beliefs and make us their slaves."

Mr. Wall snorted. "Christianity is a Jewish plot? Oh Lord, kill me now!"

"We will prove it!" Neumann said, pointing at Mr. Wall with a shaking finger. "What is beyond this door will prove it."

Mr. Wall turned to Moustafa. "And you wonder why I hate the world?"

Moustafa couldn't think of anything to say to that.

"Enough of this," Baumer said. "You will see soon enough. Let's get back to the matter at hand. Who was this Psamtik III? One of the later pharaohs, was he not?"

Moustafa couldn't believe his ears. This man claimed to be an archaeologist?

"He was the last pharaoh of the XXVI Dynasty," Moustafa explained. "He was defeated by the Persian king Cambyses II and carried off in captivity to Susa in 525 BC."

"I focused my study on learning to read hieroglyphs," Baumer said defensively. Moustafa couldn't help but smile.

"So it appears our man Psamtik III decided to seal up this temple, and probably cover it up with sand, to avoid the Persians finding it," Mr. Wall said. "And from the looks of it they never did, nor any of Egypt's other occupiers. Congratulations, you've found a perfectly preserved subterranean temple. You were right, Herr Neumann. You have made the greatest Egyptological discovery of the century. Pity you shan't be sharing it with the world at large."

"In time, all will know the truth about our glorious past," Neumann said. "Let's get in there."

Baumer produced a trowel and tried to pry the seal off from the doorway. It cracked into pieces.

Moustafa gave a hiss of disapproval. "Stupid man!"

Baumer glared at him. "Watch it. You are only alive because we want your master's cooperation."

Master? Moustafa almost punched his face in, but something held him back. It wasn't the submachine gun Otto had trained on him, but rather the aching curiosity about what lay beyond that door. Once his curiosity was satisfied, he'd go down fighting, like those brave, misled men at Omdurman. They had died in the thousands, but at least they had taken some of the British with them, and in their last moments they had seen fear and respect in their enemies' eyes.

Neumann gave a curt order and a couple of the workmen grabbed guns and headed up to help guard the entrance. Otto stayed where he was, along with two of the other workers, who picked up rifles. Baumer scraped the last of the sand away from the threshold and with Neumann's help pulled open the door. It gave way reluctantly with a grinding creak.

One of the workmen lit a lamp. Neumann and Baumer produced

electric torches and gave Mr. Wall back his own. Together they shone light into a space that no man had seen in three thousand years.

Beyond the doorway they saw a corridor about ten feet wide stretching off out of sight. The ceiling was about eight feet from the floor and painted blue with golden stars. It reminded Moustafa of some of the decorations found in various tombs. On either wall stood life-size statues of gods and goddesses. Isis and Osiris stood closest to the door, then jackal-headed Anubis and Horus with the head of a hawk. Beyond stood more, dozens of them. It looked to be all the major deities of ancient Egypt.

The Germans and their captives stood in silent awe for a full minute. It was Baumer who spoke first.

"Here's where the ancient Aryans had their font of power, and it is here where we will regain our heritage." He turned to the captives. "Mr. Wall, you may join us, but your ape must stay behind. Only those of a pure race may enter this holy place."

With that, Baumer crossed the threshold. The flagstone just beyond it lowered an inch under his weight with a loud click.

A row of bronze spikes thrust out from the wall and impaled him. One pierced his skull, and four more ran right through his body. The archaeologist ended up suspended from the spikes, which extended from niches in the side wall to reach halfway across the entrance before screeching to a stop like a horizontal portcullis. His eyes and mouth were wide open as if in shock, but he felt nothing. He had been killed instantly.

"*Mein Gott!*" Neumann exclaimed.

"Shouldn't you be shouting out to Isis and not that nefarious invention of the Jews?" Mr. Wall asked dryly.

"Silence!"

Neumann peered at the entrance. Moustafa did the same. The spikes had emerged from the right side of the doorway from holes hidden directly behind the jamb and thus hidden to anyone entering. Peeking around the corner, they saw a series of identical holes ran down the left-hand wall. The tips of another row of bronze spikes were just visible inside.

"A bit of extra insurance," Moustafa said. "The pagans probably knew their magic didn't work, as the Prophet Moses proved to them."

"I suppose this was added by good old Psamtik III in case the Persians came prowling," Mr. Wall said.

"It is fortunate only half of the spikes still worked, otherwise our way would be blocked," Herr Neumann said. Beyond his initial shock, he seemed not the least bit discomfited by the death of his companion.

"We're dealing with the Late Period," Mr. Wall said. "They didn't make traps the way they did in the good old days."

Herr Neumann turned to Moustafa. "You! You will walk ahead."

A pickle of fear turned Moustafa cold. He took care not to show it. "I thought only pure Aryans were allowed in this sacred place?"

"Don't toy with me. Get in there!"

Moustafa saw Mr. Wall tense and glance at Otto, who stood just out of reach with the submachine gun. Moustafa motioned to his employer.

"Don't. I will go ahead."

He gazed down the corridor. Unlike most subterranean tombs and temples, which had floors of solid stone cut out of the bedrock, as far as the eye could see the floor was covered in square flagstones about two feet to a side.

"Herr Neumann, give me a shovel."

"What for?" the diplomat demanded.

"So I can probe ahead of me for more of those moving flagstones. I will not walk blindly into a trap no matter how much you threaten me, and while I know my life means nothing to you, think what will happen if I get killed. I suppose you will make Mr. Wall take my place, but if he gets killed, what will you do then? Send one of your precious Germans? I doubt they respect you enough to volunteer. Otto might even force you to go ahead."

Neumann's eyes narrowed with spite, but he visibly paled, and Moustafa could tell that the diplomat knew he spoke the truth.

Neumann grabbed a shovel and tossed it at Moustafa's feet. The Germans backed away. Neumann pulled a Luger from his pocket.

"Now get in there, and if you try anything, I will kill both you and your master."

CHAPTER TWENTY

Moustafa walked slowly, pushing each flagstone he came to with the shovel before daring to step on it. Despite the cool interior of the temple's grand entrance hall, sweat ran down his face. His eyes darted to the left and right, searching for more hidden spikes. He looked up too, not trusting the ceiling to be safe from nasty surprises.

Clunk. Clunk. The shovel banged down on each flagstone. Moustafa hit them as hard as he could, and the sound echoed down the corridor like mocking laughter. Each step made him tense. The last trap had only half worked, and there was no telling just how much force would need to be put on the flagstones to set off another one. He might have trodden on a trapped flagstone already and not triggered the aged mechanism, or his next step might be his last. He had no way of telling.

Clunk. Clunk.

Moustafa's mind raced. The temptation rose in him to whirl around and throw the shovel at Herr Neumann's head. If he threw it right, he might cut right through that scrawny neck. How he would love to see that ugly head bounce down the corridor like those footballs the ANZACs used to kick down the streets during the war. The diplomat walked only a few paces behind, following with care like the rest of them. It would be an easy throw, although in the next instant Moustafa himself would die, and Mr. Wall too.

That was of little importance. They were dead men anyway. It would be better to die fighting than risk the humiliation of a death like Baumer's.

But he knew that he could not do it. Curiosity pulled him forward, the same curiosity that had made him leave his village all those years ago, the same curiosity that made him pester Mr. Clarke with questions and risk his job to sneak peeks at Monsieur Dupris's books. He had to know what lay at the end of this corridor. The history of his people lay hidden here, the secrets of Africa's greatest civilization. It didn't matter if no one else present would appreciate it or that he would never live to tell his countrymen what he had learned. He had to know for himself.

As Moustafa continued his slow path down the grand hallway, he marveled at the workmanship of the statues flanking him. All the gods and goddess of ancient Egypt were there—Ptah and Bastet, Sekhmet and Neith. He saw a rare statue of Khnum, the ram-headed god of the earth who had fashioned men out of the clay of the Nile and who had given the great Khufu his praenomen. He even saw crocodile-headed Sobek. As they passed that god of the Nile, he heard Mr. Wall chuckle behind him, "We've certainly gotten ourselves in a fix this time, old man."

Moustafa got the impression his employer was talking to the statue, not him.

So this was how he would end his life, getting killed either by a trap or a bullet in a glorious ancient temple accompanied by a bunch of European madmen? He had hoped for something better.

The searching light of the electric torches illuminated something up ahead. Gold gleamed in the faint light. The corridor was finally coming to an end. Beyond he could dimly see that it opened up into a large chamber. Moustafa had to resist the urge to rush ahead to see it. At the last minute, he remembered himself and continued his slow progress with the shovel.

Clunk. Clunk.

He almost didn't see it in time. The flagstone gave way under the pressure of his shovel. Moustafa leaped back just as a large stone dropped from the ceiling and hit the floor with a crash. The entire hallway reverberated from the impact.

Moustafa stumbled back. Dust poured from the ceiling, and he heard an ominous crackling all around him.

Coughing and blinking his eyes as they teared up from the grit, Moustafa looked around. The stone was a full-size building block, a good two hundred pounds. He would have been smashed into pulp. Around it spidered a network of cracks in the flagstones. Cracks had appeared on the walls and ceiling too.

"All you all right?" Mr. Wall said, coming up beside him.

Moustafa nodded. "This corridor doesn't look stable. I thought it was all bedrock on the Giza Plateau."

"There are faults here and there," Mr. Wall said. "See those seams? These walls are facades, and the roof a lintel. They probably hide cracked and weakened stone."

"I should have noticed that, but I had eyes only for the floor."

"And I daresay these beautiful statues."

Otto shouted something in German.

"What did he say?" Moustafa asked.

"He said another stone like that might bring the entire roof down around our ears, and I must say I agree. Please don't do that again, or I might be forced to sack you."

"Considering the working conditions at this job, I doubt you'll find a replacement."

"True enough."

"Stop chattering like a pair of old women and get moving," Neumann said, gesturing with his pistol.

Moustafa picked up the handle of the shovel, which had broken off when the stone came down. The handle was splintered and useless.

"Give me another shovel."

"Move," Neumann ordered.

"No."

Neumann raised his pistol.

"Wait," Mr. Wall said. "Fetch me my walking stick. It's just at the top of the pit outside. It's metal and will work well as a probe. I can put more pressure on a single spot than I could with a shovel."

Neumann hesitated for a moment, then nodded and said something in German to one of the workmen, who ran off down the corridor.

When the man returned with the cane, Mr. Wall said, "Let me take the lead."

Moustafa didn't argue and neither, to his surprise, did Neumann. They were so close to their goal it probably didn't matter who took the risks now. They'd be disposed of soon enough.

Mr. Wall pushed hard on each flagstone, and then he tested them with his foot, ready to leap back.

They made it to the end of the corridor and beheld the chamber at its end. Before them stood a great altar covered with the desiccated remains of loaves of bread and what might have once been fruit. Behind the altar stood a beautiful alabaster statue of Isis with a dress and eyes made of gold foil. It was the gold that had first caught their torchlight. Flanking her stood Osiris and Anubis. The pure white stone shone in the light with a warm glow. In niches all around the room stood alabaster statues of pharaohs. Moustafa recognized the cartouches of Khufu and his predecessor Snefru. Turning his gaze around the room, he went back in time through the great III Dynasty of Huni and Khaba and Sekhemkhet to Djoser, builder of the first step pyramid at Saqqara. The names of all but Huni were written in the square serekh, a stylized drawing of a palace, for the cartouche had not yet come into fashion. Beyond Djoser stood a statue of his predecessor Sanakhte, founder of the III Dynasty, and then the little-known rulers of the II Dynasty. On the far wall stood the earliest pharaoh of a united Egypt, the legendary Narmer.

Moustafa's gaze roved around the room for more statues. Virtually nothing was known about the predecessors of Narmer, and he hoped to see their likenesses and names, but sadly the builders did not think them worthy of inclusion.

Then his heart raced at the implication. This proved Narmer really was the unifier of Upper and Lower Egypt and the land's first true pharaoh. This had been argued back and forth in the academic journals for years. A long debate was finally put to rest in this chamber.

Moustafa turned back to the Europeans to find them as entranced as he was. Even the soldiers looked overawed, although perhaps more by the gold decoration on the statue of Isis than by the chamber's historical significance.

"What a pity Baumer didn't live to see the final proof of all we knew to be true," Neumann said.

"Whatever do you mean?" Mr. Wall asked.

"Here are the true representations of the early pharaohs. As you can see, they were white, with noble Aryan features."

"You donkey's ass!" Moustafa shouted. "These statues are made of alabaster. Of course they're white. When I was digging at Abusir in the 1913 season I came across fifty ushabti made of faience. Does that prove the ancient Egyptians were blue?"

"Bah, you know nothing of real history." Neumann turned and gazed at the altar, which was covered with hieroglyphs. "What does this say?"

Moustafa shook his head. This carbuncle claimed he didn't know anything about history but needed him to translate the inscription?

Nevertheless he approached the altar, drawn by the old text. Mr. Wall joined him. Neumann stood just behind them with his pistol at the ready. Otto stood a little to the right with the submachine gun and the two soldiers a bit behind.

Moustafa studied the writing for a moment and started to read. "Oh, Isis, protector of my house, hear me! Through my power I heal the sick and make the meek stand proud. I bring power to the land of the sedge and the bee. From the northern waters to the southern cataracts, I rule."

"Oh, you missed something there, Moustafa," Mr. Wall said, pointing with his cane. Moustafa noticed that for some reason he gripped it by its end and pointed with the head. "That line there doesn't say 'make the meek stand proud.' It says 'make the forgetful remember their noble birthright.'"

"Really?" Neumann said, stepping forward. "Which line?"

"That one," Mr. Wall said, pointing with the head of his cane.

Moustafa stared at the line. It said no such thing.

Mr. Wall pulled back his cane, gripped the head, and did a remarkable thing. He twisted the cane and pulled a sword out from it.

With a single thrust, he ran Neumann straight through. In the same movement, he spun around just as Otto was aiming the submachine gun and struck the gun with the metal shaft of the cane. The gun jerked to the side and fired a burst of bullets that stitched a line of pockmarks into the wall.

Mr. Wall yanked the sword out of Neumann, smacked Otto upside the head with the shaft of his cane, and then stabbed him.

The veteran got stunned by the blow to the head but had enough awareness to dodge to the side and was only scraped along the ribs by the blade.

Then Moustafa was too busy with his own fight to see what his boss did next. He ducked down, grabbed Neumann's gun, and without taking the time to rise pumped a bullet into one of the workmen. The German doubled over, clutching his belly, and Moustafa rolled away to avoid a shot from the other man. A hot pain along his shoulder told him he hadn't quite made it. He fired again, but his shot went wild, and the workman backpedaled, firing a bullet that hummed by Moustafa's ear and planted itself into the leg of a statue.

Another burst of submachine gun fire, and a rain of stone fragments fell from the ceiling. Out of the corner of his eye, Moustafa saw his boss and Otto struggling for the weapon.

Moustafa fired at the workman three times in rapid succession. The man was already bolting down the hallway, shouting for help. The first shot missed. The second thudded into his back and the man stumbled. The third shot cut a leg out from under him and he landed hard on the floor.

Moustafa turned to the fight beside him just in time to see Otto kick Mr. Wall in the knee and make him drop to the floor, losing his grip on the submachine gun. They stood only a step away. Moustafa leaped at them and before Otto could bring his weapon to bear, Moustafa had the pistol up against his temple.

Otto froze. The submachine gun dropped to the floor with a clatter.

Mr. Wall scooped it up, then suddenly turned and fired a burst down the hallway.

The man Moustafa had wounded had turned around and was just aiming his rifle at them when he caught a full burst from the submachine gun to his chest. Blood burst all around, spattering the statues of the gods and even the starry sky painted on the ceiling.

"Attack! Get in their trenches, men, and secure the communication lines!" Mr. Wall shouted, running down the corridor.

"Captain! Major! Whatever you once were, we have a prisoner!"

Mr. Wall stopped and turned.

Moustafa thought fast. "We're trapped alone in the enemy trench, sir, just the two of us. But we have this prisoner. We might be able to use him to escape."

"And bring the plans back to HQ. Good idea."

"Take your sword cane, sir. It's a clever trick, and you wouldn't want to be without it when you walk the streets of Cairo." Moustafa clapped his hand over his mouth at this slip.

"Cairo, um . . ." Mr. Wall looked confused, gazed around him for a moment, and retrieved his sword cane. Otto stared at him, his expression turning from confusion to understanding to sympathy.

"The war is over, *Kamerad*," the veteran said in a soft voice. "Enjoy your rest before the next one starts."

The sound of running feet echoed down the hall. Moustafa pushed Otto to the side of the room so they would be out of sight. Mr. Wall hesitated for a moment, looking around him before he followed.

Moustafa glanced at his shoulder. It was only a graze and did not bleed too much. He'd be all right for the moment.

Except for the unknown number of Germans blocking their only path to escape.

And Mr. Wall trembling all over and slowly sinking to the floor.

"Are you hit?" Moustafa asked.

"Hit?"

"Are you injured?"

"How could I be? The war is over. Then why the guns? Why this strange trench? I don't need this." Mr. Wall dropped the submachine gun.

Otto tensed. Moustafa pressed the muzzle of the pistol against his head to keep him from temptation and looked Mr. Wall in the eye.

"The war is not over. We are trapped in an enemy trench with a German prisoner. The only way out is that way, and the Germans are blocking it with a superior force. If we want to get the plans back to HQ, we must negotiate our way out of here. They don't know we have the plans, so they might let us go. This man is an officer so they will listen to him. I don't speak German, and we can't trust Otto, I mean this officer, to say the right thing. You speak German. You must negotiate with them."

"We're still fighting? I don't understand. Isn't it 1919?"

Moustafa hated doing this, but he had to be cruel in order for them to have a chance at survival.

"No, Mr. Wall, I mean, sir. It's 1917, and I am a colonial soldier assigned to help you on this mission. You must speak with them."

Suddenly the doorway and altar were bathed in light.

Gripping Otto tight, Moustafa glanced down the corridor. The Germans had placed several electric torches on the floor facing them. With the glare of the light, what lay beyond them was shrouded in darkness. No doubt they hid there with their rifles, waiting. They would have a clear shot while Moustafa and his boss would be shooting blind.

Assuming he could get his Mr. Wall's mind back together enough for him to be any more use in this fight.

Mr. Wall straightened up, gripping the submachine gun once more. He pulled out the magazine and checked it before snapping it back into place. Moustafa tried to remember how many rounds the magazine held and tried to estimate how many shots it had already fired. He couldn't be sure, but he thought there couldn't be more than one or two more bursts left in it. And Moustafa probably had only a couple of bullets in his pistol. The two rifles lay exposed to fire and thus out of reach.

Mr. Wall called out in German and was greeted with silence. He called out again. Moustafa glanced at their prisoner, to find him looking back at him, studying him. Moustafa glared at him and pressed the gun harder against his temple. Otto only chuckled. Moustafa could feel his wounded arm, the one gripping Otto, slowly weakening. He wondered if the German noticed it too.

A call came from down the hall. Otto gave a brief reply, mentioning Neumann's name.

There was a pause. Moustafa looked nervously from his prisoner to his boss. He could tell Mr. Wall was a thousand miles away. He did not see what was really around him. Moustafa couldn't worry about that now. At least in this state he could fight.

Finally another call came from down the hallway. It sounded like assent.

"They say we can pass as long as we leave them the temple and drop off Otto unharmed in the desert. This is a temple?"

"The Germans have invaded Egypt, sir. What will they do with the temple? Bury it again? They know its secret is not safe as long as we live."

"Yes, they'll come after us, but perhaps we'll make it out into the open desert before they do."

Moustafa nodded. Mr. Wall may not be clear on where he was, but he grasped the essentials well enough.

"There's a hotel less than a mile from here. Do you think anyone there heard the shots?" Moustafa asked.

"Hard to tell. All the shots were fired underground."

"If the Germans think the people in the hotel haven't noticed the firefight, they'll probably try to kill us at the first opportunity."

"Best to assume that in any case."

Moustafa let out a sigh. "Ready?"

"Ready."

They edged around the corner and into view, keeping Otto in front of them as a human shield. No shots came. As they passed one of the discarded rifles, Moustafa moved to pick it up but got stopped by a barked command in German.

"Let's not push our luck," Mr. Wall replied.

They moved slowly forward, trying to hide behind Otto as much as they could. Despite the gash on his side, the German didn't seem badly hurt.

"How many are there?" Mr. Wall whispered.

"I don't know. Four, I think. Maybe a few more."

"Only four? Are we at an isolated outpost? A listening station?"

"Just focus on what is at hand, sir. I'll explain everything later."

Otto cut in. "You're not actually in battle. You're—"

Moustafa silenced him by nudging him in the head with the muzzle of the pistol.

Mr. Wall shouted something to their invisible opponents and then translated for Moustafa's sake. "I told them to move back. What are all these statues?"

"Focus on the enemy, sir."

Moustafa tried to peer beyond the light of the electric torches sitting on the floor. He thought he caught some movement.

They passed the torches and could see better. Five Germans, each carrying a rifle, were about twenty paces from them, edging back and darting from one statue to the next for cover. Moustafa felt terribly exposed. If they decided Otto's life wasn't worth saving, they could kill them all with a single volley.

The Germans backed off to the entrance and moved up the sides of the pit and out of sight.

"Let's move with care," Mr. Wall said. "They're up to something. I can feel it."

"Do you remember your bag, sir?" Moustafa said with a whisper.

"My bag? Oh yes. That has the plans. Um, no. It has—"

"Best not to say, sir. I believe they left it just past the opening. You should grab it."

"Yes."

Moustafa looked all around as they moved up and out of the pit. The Germans had taken up position in a wide semicircle facing them, lying prone in the sand and several yards away, half-invisible in the shadows. Moustafa and the others, however, were illuminated from behind by all the light in the tunnel. Moustafa glanced at the tarpaulin that blocked the light from view of the hotel. Was a German lurking behind there?

"I'll tell them to back off toward the pit," Mr. Wall said, picking up the bag from where it lay not far from the entrance. He shouted something in German. There was a brief argument, and then the Germans moved to either side and around them as they advanced. They kept their guns leveled as they moved toward the entrance.

Then Otto made his move. When Moustafa turned his head to look around the desert for any hidden enemies, Otto slapped his pistol arm away and drove a punch straight into Moustafa's face. The veteran may have been smaller than Moustafa, but his fist was like iron. Moustafa stumbled back and fell to the ground as a well-placed kick got him straight in the stomach.

Otto shouted something, and suddenly the air was filled with bullets.

Moustafa went prone. His employer dove down next to him. Rifles blammed from several locations in and around the pit. Mr. Wall let out a burst of submachine gun fire. Moustafa thought he saw one German go down but couldn't be sure. He fired his own weapon at the muzzle flares as bullets kicked up sand all around him.

After two shots, his gun did nothing but click.

A moment later, Mr. Wall ran out of ammunition too.

Mr. Wall cried out. Moustafa glanced over and saw him grasping his forearm.

"We have to run," Moustafa said as a bullet plowed through the sand between them.

"Retreat? We'll never make it. Here." Mr. Wall emptied the bag and out spilled several grenades. "Were you trained in these?"

"No."

"It's simple. Pull this pin here and throw."

Moustafa grabbed one, put his finger through the metal ring his employer had indicated, and gave it a swift yank, half expecting it to blow up in his face.

He threw it as hard as he could. Mr. Wall did the same beside him. Moustafa felt a hot streak on his hip and fell down hard.

"Got me again!"

Mr. Wall wasn't listening. He was already throwing another grenade, and another and another. They went off in rapid succession, a series of thuds and blinding flashes in the night. Only when he ran out did he fling himself back down.

The sand trembled. A low rumble shook the desert. Blinking and trying to see past the afterimages of the blasts, they saw the sand shift. The pit the Germans had dug was no more. The entire area was shifting, sand moving inward on the blast site.

The sand they lay on started moving too, pulling them toward where the grenades had gone off.

They got up and ran, Moustafa limping as fast as he could with his injured hip. The rumbling continued, along with several deep booms as the great masonry of the subterranean temple collapsed. Moustafa imagined priceless statues toppling over and smashing on the flagstones, the roof caving in, and sand pouring through the gaps.

The rumbling stopped, followed by a loud hiss of the sand rearranging itself. After a minute, they looked out on a featureless desert. In the distance, they could see the tourists on the brightly lit porch of the Mena House Hotel staring into the night, wondering about the noise and unable to see what was happening. Moustafa clearly saw the two soldiers on guard start hustling everyone inside.

Otto's distant voice came to them from out of the night. "Well fought, *Kamerad*, but we will win the next one!"

"How did he survive?" Moustafa asked.

"People like us always do," Mr. Wall muttered, cradling his injured forearm. "Let's get out of here before the Germans launch a counterattack."

"You mean before the police arrive."

"What? The, um, oh yes."

"Come, Mr. Wall."

The two helped each other through the darkness of the Egyptian desert, making a wide circle away from the vanished temple before heading for the light of the distant hotel.

CHAPTER TWENTY-ONE

Augustus found Sir Russell standing in the hallway in front of his office door at police headquarters talking with a correspondent from the *Times*.

"Is it true that a soldier was killed in the rioting?" the reporter asked.

Russell nodded grimly. "Yes, unfortunately it is true. Private Declan Andrews got separated from his unit and was set upon by some cowardly thugs in the crowd. They literally tore his limbs from his body. My officers tell me that one big brute of a Soudanese actually charged our line wielding poor Andrew's leg as a club. I'm happy to say that he was killed with a single shot to the head."

"Were any other natives killed in this engagement?" the correspondent asked, writing in his notebook.

"None," Sir Russell replied with an authoritative shake of the head. "The other culprits had all slunk away, and it is the policy of the British army not to fire on unarmed protestors. We only shoot when we're attacked."

"Do you anticipate further disturbances?"

"A few, perhaps. I think the natives have learned their lesson, at least here in Cairo. The fellahin in the countryside are a bit slower in getting the message no matter what it is."

"Fellahin?"

"The Egyptian term for peasant."

The reporter smiled. "Aren't they all?"

Russell smiled in return. "Quite right. In any case, I think Cairo has been more or less pacified. And by the time your readers see your article and book passage to come visit Egypt's many wonders, I have no doubt the countryside will be well in hand."

"Thank you, Commandant. Most kind of you to meet with me."

"Not at all. I am always happy to meet with representatives of the press."

The reporter left. Russell spotted Augustus waiting a few steps away and signaled for him to enter his office. He closed the door behind them and settled behind his desk with a sigh. Augustus took one of the comfortable leather chairs facing him.

"What happened there?" Russell asked, pointing the Augustus's arm in a sling.

"Spot of bother with the murderer."

"Well, I daresay you've had a livelier time of it than I. What a bore these press interviews are," Russell said, reaching for a decanter of whiskey. "Hacks and sycophants, the lot of them. Who are these journalists, anyway? Failed novelists, I suppose."

"I haven't the slightest idea," Augustus replied, taking the glass the commandant offered him. "So is the situation really in hand?"

"More or less," Russell said, an enthusiastic grin cutting through his fatigue. "Oh, we've had a fine time of it, chasing the Cairo riffraff down alleys and throwing them in the wagon. The jails are fit to burst."

"Can they hold a few more?"

"You found the murderer?" Russell asked.

"I did, but I had to shoot him. Self-defense."

"Oh dear. I'm afraid I'll have to launch an investigation. Simple formality, you understand," Russell said, taking a sip of his whiskey.

"I understand. No, the fellow I mean is an Egyptian by the name of Hassan who's causing trouble in my neighborhood. Quite the local rabble-rouser. He tried to break into my house, and when that didn't work he tried to start a riot against me. His cousins are in on the game as well."

"Point them out to me and I'll give them five years hard labor."

"Most kind."

"Now do tell me more about this shooting."

Augustus did, leaving out as much as he dared. There was no mention of the underground temple on the Giza Plateau or of the involvement of the German diplomatic corps or of the shootout in the house. Augustus knew that to mention any of this would lead to nothing except trouble. Russell was on side as far as these matters went, but he was still a police commandant, and he could not ignore civilians shooting at diplomats or one of His Majesty's subjects keeping a large cache of weapons in his house.

Sir Russell seemed satisfied with the explanation and poured them another whiskey before launching into a long, boastful account of suppressing the riots. Augustus listened with half an ear as he wondered how the German embassy would explain Herr Neumann's disappearance. Did they know what he had been up to? Probably not. And if the diplomat had kept it secret, then his disappearance would remain a mystery to them. No doubt they would assume the rioters had killed him.

At last Russell declared that he had to get back to work, which suited Augustus just fine. He hadn't wanted to speak with the man anyway.

"I'll have some officers come over this afternoon to take away this Hassan fellow and the rest. As for the shooting, have no fear. We'll get it sorted. I have enough to worry about at the moment, however. Did you know there was a big shootout reported in the Zamelek neighborhood night before last? Some old house rented under a false name. My men were too busy to get to it in time and when they did, everyone had cleared out. Bloodstains and bullet holes everywhere."

"Did they find anything else?"

The police commandant shook his head. "A few personal effects. Nothing of value. Wouldn't be a bad case for you, eh?"

"Perhaps so."

"Indeed, but here's something a bit more up your street. The staff at the Mena House Hotel reported another gunfight near the pyramids last night, and some explosions too."

"Probably grave robbers taking advantage of the chaos in town to do a bit of looting," Augustus said, shifting in his seat. He felt terrible about what he had done to the temple, not that he had been given much choice. At least he couldn't remember most of it.

"That's what I thought, but Monsieur Dupris went over the ground and couldn't find anything."

"Why doesn't that surprise me?" Augustus muttered.

Sir Russell cocked his head. "I beg your pardon?"

"Oh, nothing. Good luck with your investigations, Sir Russell."

Augustus took his leave and caught a taxi back to his house on Ibn al-

Nafis Street. As Sir Russell had predicted, the streets were calmer today. The roadblocks remained up, and there were still protests in some more remote neighborhoods, but the movement seemed to have lost its steam, at least for now. Augustus didn't think it was over by any means. Too much blood had been shed.

As he went to his front door, Faisal popped out of hiding.

"Hello, Englishman!"

"Hello. I took care of Hassan and his cousins for you. The police will get them today, and you won't have to worry about them until you're big enough to take care of yourself."

Faisal leaped up and spun around.

"Great! They'll be breaking big rocks into little ones for years! I hope they get sent to the mines in the Sinai. That's the worst place for prisoners to go. Everyone says so."

"I have to admit you are a font of unusual and occasionally useful information," Augustus said, opening his door.

Karim the watchman came up to them, brandishing his club.

"I am sorry, sir. I told this beggar boy to stay away from here. I'll teach him a lesson."

"That's quite all right, Karim. He's with me."

Faisal made an obscene gesture. "That's right. I told you he was my friend. Now go back to the mangy jackal that sired you!"

The watchman glared at Faisal and stalked away, muttering under his breath.

"Some of Moustafa's language seems to have rubbed off on you," Augustus observed.

Faisal grinned. "We sure had fun, didn't we?"

"I'm not sure 'fun' is how I would describe it," Augustus said, although he couldn't suppress a smile.

Faisal looked beyond him into the house.

"Do you like your new house?"

"Yes."

"Do you ever see any jinn?"

"There's no such thing as jinn."

Faisal gave him a knowing grin.

"Not in your house there aren't. Not anymore."

THE CASE OF THE PURLOINED PYRAMID

"I'm not sure what you mean."

Faisal was still looking beyond him, into the front hallway and the courtyard beyond, where the fountain bubbled with water, sparkling as it caught the sunlight.

"It's an awfully big house for one person."

"That's the way I like it. I enjoy my privacy."

"You don't have anyone to clean for you? Or cook for you?"

"An old woman comes twice a week to clean and do the laundry. And I cook for myself or eat out."

"But who shines your shoes?"

"I got quite accustomed to doing those things for myself in the army."

"What about the shop? You don't need any help in the shop?"

"Oh, Moustafa is quite efficient at all that."

"Oh."

They fell into silence, staring at each other. Augustus pulled out his wallet.

"Here. For all your help," he said, handing over a note.

Faisal's face lit up. "Fifty piastres!" Then he grew serious. "This will only get stolen. When you have to sleep outside, things always get stolen."

"I see." Augustus took back the note and gave him ten piastres. "I'll tell you what I'll do. What's that falafel seller's name down the street?"

"His name is Mohammad."

"Of course it is. I'll give him enough money that you can have a falafel every day for a month. And who's that woman who sells fruit next to him?"

"Raisa. She's Mohammad's aunt."

"Well, I'll do the same with Raisa, so you'll have food every day for a month. For all you've done for me."

Faisal grinned. "Thanks."

"Good luck," Augustus said, putting his hand on the doorknob.

"Will you be borrowing your friend's motorcar soon?"

"I don't know. I think he might be a bit reluctant to loan it to me."

They both laughed. Faisal stopped first.

"The trip to the pyramids was fun," Faisal said wistfully.

"Except for the mob of village children throwing stones at us."

"Why do you always think of the bad things?"

"Now you're sounding like Heinrich. I'm glad you enjoyed the pyramids, but now I really must go. It's been a long few days and I must rest."

Faisal looked beyond him again.

"Sure is a big house. I bet ten people could live in there and never get in each other's way."

"Yes, Faisal. It's a big house."

They stared at each other for a moment longer.

"Good luck to you, Faisal."

Augustus shut the door.

***

The chatterers at the Sultan El Moyyad Café had much to talk about. The protests were the main topic of conversation, and speculation was rife that London would finally relent and set the independence leaders free. Ali's son, the university student and protest leader, had even made a brief appearance to fill them in on the latest news before returning to the struggle. He read French and had scoured the foreign press, discovering that all the powers were against England in this matter.

"They'll put pressure on London and soon all our comrades will be free," the youth declared.

"And once Sa'ad Zaghloul and the rest are free, the whole country will soon be out of its jail!" Ali said, beaming with pride at his son.

But the café goers on Ibn al-Nafis Street had more to talk about than most Cairenes. The café sat right opposite the Englishman's house, and there were endless opportunities to gossip and speculate about that place. First there had been the party, with all its fine guests and that stunning Turkish woman who dressed like an Ottoman but acted like a European, and then there had been the shooting. But even that hadn't been all. There had been much coming and going during the day and in the middle of the night, which had made for many wild theories and comments in the café, and the motorcar parked out front led to more comment. When one morning Anwar the waiter opened the café while his father dozed in the back corner, he had seen that the car had obviously been in an accident. In fact, it looked like it had been in several accidents.

Anwar assumed, like everyone else, that the Englishman had been attacked by the protestors.

"Too bad we weren't there to protect him again," Ali said as Anwar brought him his first coffee of the day. "Hassan was ready to tear him apart.

A good thing Youssef and Mohammed were with me, or we would have never freed him."

"May God protect him," Mohammed said as he set up the backgammon board. "As your fine son says, Ali, it is the British government we are against, not the British themselves."

"Except for the soldiers," Ali responded.

"Beasts in uniform," Youssef called over from next door, where he was opening up his barbershop for the day's work.

"When the colonial government goes, the soldiers will go," Ali said with a nod. "And once they do, I suspect the British civilians will be a little less haughty."

Mohammed chuckled as he set up the pieces, and Ali shifted his chair to play with him. "No, Ali, that won't happen. Look at the French. Their soldiers left a hundred years ago and they still act like they own Egypt. The Germans and the Italians aren't much better."

"Ah, just in time to see Ali get beaten again!"

This was from Bisam the water seller, who set down his big keg of sweet well water from a village outside Cairo and sat down next to them.

"May God grant you long life. I'll beat him this time," Ali said.

"May God grant you good luck." Bisam chuckled. "He's already granted me some."

"How so?" asked Mohammed, picking up the dice.

"Hassan and his cousins are in jail, praise be to God. They always made me give them water for nothing."

Anwar leaned over, bringing Bisam his morning tea.

"I saw the whole thing," he said with a grin. "It was the best sight I've ever seen!"

Hassan had been dragged away by two colonial policemen, screaming and struggling the length of Ibn al-Nafis Street. His cousins had been rounded up as well. Zaki had managed to knock out two policemen before they had managed to subdue him, and this while he had been laid up in bed with a broken leg. Qamar had fought hard as well and had to be beaten senseless.

As Mohammed crushed three different opponents in three consecutive games of backgammon, everyone argued about what they had been arrested for. Some said it was for the murder of a spice merchant. Others for the theft of a jewelry shop. The conversation turned into a long list of the evils that accursed family had committed in the neighborhood, and each crime had its supporters as the one that finally laid them low. No one suspected that the Englishman had been responsible.

No one, that is, until the café got a new customer.

Everyone immediately recognized the Nubian who worked at the Englishman's shop.

He greeted everyone, sitting down rather stiffly. His employer had sent him to the hospital and he had been well cared for, but his shoulder and hip still stung. He ordered a coffee. After the usual pleasantries and questions after family, all of which had to be repeated any time another of the café crowd made their appearance, they finally got to ask the question they really wanted to ask him.

"So what kind of a man is this Englishman?" asked Mohammed al-Hajji, who had just come from the mosque. Of course he had finished calling the dawn prayer two hours before, but it was his habit to stay in the mosque and study the Koran before coming to the café.

"He's a strange one, to be sure," Moustafa said. "The war has left him a bit of a recluse, and he has little love for his own kind. But he will be a good neighbor to you. Don't worry about that. He was the man who got Hassan and his cousins arrested."

Everyone gasped.

"Really? Was it because of that riot Hassan tried to start? I was surprised that he didn't have him arrested right away."

Moustafa shook his head. "No, their troubles started well before that. And he wanted me to express his thanks to you for helping him. He would have done so himself, but he was busy investigating the murder in his house."

Actually Mr. Wall had done no such thing. Europeans often forgot to thank people. Moustafa had become so accustomed to that he didn't expect them to remember anymore. But what Moustafa really wanted to tell them, the reason he had come over to this café, was about how Mr. Wall got in a fight with Hassan and his entire gang and defeated them all. He'd gotten the tale from Faisal, no doubt in an exaggerated form, and Moustafa exaggerated it further, placing him in the scene as a witness to add some veracity. In this version, Mr. Wall faced a dozen thugs, not just four, all armed with swords and guns. Mr. Wall had fought them all off with only his fists and his cane, which Moustafa neglected to mention could turn into a sword.

The men at the café listened with rapt attention. Moustafa was a natural storyteller, a talent born from the village where he grew up, where there was little to do but regale each other with tall tales after the day's work was done. He had been raised on the stories of the south, and now he was getting new ones in the north. He told them all about the fight, and even gave some details of how Mr. Wall tracked down and shot the murderer. While he had to leave out much of that story, he did mention how he had saved Faisal and stopped the Germans from looting Egypt's antiquities. He did not mention the destruction of the underground temple. That pained him deep in his heart and gave him a seething anger toward the Germans whose foolishness had led to it. He supposed someday someone would discover it and painstakingly restore it to its former glory like so many other ancient monuments. He wondered what those future archaeologists would make of Baumer's skewered skeleton.

"This is a man who believes in justice," Mohammed al-Hajji said approvingly. The others nodded in agreement.

Moustafa smiled. That was all he wanted to hear. He had cemented Mr. Wall's reputation. His boss was an outsider and always would be, but he had contributed to the neighborhood and shown himself to be honorable. That would earn him respect, and he would not be molested by anyone living here. At least no one honest.

Moustafa sipped his coffee as the conversation turned to other things. This wasn't a bad café. Perhaps he should come more often. He deserved a break every now and then, and there was a nice bunch of fellows here. He got a feeling he'd have more stories to tell them before long.

***

It was a tough climb to get everything he needed up to the Englishman's roof. Faisal had to make five trips to get his blanket, some wood he had scrounged, a tarpaulin he had stolen from the market, and some straw stuffed in burlap bags up the three floors to the rooftop. He had watched carefully and saw that the Englishman never came up here. His laundry was all taken away by the washerwoman, and so he didn't even come up to use the line.

That suited Faisal just fine. He still took care, however. When he cleared out the old shed on the roof, he left a heap of old wood and broken furniture against the doorway like it had been before, so no one would see the little bedroom he made inside. He cleared out the rest of the junk, lowering it painfully down the side of the building and disposing of it, so that the shed was about half-empty. He swept it out with a bundle of reeds, stomped on a few bugs so he'd have the place all to himself, laid down the burlap sacks filled with straw, covered them with the tarpaulin, and then laid his blanket over it.

Faisal stood back and admired his handiwork. This was the best place he had ever lived. It was safe from thieves and bullies, free of vermin, and would be warm in the winter. In the summer, he could sleep outside under the stars, although if he did that he would have to wait until the Englishman went to sleep every night to be sure he didn't come up here and catch him.

And not only did he have his first home, he had his first job. The Englishman didn't know about all the dangers around him. Who saved him from Hassan? Who saved him from the jinn? And if Faisal wasn't around, who'd save him the next time?

Yes, Hassan wasn't the only thief in the neighborhood. Others would be prowling around the house soon enough. Faisal needed to guard the rooftop to keep anyone from coming up here and squeezing through the window like he did. Plus he had to make sure that amulet stayed put so the jinn didn't haunt the house again.

Of course a job meant pay, so when the Englishman was sleeping like a dead man, Faisal could sneak down and get some food from the pantry. Not too much, mind you. He'd be fair. Just enough to eat well. And maybe a little extra to sell. He needed a new jellaba. And perhaps some sandals. And sweets. Definitely some sweets. The Englishman never kept sweets in the house. Silly Englishman.

But better than his little bedroom and the food and the new jellaba and the sweets, he would be able to keep an eye on everything that happened in the house. If he hid out of sight beside the rooftop windows, he could hear the conversations filter up. The Englishman and Moustafa often spoke in Arabic and Faisal could tell what they were saying. Also, he could peek over the front of the rooftop and watch who came and went from the antiquities shop. He'd know everything that happened and everything they were planning.

That would be the best, Faisal thought as he watched the moon rise over the Mokattam Hills and Mohammed al-Hajji, the muezzin from the mosque at the corner of the street, made the call for evening prayer. Faisal could see him, a dark figure standing on the walkway of the minaret a block away and a little above him, silhouetted against the moonlit sky.

Yes, knowing what went on downstairs would be the best. Because the next time the Englishman and Moustafa went on one of their adventures, he wouldn't miss any of it.

HISTORICAL NOTE

While the main characters and story in this novel are pure fiction, the historical background is as accurate as I could make it. The events of the Egyptian Revolution of 1919 unfolded as they are portrayed in the novel, from the arrest of the independence leaders who were pressuring the British Empire to make good on its promises, to the mass protests and their bloody suppression. This was a key moment in modern Egyptian history and marks the beginnings of an effective independence movement, one that would see completion in the following generation.

A couple of the minor characters are also real, such as Sir Thomas Russell Pasha, commandant of the Cairo police. His racist and arrogant attitudes toward the "natives" in my novel are sadly all too accurate. In fact, I think I might have gone a bit easy on him. His personal correspondence from this period makes for appalling reading.

Another real figure is that of Heinrich Schäfer. I am glad to say he finally did finish his *Principles of Egyptian Art*, which, while a weighty academic tome, is still one of the most thorough introductions to understanding the art of ancient Egypt almost a hundred years after it was written.

Sheikh Moussa el Hawi, the renowned snake charmer who cleared out Augustus Wall's home of deadly serpents, may or may not be a real figure. He is discussed in Paul Brunton's *A Search in Secret Egypt*, but so much of that mystical book is exaggeration or pure invention (although of the most entertaining sort) that I have no idea if the snake charmer actually existed.

Besides Schäfer's *Principles of Egyptian Art*, two other excellent books that helped with researching this novel are *Grand Hotels of Egypt in the Golden Age of Travel* and *On the Nile in the Golden Age of Travel*, both by Andrew Humphreys.

I must admit to one spot where I played with history. The mastaba of Idu is exactly as I described, but it was not excavated by a French archaeologist named Pierre Dupris, who is my own invention. The mastaba was actually excavated in 1924 and 1925 by George Andrew Reisner, director of the Harvard University-Museum of Fine Arts, Boston, Expedition.

I changed this, with no disrespect to Mr. Reisner, because I wanted an interesting site I was personally familiar with that my readers could actually visit, one discovered by a fictitious character I didn't mind disparaging. I'll give Mr. Reisner the benefit of the doubt and assume he was a better man than Pierre Dupris! The fact that a curse is written on the doorjamb was an added bonus, for what book about Egyptology would be complete without a curse?

Even stranger than the curse of Idu was the Thule Society, one of the many esoteric societies that emerged in Germany after World War I. Some added racist elements to their outlandish occult theories, and the Thule Society was the foremost among them. Many of the early members of the Nazi Party were also members of the Thule Society. Like most secret societies, they had a fascination with the mysteries of the Orient, and while there is no record of their searching for the lost inscription on the Great Pyramid of Cheops, it would come as no surprise if it was on their to-do list.

About that inscription. The Great Pyramid really was encased with blocks of polished white limestone, and early travelers reported that it really did bear an inscription. Most of the stone was robbed after a disastrous earthquake in 1303 AD destroyed much of Cairo. The stone was used to rebuild many mosques and palaces. Not wanting to have a pagan inscription on their buildings, the architects placed the stones face-to-face to hide the writing.

So the last statement of the great Pharaoh Cheops really does lie hidden within the walls of Cairo's medieval buildings.

ABOUT THE AUTHOR

Sean McLachlan worked for ten years as an archaeologist in Israel, Cyprus, Bulgaria, and the United States before becoming a full-time writer. He is the author of numerous fiction and nonfiction books, which are listed on the following pages. When he's not writing, he enjoys hiking, reading, traveling, and, most of all, teaching his son about the world. He divides his time between Madrid, Oxford, and Cairo.

To find out more about Sean's work and travels, visit him at his Amazon page: http://www.amazon.com/Sean-McLachlan/e/B001H6MUQI/ or his blog: http://midlistwriter.blogspot.com/, and feel free to friend him on Goodreads: www.goodreads.com/author/show/623273.Sean_McLachlan, Twitter: @writersean, and Facebook: www.facebook.com/writersean.

You might also enjoy his newsletter, *Sean's Travels and Tales*, which comes out every one or two months. Each issue features a short story, a travel article, a coupon for a free or discounted book, and updates on future projects. You can subscribe using this link: http://eepurl.com/bJfiDn. Your email will not be shared with anyone else.

FICTION BY SEAN MCLACHLAN

Trench Raiders (Trench Raiders Book One)

September 1914: The British Expeditionary Force has the Germans on the run, or so they think.

After a month of bitter fighting, the British are battered, exhausted, and down to half their strength, yet they've helped save Paris and are pushing toward Berlin. Then the retreating Germans decide to make a stand. Holding a steep slope beside the River Aisne, the entrenched Germans mow down the advancing British with machine gun fire. Soon the British dig in too, and it looks like the war might grind down into deadly stalemate.

Searching through No Man's Land in the darkness, Private Timothy Crawford of the Oxfordshire and Buckinghamshire Light Infantry finds a chink in the German armor. But can this lowly private, who spends as much time in the battalion guardhouse as he does on the parade ground, convince his commanding officer to risk everything for a chance to break through?

Trench Raiders is the first in a new series of action novels that will follow the brave men of the British Expeditionary Force through the major battles of the First World War a hundred years after they happened. The Battle of the Aisne was the start of trench warfare on the Western Front, and it was there that the British and Germans first honed their skills at a new, vicious brand of fighting.

Available in electronic edition!

Digging In (Trench Raiders Book Two)

October 1914: The British line is about to break.

After two months of hard fighting, the British Expeditionary Force is short of men, ammunition, and ideas. With their line stretched to the breaking point, aerial reconnaissance spots German reinforcements massing for the big push. As their trenches are hammered by a German artillery battery, the men of the Oxfordshire and Buckinghamshire Light Infantry come up with a desperate plan—a daring raid behind enemy lines to destroy the enemy guns and give the British a chance to stop the German Army from breaking through.

Digging In is the second in a new series of action novels that will follow the brave men of the BEF through the major battles of the First World War a hundred years after they happened. The Battle of Ypres was the first of many great slaughters on the Western Front, and it was there that both sides learned the true horror of the world's first global conflict.

Available in electronic edition!

No Man's Land (Trench Raiders Book Three)

No Man's Land—a hellscape of shell craters and dead bodies. Soldiers have fought over it, charged across it, and bled on it for a year of grueling war, but neither side has dominated it.

Until now.

An elite German raiding party is passing through No Man's Land every night, attacking the British trenches at will. The Oxfordshire and Buckinghamshire Light Infantry needs to reassert control over their front lines.

So the exhausted men of Company E decide to set a trap—a nighttime ambush in the middle of No Man's Land, where any mistake can be fatal. But the few surviving veterans are leading recruits who have only been in the trenches for two weeks. Mistakes are inevitable.

Available in electronic edition!

Christmas Truce

Christmas 1914

In the cold, muddy trenches of the Western Front, there is a strange silence. As the members of a crack English trench raiding team enjoy their first day of peace in months, they call out holiday greetings to the men on the German line. Soon both sides are fraternizing in No Man's Land.

But when the English recognize some enemy raiders who only a few days before launched a deadly attack on their position, can they keep the peace through the Christmas Truce?

Available in electronic edition!

Warpath into Sonora

Arizona 1846

Nantan, a young Apache warrior, is building a name for himself by leading raids against Mexican ranches to impress his war chief, and the chief's lovely daughter. But there is one thing he and all other Apaches fear—a ruthless band of Mexican scalp hunters who slaughter entire villages.

Nantan and his friends have sworn to fight back, but they are inexperienced, and led by a war chief driven mad with a thirst for revenge. Can they track their tribe's worst enemy into unknown territory and defeat them?

Available in electronic edition!

A Fine Likeness (House Divided Book One)

A Confederate guerrilla and a Union captain discover there's something more dangerous in the woods than each other.

Jimmy Rawlins is a teenage bushwhacker who leads his friends on ambushes of Union patrols. They join infamous guerrilla leader Bloody Bill Anderson on a raid through Missouri, but Jimmy questions his commitment to the cause when he discovers this madman plans to sacrifice a Union prisoner in a hellish ritual to raise the Confederate dead.

Richard Addison is an aging captain of a lackluster Union militia. Depressed over his son's death in battle, a glimpse of Jimmy changes his life. Jimmy and his son look so much alike that Addison becomes obsessed with saving him from Bloody Bill. Captain Addison must wreck his reputation to win this war within a war, while Jimmy must decide whether to betray the Confederacy to stop the evil arising in the woods of Missouri.

Available in print and electronic editions!

The River of Desperation (House Divided Book Two)

In the waning days of the Civil War, a secret conflict still rages . . .

Lieutenant Allen Addison of the *USS Essex* is looking forward to the South's defeat so he can build the life he's always wanted. Love and a promising business await him in St. Louis, but he is swept up in a primeval war between the forces of Order and Chaos, a struggle he doesn't understand and can barely believe in. Soon he is fighting to keep a grip on his sanity as he tries to save St. Louis from destruction.

The long-awaited sequel to *A Fine Likeness* continues the story of two opposing forces that threaten to tear the world apart.

Available in electronic edition!

Radio Hope (Toxic World Book One)

In a world shattered by war, pollution and disease . . .

A gunslinging mother longs to find a safe refuge for her son.

A frustrated revolutionary delivers water to villagers living on a toxic waste dump.

The assistant mayor of humanity's last city hopes he will never have to take command.

One thing gives them the promise of a better future—Radio Hope, a mysterious station that broadcasts vital information about surviving in a blighted world. But when a mad prophet and his army of fanatics march out of the wildlands on a crusade to purify the land with blood and fire, all three will find their lives intertwining, and changing, forever.

Available in print and electronic editions!

Refugees from the Righteous Horde (Toxic World Book Two)

When you only have one shot, you better aim true.

In a ravaged world, civilization's last outpost is reeling after fighting off the fanatical warriors of the Righteous Horde. Sheriff Annette Cruz becomes New City's long arm of vengeance as she sets off across the wildlands to take out the cult's leader. All she has is a sniper's rifle with one bullet and a former cultist with his own agenda. Meanwhile, one of the cult's escaped slaves makes a discovery that could tear New City apart . . .

Refugees from the Righteous Horde continues the Toxic World series started in *Radio Hope*, an ongoing narrative of humanity's struggle to rebuild the world it ruined.

Available in electronic edition!

We Had Flags (Toxic World Book Three)

A law doesn't work if everyone breaks it.

For forty years, New City has been a bastion of order in a fallen world. One crucial law has maintained the peace: it is illegal to place responsibility for the collapse of civilization on any one group. Anyone found guilty of Blaming is branded and stripped of citizenship.

But when some unwelcome visitors arrive from across the sea, old wounds break open, and no one is safe from Blame.

Available in electronic edition!

The Scavenger (A Toxic World Novelette)

In a world shattered by war, pollution, and disease, a lone scavenger discovers a priceless relic from the Old Times.

The problem is, it's stuck in the middle of the worst wasteland he knows—a contaminated city inhabited by insane chem addicts and vengeful villagers. Only his wits, his gun, and an unlikely ally can get him out alive.

Set in the Toxic World series introduced in the novel *Radio Hope*, this ten thousand-word story explores more of the dangers and personalities that make up a post-apocalyptic world that's all too possible.

Available in electronic edition!

The Last Hotel Room

He came to Tangier to die, but life isn't done with him yet.

Tom Miller has lost his job, his wife, and his dreams. Broke and alone, he ends up in a flophouse in Morocco, ready to end it all. But soon he finds himself tangled in a web of danger and duty as he's pulled into scamming tourists for a crooked cop while trying to help a Syrian refugee boy survive life on the streets. Can a lifelong loser do something good for a change?

A portion of my royalties will go to a charity for Syrian refugees.

Available in electronic edition!

The Night the Nazis Came to Dinner and Other Dark Tales

A spectral dinner party goes horribly wrong . . .

An immortal warrior hopes a final battle will set him free . . .

A big-game hunter preys on endangered species to supply an illicit restaurant . . .

A new technology soothes First World guilt . . .

Here are four dark tales that straddle the boundary between reality and speculation. You better hope they don't come true.

Available in electronic edition!

The Quintessence of Absence

Can a drug-addicted sorcerer sober up long enough to save a kidnapped girl and his own duchy?

In an alternate eighteenth-century Germany where magic is real and paganism never died, Lothar is in the bonds of nepenthe, a powerful drug that gives him ecstatic visions. It has also taken his job, his friends, and his self-respect. Now his old employer has rehired Lothar to find the man's daughter, who is in the grip of her own addiction.

As Lothar digs deeper into the girl's disappearance, he uncovers a plot that threatens the entire Duchy of Anhalt, and finds that the only way to stop it is to face his own weakness.

Available in electronic edition!

HISTORY BOOKS BY SEAN MCLACHLAN

Wild West History

Apache Warrior vs. US Cavalryman: 1846-86 (Osprey: 2016)
Tombstone: Wyatt Earp, the O.K. Corral, and the Vendetta Ride (Osprey: 2013)
The Last Ride of the James-Younger Gang (Osprey: 2012)

Civil War History

Ride Around Missouri: Shelby's Great Raid 1863 (Osprey: 2011)
American Civil War Guerrilla Tactics (Osprey: 2009)

Missouri History

Outlaw Tales of Missouri (Globe Pequot: 2009)
Missouri: An Illustrated History (Hippocrene: 2008)
It Happened in Missouri (Globe Pequot: 2007)

Medieval History

Medieval Handgonnes: The First Black Powder Infantry Weapons (Osprey: 2010)
Byzantium: An Illustrated History (Hippocrene: 2004)

African History

Armies of the Adowa Campaign 1896: The Italian Disaster in Ethiopia
(Osprey: 2011)

Printed in Great Britain
by Amazon